BLACKWING

FIRST ORDINANCE SERIES, BOOK THREE

CONNIE SUTTLE

Print Second Edition (2018)
Print ISBN: 1-63478-045-0
Print ISBN-13: 978-1-63478-045-2
eBook ISBN: 1-93975-933-1
eBook ISBN-13: 978-1-93975-933-7

Published by:
SubtleDemon Publishing, LLC
PO Box 95696
Oklahoma City, OK 73143

Cover art by Renee Barratt @ The Cover Counts

*To Walter, Joe, Larry, Lee, Dianne, Sarah and Mark.
Thank you.*

ACKNOWLEDGMENTS

As always, this book is the result of collaboration. If it weren't for the support of my editor, my cover artist and my beta readers, it would be less than it is. All mistakes, as usual, are mine and no other's.

About the Author:
Connie Suttle lives in Oklahoma with her husband and a conglomerate of cats. They have finally banded together to make their demands, which has proven disconcerting to all humans involved.

You may find Connie in the following ways:
Facebook: Connie Suttle Author
Twitter: @subtledemon
Website and Blog: subtledemon.com

Blood Destiny Series:

Blood Wager

Blood Passage

Blood Sense

Blood Domination

Blood Royal

Blood Queen

Blood Rebellion

Blood War

Blood Redemption

Blood Reunion

Blood Destiny Series Boxed Set (Books 1-10)

Blood Recall

Blood Alliance*

Legend of the Ir'Indicti Series:

Bumble

Shadowed

Target

Vendetta

Destroyer

Legend of the Ir'Inditi Boxed Set

High Demon Series:
Demon Lost
Demon Revealed
Demon's King
Demon's Quest
Demon's Revenge
Demon's Dream

God Wars Series:
Blood Double
Blood Trouble
Blood Revolution
Blood Love
Blood Finale

Saa Thalarr Series:
Hope and Vengeance
Wyvern and Company
Observe and Protect*

First Ordinance Series:
Finder
Keeper
BlackWing
SpellBreaker
WhiteWing

~

R-D Series:

Cloud Dust

Cloud Invasion

Cloud Rebel

~

Latter Day Demons Series:

Hot Demon in the City

A Demon's Work is Never Done

A Demon's Due

~

Seattle Elementals Series:

Your Money's Worth

Worth Your While*

~

BlackWing Pirates Series

MindSighted

MindMage

MindRogue

MindMaster*

~

Black Rose Sorceress Series

The Rose Mark

Rose and Thorn

Black Rose Queen

Queen of Thorns and Roses

Future Wars Series

Buffer Zone

Black Zone*

Other Titles from SubtleDemon Publishing:

Malefactor

Transgressor

Underhanded*

by Joe Scholes

*Forthcoming

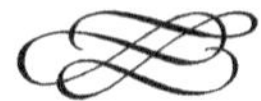

 ogeffa II
Quin

Heavy footsteps on cobbled streets invade my dreams, now. I will never forget my first night on the non-Alliance world of Vogeffa II—if I'd fallen into the hands of any besides LaFranza of the Falchani, I may not have survived.

By the time he made his way back to the small shop he owned on a back street of Gungl, Vogeffa II's major city, I was terrified, exhausted and overcome with grief. There was no mistaking the last sound I heard before I'd entered the blackness of the gate—Siriaa had exploded behind me, taking those I loved with it. My call to Queen Lissa had come too late to save them.

When LaFranza pulled me through the back door of his tattoo parlor, I was shivering, too—from the rain that fell outside. His hair, blacker than night and braided down his back, dripped on the rug inside the door as he frantically searched through drawers in a tiny back room to find something warm to drape over me.

That's when I saw the second person after my arrival. It was only because I recognized him immediately that I flung my arms about his neck and wept.

Terrett had walked into the small room at the back of LaFranza's shop to see what the noise was. Somehow, against all odds, he was staying with the man who'd rescued me from Gungl's dark streets that night. Strangely (and perhaps just as well), the Orb had disappeared.

Although Terrett was unable to speak, he did perform a soothing hum in his throat as his arms wrapped around me.

My life in Gungl began a moon-turn later, when I was finally able to pull myself out of bed without crushing grief slamming into me and causing me to collapse.

The following day, my plan for revenge against Vardil Cayetes, the man responsible for Siriaa's destruction, began.

"Call me Lafe—it's shorter and better," LaFranza instructed. His language was one I'd never heard before; nevertheless, I understood it perfectly. He was tall, with bulging muscles in his arms and dark eyes that held a strange fold at the corners, lending them a mysterious, unusual shape.

Still, he was pleasing to the eye and when he removed his shirt whenever the temperature warmed inside his living quarters, I discovered he was covered with the evidence of his art.

Eagles, such as I'd never seen, decorated arms, chest and back, with colors so vibrant the sight almost made my breath stop. "I didn't do the back tattoo—my best apprentice did that one with my inks. Do you know anything about the art of tattooing skin?" he asked, the corners of his mouth curling in an almost-smile.

"No, but I imagine I can learn anything with proper instruction," I said, embarrassed by my fascination with the art on his body.

"Can you hand the proper ink cups to me?" he asked.

"I can find anything," I shrugged. "Including the proper ink colors."

"If you're going to be my assistant in the shop, we'll have to do something about your wings," Lafe mused while studying my feathers. I pulled them tighter against my body, suddenly terrified. Would he cut them away? I backed up and into Terrett.

Waving a hand and shaking his head, Terrett let me know that cutting my wings wasn't an option. Lafe confirmed Terrett's denial. "I think we should dye them, perhaps. Along with your hair. What you have will stand out anywhere. We don't need to stand out. I imagine that black wings won't raise such a fuss—I know of some who've had mechanical black wings grafted upon their backs and they fly—after a fashion."

"But," I began. How was he going to dye my wings black? Dyed hair was common; wings were not.

"I'm a master at mixing inks and dyes," Lafe lifted a dark eyebrow as he studied me. "My tattoo colors are the best. That's why my business is so good. I figure we'll have to dye your feathers every three or four eight-days, just to ensure that they stay black," he mused as he walked around me.

"What's your name?" he asked as he faced me once more. For a moon-turn, he'd allowed me to mourn while Terrett did his best to feed and clothe me properly. Now, it was time to repay Lafe's generosity.

"Uh, Quin," I hung my head.

"No. Quin it is not. After we dye your wings black, that will be your name. BlackWing."

I wanted to tell him about real Black Wings. Justis in particular, but somehow, that would make me cry and I knew I couldn't. I'd read something else in Lafe's face as well as Terrett's. Time was different, here, as if the gate I'd been shoved through had flung me forward—years or sun-turns, it no longer mattered.

"Why are you helping me?" I asked, pulling my thoughts away from painful subjects.

"I was placed here to cause as much trouble for Cayetes as possible. I was told I'd have unusual help. I can't think of anything more unusual than a mute Sirenali and a winged girl."

"You knew I was coming?" I frowned at him.

"Not you specifically, but I don't argue with the gods when they say my help is needed. If they hadn't, I'd still be doing battle and tattoos on Falchan."

"Who is Cayetes?" I asked.

"Vardil Cayetes," Lafe amended. "The one who blew up the planet they called Siriaa. Also the one who became ill and went looking for a rogue warlock or two to perform a transference. Once it's done the first time, it has to be done again every few days, before the new body begins to die. It's forbidden spellwork and outlawed by the Karathian King. That doesn't stop a few powerful rogues from doing it now and then—for the right price, you understand."

"This Cayetes destroyed Siriaa?"

"Yes."

"Then he is my enemy."

"Mine, too, young one," Lafe nodded. "Terrett, find our BlackWing a knife and show her how to use it. We'll dye her hair and feathers tonight and you can take her to the market tomorrow."

"Smoke green." I handed the proper ink cup to Lafe. His customer, who looked as if he could crush rocks in his bare hands, stared at my wings while Lafe worked on his shoulder, tapping ink by hand into the man's skin. My white wings were now a sleek black, although still not as handsome as Justis' had been. No dye would ever compare to the real thing, I think.

Biting my lip, I let my mind go blank—it was a technique Lafe was teaching me—to let my troubles go by clearing my mind of all thoughts. It had become a regular practice whenever painful memories threatened to overwhelm me.

At times, too, I thought about Daragar and whether my mindspeech would reach him, but he would likely attempt to take me away from my intended revenge against Vardil Cayetes. Calling the Larentii could wait. Kaldill, too, if he survived, would only take me away, convincing me that Cayetes should be hunted by someone else.

I wanted that job for myself.

Lafe wasn't yet aware of all my talents, and he'd already said on several occasions that only those closest to Cayetes would be able to identify his latest incarnation.

That's where Lafe was wrong.

With my strange gifts, I would know him the moment I saw him. That's why I was determined to learn knife and blade skills from Lafe and Terrett—I needed every advantage if I were to make Cayetes pay.

"Crimson," Lafe brought me back to the present. I handed him the proper cup and took the smoke green away to cap it tightly.

Other tattoo artists used a mechanical tool to place the designs and colors on the skin—Lafe did his the old way, by tapping it in with long needles by hand. Yes, it was somewhat slower, but just as he said, he had the best colors and his artistry was unsurpassed.

A faster, cheaper tattoo could be gotten a few streets over. If you wanted a work of art on your skin, you came to Lafe.

"Now," Lafe said, after the shop was closed and dinner consumed, "We begin. I am your sursee—the master. You are the virsee—the student. I have taught Terrett many things since he came to live with me, so he will help you learn."

"Yes, sursee," I dipped my chin respectfully.

"Ah, you do know what to do," Lafe inclined his head in reply. "I wish I could promise no bruises—or at least no hard bruises, but anyone who learns to fight—either with sword or hand, will tell you a different story."

Earlier, Terrett had handed me a training outfit—made of white fabric. White was the beginner's color, a blank canvas for the master to create. Lafe was dressed all in black, the color of the one who'd mastered the art of the blade and of hand combat.

I merely wanted to learn enough to destroy Cayetes.

"There are no shortcuts," Lafe said, as if reading my mind. "You will learn thoroughly or I will not teach. Is there anything you wish me to know before we begin?"

"My bones," I said, lowering my eyes. "They are not as thick as most humanoids. It makes it easier to fly."

"Ah. Like the birds. Their bones are hollow, did you know? This is good information. I do not wish to break bones; therefore, we will temper the blows until I understand how strong your bones are."

No blows landed that night. We began by stretching. Then I learned to position my elbow to make the best strike against an attack from behind. "There is no shame in any blow, no matter how clumsy, if it achieves the desired result against an enemy," Lafe informed me. "However, we will work to ensure you know how to land the most effective blows with the smallest amount of force. Fighting a larger, stronger opponent will tire you if you do not land your blows efficiently."

He was right—few in Gungl were as short or as thin as I. Like the jungle the city was named after, it was survival of the fittest. Whenever I went to the market with Terrett, we watched carefully so we wouldn't be targeted for an attack.

The city itself was crumbling with age and disinterest—its inhabitants were more concerned with keeping their lives than rebuilding something that was falling to dust about them.

Streets had bricks missing; wagons, horses and any other conveyance had to be driven around patches of exposed ground as they made their way past those who walked warily in clumps and bunches.

The market was fifteen blocks away; it was the only place where one might buy food in the city. New bricks and older, used bricks from the streets could be bought, too, if one were interested in repairing one's house to keep out the cold during winter months.

Most of the vegetable and meat vendors knew Terrett, and were quite surprised to see me when I went with him the first time. After all, he could only point and gesture to let them know what he wanted.

He and I—I could see what he wanted and knew what he wanted to say, although he couldn't do that for himself. He would nod emphatically whenever I relayed a message to any vendor. If they asked too much, thinking to take advantage of a girl and her mute companion, Terrett would offer a rude gesture and go to the next stall.

Eventually, they learned to give us what we wanted; Lafe was willing to pay a reasonable price for it.

"Terrett," I said the following morning as we walked to the market, "Do you have mindspeech? Have you ever tried it?" I turned to look into his dark-green eyes. To me, they resembled the color the sea would turn on a cloudy day.

His steps faltering as he considered my question, he eventually shook his head. I understood that to mean he'd never tried it. Whether I saw something in him or in his background, I urged him to try.

"Just think what you want to say and direct it toward me," I said as we continued on our way.

Don't know how, filtered into my mind.

"Terrett, you have mindspeech," I said. "I heard you clearly just now. You said *don't know how*."

His eyes widened and his steps slowed a second time. *You're making good progress in your lessons. Sursee told me this.*

"Really? I thought I was doing poorly." I had the bruises to prove it, too. I'd failed to block a blow and slip away from Lafe's grip when he came at me from behind. He'd pronounced me dead as I lay on the mat at his feet, blinking up at him while my cheeks flooded with heat.

You try hard. He sees this. I cannot say how grateful I am to be able to talk with you, he added.

Terrett, if I could, I'd see to it that you could talk to everyone, I returned. Again, his eyes widened when he heard my mental voice.

I thank you for that. Most who know what I am are grateful I cannot speak.

"They're fools," I rubbed his back as we began to walk again. "I didn't speak for sixteen years," I added. "Because I was too afraid to say anything."

You must tell me this story, he said.

Someday, I promised. *When the telling won't make me weep.*

"Ah, you make your sursee happy," Lafe accepted the steaming bowl of rice with fish and sauce for his midday meal. Rice was difficult to come by, but the vendor who sometimes had it saved all he had for us.

I liked rice, too, but seldom ate it because I knew Lafe liked it so much. Terrett had his fish seared lightly with some of the green vegetables I'd cooked for myself. We sat cross-legged around Lafe's low table, enjoying a short meal break before he had to go back to work.

Part of my job was keeping the bedrooms clean, although Terrett helped with the living quarters and any heavy lifting. Lafe liked his quarters clean and uncluttered, and I didn't mind dusting beneath his bed.

At least there were none waiting to hit me out of a fit of jealousy.

Terrett handled most of the cooking, although I helped as much as I could and cleaned the table and kitchen after meals.

Then, whenever Lafe had a complicated tattoo to ink, I helped in the shop, handing him ink and tools. I cleaned the needles afterward, and sterilized them before his next appointment.

I'd lived with Lafe and Terrett for six moon-turns before Cayetes' men returned to Vogeffa II.

"He doesn't come often—he's smart enough to know that if he targets a world continuously for his bodies, the ASD will send someone in to track his men back to his current compound," Lafe said. I watched as he pulled his blades from a high shelf in his closet and unsheathed them.

They gleamed in the dim light of evening—he kept them polished and sharp. Lafe intended to pick off some of Cayetes' kidnappers while they hunted the streets of Gungl.

That's what he'd been doing the night I was dumped in Gungl—almost on his head. He'd saved my life by keeping me quiet and pulling me away from Cayetes' Storm.

Cayetes' Storm—it was what the people of Gungl called the army of kidnappers and murderers Cayetes employed. Nobody was safe when the Storm rolled in. While Cayetes preferred young, male bodies, he'd been known to take strong women or anyone else, as long as those bodies were only temporary.

Wanting to weep for the souls he displaced in order to take a body for a few days before discarding it, I watched as Lafe dressed head to toe in black leather, strapped his blades to his back, walked silently out the back door and disappeared into the night.

He is a master of the blade and of stealth. He'll be fine, Terrett reassured me when I began to fret hours later.

"Has he ever been out this long?" I whispered. Terrett and I were locked inside Terrett's small room, huddled in a corner. Lafe had instructed us to disappear into the attic if anyone tried to break into the shop to capture anyone inside. It wasn't our capture that I worried about that night.

Cayetes only hired the worst of the worst—one only had to walk the streets of Gungl to see the damage they left behind, provided the one wounded in the attack survived. Missing limbs were a specialty of Cayetes' men, led by a hulking giant called Bleek. Rumor had it he belonged to a four-armed race and could wield four blades at once.

The thought of such a man terrified me.

The sound of the back door closing had me off the floor and running. Without doubt as to who it was, I also understood he was wounded.

Lafe didn't know until that night just what it was I could truly do.

Terrett keened behind me as we slid into the small kitchen—Lafe lay huddled on the floor, his blood everywhere as he clutched his arm and side.

"Get back—I'm dying," Lafe gritted. "There's nothing you can do."

"Sometimes, it pays to know the strengths of your allies," I said, dropping to my knees. Already I was glowing with light as I gripped Lafe's arm and devoted all my energy to healing his wounds.

~

"Master LaFranza is ill, come back next week," I said. This customer, ignoring the closed sign on the door, knocked anyway, and kept knocking until Terrett and I went to answer it.

"Huh," the customer, a man already drunk at midday, blinked hazy eyes at me.

"Turn around and go," I ordered, pointing toward the street. "Huh," he said again and wobbled away.

"Drunks and fools," I muttered, shutting the door and locking it again.

Both, Terrett informed me.

When we got back to Lafe's bedroom, he was awake and sitting up on the bed. I wasn't surprised; the drunk's knocking would have wakened the dead and the deaf.

"You're more talented than I thought," Lafe lurched to his feet.

"I can't manufacture the blood you lost; that's why you're still weak," I pointed out as sternly as I could. "You really ought to get back in bed."

"The virsee ordering the sursee?" he lifted a dark eyebrow and managed a scowl.

"Where your health is concerned, I may be the sursee," I snapped.

"Is that how it is?" I followed close behind him as he walked unsteadily toward the kitchen, then sat on the stool in the corner. He and I both knew the short walk had drained him.

"Fish and rice?" Lafe asked, his voice hopeful.

"Lamb and rice," I replied. "Terrett worked hard on the lamb. It should be quite tender in the sauce."

"Good." Lafe ended up eating one-handed from his bowl after I scooted his stool to the kitchen counter. The arm I'd healed lay in his lap—it would take a few days for him to comfortably use it again. At least the hole in his side was healed and didn't bother him as much, although his breath hitched now and then.

"Well, sursee healer, when will I be well enough to get back to work?" he dropped his chopsticks with a sigh.

"Perhaps four days—if you push it—and I know you will."

"You know me that well already?"

"I can see it in your face. The scowl you're wearing says it all."

"Well, then, four days it is. Terrett, will you lend a shoulder to help me back to bed?"

I watched as Terrett draped Lafe's good arm over his shoulders and then walked slowly down the hall with his charge. I shook my head and went to the sink to wash Lafe's bowl.

I heard something at the market today, Terrett informed me later, as we sat together on the stoop outside the back door. *To them, I am just a mute who cannot carry tales,* Terrett added. I nodded—I understood his frustration at being overlooked simply because he didn't speak—my past had seen to that.

What did they say? I asked.

There is a meeting at dark hour tonight. I overheard one vendor telling another. The meeting is to be held behind the abandoned magistrate, he added.

Once, Vogeffa II had been a reasonable world, until it was overrun by criminals; most of them fleeing Vogeffa I when a stronger faction gained control. Now it was a difficult place to live, unless you were different in some way. It was better if you frightened others—they tended to stay out of your way and were less likely to attempt to cheat you.

To say that Vogeffa II and Gungl in particular drew an unusual crowd would be putting things in extremely mild terms.

With my hair and wings regularly dyed black, I fit right in. Of course, most thought my wings mechanical in nature, but none had seen me fly. More than once, though, I'd knocked the curious in the nose with a wing when they thought to get too close to my feathers.

Terrett, too, had to show his other side upon occasion, and that in itself served to frighten even the toughest he might meet.

Sirenali were amphibious, as well as capable of shifting. Terrett could grow dark scales and sharp teeth if he chose to do so. It made me glad to be his friend and not his enemy.

I can fly to the meeting and watch from a rooftop, I said, coming back to our conversation.

Dangerous, Terrett shook his head.

Don't we need to know what the meeting is about?

Probably.

Then I should go. I can glide in—they'll only think it an owl chasing mice if they hear anything.

The last thing I want is for you to be in danger, Terrett insisted.

I can fly away just as easily as I fly in, I reminded him. *I might even be able to carry you with me.*

Do you think so?

It's not far, I said. It wasn't. The abandoned magistrate was once a court of law—when such a thing was accepted on Vogeffa II.

Now it was street law and strong fists, guns or steel.

Lafe will kill us, Terrett pointed out.

Lafe can barely walk to the kitchen, I said.

True. We have an hour, Terrett said. *How long will it take you to fly if you carry me?*

Only a few minutes, as you measure time, I said. *We don't have to stay for the whole thing if we learn what we want in the first few moments.*

Agreed.

Good.

With his arms and legs wrapped around my body, I carried Terrett with me while I flew to the designated meeting place. We were early enough and my gliding silent enough that none heard when we dropped softly onto a nearby rooftop.

A fire burned at the center of an old, broken fountain, allowing us to watch as a crowd gathered below us. Some brought their drink with them, passing a bottle around while the crowd grew larger.

Firelight glittered in eyes and on bottles as the courtyard filled with people.

What I knew was this—Lafe hadn't been approached. I noticed that many others were also missing. This crowd had been chosen by someone, and that immediately made me suspicious. When I relayed my thoughts to Terrett, he agreed.

"Thank you for coming," a man stepped forward so he could be seen easily. I touched Terrett's shoulder and pointed—on the outskirts of the crowd and hidden in the shadows were several men.

They were armed. I could see the gleam of metal here and there as the light of the fire reached them for a moment.

Terrett nodded—the spokesman had his guards present. I'd never seen this man before and when I asked Terrett, he shook his head. This one was a stranger.

"As you know," the man began, "Gungl suffered another raid by Cayetes' Storm last night."

Many in the crowd grumbled—everyone in Gungl knew what Cayetes' men had done. Terrett knew of at least six bodies dumped in the open sewer that ran through the outskirts of the city.

"I have a solution," the man said.

"What's that? We don't have an army to stand against Cayetes. Last night proved it," someone called out.

"We don't need an army. If we have money, though, we can buy weapons to build an army."

"Right. Why don't you buy a few star ships and freighters, too, while you're at it?" That question drew laughter.

"All in good time," the man said. "We are men of Gungl. There are outlying villages and towns, where Cayetes' Storm never goes. They always strike here. Don't they?"

General agreement was voiced by the crowd.

"Yet," the man continued, "in those outlying villages, strong, young men, perfect for Cayetes' tastes, plow the ground. In fact, they're breeding like rabbits, out there."

"What good does that do us?" someone hooted.

"This is my suggestion," the man said. "We strike the villages. Take what Cayetes would choose for himself, place the other villagers under our thumb and sell the men to Cayetes when his Storm returns. I'd think he'd be happy to pay a fee for what he didn't have to hunt himself. Then we buy our weapons and arm ourselves better."

"This is outrageous," someone stepped from the crowd to confront the man. "You're talking murder and selling our own to Cayetes."

Before he could continue, a bowstring vibrated and an arrow pierced his throat. Terrett's hand was over my mouth as we watched the poor man die, clutching at the arrow and choking on his own blood.

"Are there any others who wish to disagree?" the man asked.

When nobody responded, he nodded. "First," he said, "We must take care of some business. Who wants to deal with LaFranza? He'll never agree to this and I hear he was wounded last night. Probably won't be too much of a fight, since he almost lost an arm."

My heart stopped. They intended to kill those who hadn't been invited to this meeting. I had to do something.

Quickly.

Gathering my courage and struggling to stop my hands from trembling, I sent the call.

They all answered. The rumbling started while the men gathered below turned about in surprise, searching for the source of the noise. When the squeaking began, they understood what was coming.

It was already too late for them to flee.

That night, those men were overrun by rats, mice and other vermin. Some men fell and were bitten when huge rats attempted to claw their way up cowering bodies—I didn't care.

Amid the squeaking, scrabbling, cursing and shouting below, I hugged Terrett to me, lifted off the rooftop and flew toward Lafe's shop as fast as I could.

It took moments for me to reach Lafe's shop. It would take longer to get him away. Terrett and I had to save his life or die defending it.

CHAPTER 2

*C*alling three horses to me is nothing compared to calling an army of rats and mice. A stable wasn't far from the shop; I could hear the horses galloping toward us as Terrett helped Lafe out the door and down the steps.

He'd insisted on carrying his blades himself. Without stopping to gather anything else except Lafe's money chest, we climbed onto the backs of horses and held on tightly while I asked them to run.

By the time we reached the outskirts of the city, half of it was burning behind us. I wanted to weep for Lafe's carefully collected tools and supplies—they'd be nothing but ash and warped metal by morning.

I did know one thing, however. The man who'd called the meeting? He wasn't looking to appease Cayetes by selling able-bodied prisoners to him. He was already in Cayetes' employ. My enemy was stretching out his hand to destroy another world.

Quin?

Terrett's voice filled my mind.

"Hmmm?" I mumbled.

Wake, please. There's a root in my back.

"Oh. Sorry." I discovered that I'd slept against Terrett's shoulder following a long ride on horseback into the countryside. Lafe snored softly nearby, stretched out on spring grass that was beginning to grow nicely.

Pulling stiffly away from Terrett, I watched as he dislodged himself from the tree we'd chosen to sleep under, once we were far enough away from Gungl that we didn't worry about followers.

A river is near. Terrett walked a short distance before bending his back to get the kink out of it. *I'll fish for breakfast*, he added before heading in that direction.

I'll check on Lafe, I said. Kneeling beside the prone Falchani, I listened carefully to his regular, deep breathing. He appeared to be fine, so I let him sleep while I went in search of wild onions and anything else I could find to eat.

I could find anything, as long as there was something to find. That wasn't much in our current location. When Terrett returned, he carried two gutted fish in his hands and watercress in his shirt pocket. The plant he'd collected for me, so I could eat.

By the time Terrett had a fire going and the fish cooking, Lafe woke and sat up stiffly. "Breakfast fish will be ready soon," I said. "Need help standing?"

"No. I feel better today, even with the wild ride after midnight," he said. "I suppose the shop's gone?"

I nodded. I knew it as surely as I knew anything. I knew, too, that many men had died during the night—men who hadn't deserved their deaths.

"The man—at the meeting—he works for Cayetes," I said.

"That means Cayetes isn't satisfied with owning Vogeffa I. He wants Vogeffa II as well," Lafe muttered. "I'll check the horses," he added. "Can you use your finding trick to get us to a village?" he tossed over his shoulder.

"Oh, yes," I said. I'd already used my gift to search for the closest one.

I hadn't felt poor in a while. I recalled those memories while we rode toward the village after our meager breakfast. I'd used the end of a tiny branch to clean my teeth and chewed mint leaves I'd found to improve my breath—wild onions can be quite pungent on the tongue later if nothing is done about it.

We didn't even have saddles for the horses we'd stolen.

Yes, we were officially thieves, but those who'd forced us to leave Gungl would have stolen our lives. The theft of three horses was small in comparison, and an easy decision for me to make.

Vogeffa I

Vardil Cayetes' Compound

"We imagine LaFranza's two assistants got him away, but there's little they can do—his wounds were mortal—Bleek saw to that. He's likely dead from the ride out of Gungl." Magul offered his explanation to Vardil's most recent incarnation. "The meeting went well; we will have the other dissidents taken care of and the remaining citizens of Gungl allied with us or too afraid to disagree."

"How long before you're ready to lead them into the outlying areas?" Vardil snapped. "You and Bleek brought me only six decent bodies, and I've already used this one," Vardil tapped his chest.

"We've emptied Gungl of suitable replacements. You understand that, don't you? We've had this discussion," Magul said. "Unless you want to be easily identified by taking on deformed or mutated bodies, then we have to look outside Gungl. We've left the farmlands alone as they're feeding the city while acting without suspicion as your breeding grounds, but it's time to take what the planet has to offer. With enough bodies, we can move to another set of worlds elsewhere."

"We have to find something suitable that isn't contaminated by that fucking poison," Vardil snapped. "You know I want Vic'Law, but I have to get there, first. Two applications have been denied already. I intend to take it anyway. I have spies and plans in place, but I need time to solve the problem of my changing appearance—I've hidden myself on Vogeffa I, but I already had control of it. Taking another world for my own will require a constant, recognizable presence. I can't keep changing faces every three days."

Magul held his tongue. If Vardil hadn't dealt with Marid of Belancour when the wizard sought to sell the poison to begin with, Vardil wouldn't be searching for new bodies and new worlds that weren't tainted with it.

Marid was dead and five years had passed since Vardil destroyed Siriaa, the source of the poison. The ranos cannon he'd paid to have constructed had blasted space dust from that infected world outward to land upon other worlds, spreading the poison for which none could find a cure.

Wherever they moved, the new location would have to be checked and double-checked by Vardil's well-paid scientists, to verify that the new world was clear of the creatures responsible for manufacturing the poison. That endeavor took them away from more lucrative activities, but Vardil valued his life above designer drug production and a host of other things.

Vic'Law had already been cleared and approved by those scientists, but Vardil could have a fight on his hands—Vic'Law was already governed by crime families and he'd have to plan his takeover carefully. Likely, he would need a temporary home while his plot to take Vic'Law blossomed.

Yes, they understood the creatures and their poison better, now, but that was little consolation against the fact that it was unstoppable, once it infected a world. Vardil and his empire needed to get away now, before anyone was infected with the creatures responsible.

The poison had reached Vogeffa I; that was the primary reason Vardil searched for a new location. It was only a matter of time before Vogeffa II was also infected.

"I spoke with Bleek—he says the same thing about LaFranza—that he delivered a mortal wound," Vardil gruffed. "I'm no longer concerned about that particular problem. Take your army into the countryside; leave only those alive whose bodies I will appreciate. Make sure they're not wounded severely—I hate going into a body that's ill or not fully functional."

"I understand," Magul bowed to Vardil. "Your command will be implemented immediately."

❧

Le-Ath Veronis

Avii Castle

"Do you suppose they'll ever get tired of staring at us?" Gurnil asked. Below the castle, three tour boats floated on the waters surrounding the giant bowl, filled with tourists who were likely recording images of Avii Castle on their comp-vids.

"Jurris uses the money to fund our government and pay for incidentals," Justis shook his head. "I just wish he'd stop selling tickets for the early risers to ogle my troops when we train in the mornings."

"I hear those tickets are very expensive," Gurnil laughed humorlessly.

"I've had to do more than enough shouting at the guards, when they decided to pose for images rather than attending to their exercises." Justis expressed his displeasure by rustling ebony wings.

"At least we don't have to worry about the boats—Orik, Wolter, Deeds and the others from Fyris do that for us. Dena is very good at keeping the financial records—with help from Renée, Queen Lissa's assistant."

"Who knew a Yellow Wing would have talents for such?" Gurnil laughed. "I hear Jurris has asked Queen Lissa whether she knows if Prince Liron will have red wings."

"I hear she wisely turned his question away," Justis grimaced. "He'll have to wait until the boy is nine, just like every other child of mixed parentage."

"You came to see me for a reason other than to watch the tour boats?" Gurnil turned to Justis.

"Yes. I was made an offer—by Kooper Griff, Head of the Alliance Security Detail."

"What offer is that?" Gurnil's curiosity was immediate. He knew the ASD only employed the finest to be their agents.

"To work for him on special assignments. He says that there are ways—shield spells or such—that can keep my wings hidden. I will look as any other man who walks about. Of course, I will be forced to keep my flying ability secret, using it where I can't be seen, but the personal shields the ASD possesses will achieve that easily."

"What do you intend to do? Will Jurris say no?"

"My brother realizes that I grow bored. Any one of my Captains can do what I do. Besides, Ardis is ready for a promotion."

"This isn't a way to destroy yourself—is it?" Gurnil asked quietly.

"No. Yes, those thoughts come at times, when I miss Quin. They will retreat; they always do."

"Any idea what you'd be doing, or where? I realize you now speak Alliance Common fluently, but you still keep your Avii habits," Gurnil pointed out.

"Kooper didn't think it would present a problem. He wants more agents to hunt for Cayetes."

"Ah. Now I see why you're so eager to accept this position."

"Wouldn't you?"

"If I had the ability, perhaps," Gurnil nodded. "We all miss Quin. Every time Nina's grandchildren sniffle, she wishes for Quin. Have you spoken with Berel and Kaldill?"

"Yesterday. Berel wants to come with me, just to keep my temper in line. Kaldill says he's ready for his son to take over Gaelar N'Seith for an extended period."

"I'd feel better if those two were with you," Gurnil said, focusing on the tour boats again. "I'd feel even better if the Larentii accompanied you. Where, do you think?"

"He says there is activity on Vogeffa II, which worries him. Kaldill can get us onto that world without any trouble."

"You know it's an outlaw planet, don't you?"

"Yes."

"Even Vogeffa I is better off—it has a government, at least."

"As such, Vogeffa I's laws are more stringent than many Alliance worlds—with punishments far more severe for breaking government rules," Justis snorted. "Yes, I've done my research. Berel says it's much like Campiaa was at one time, ruled by criminals with steel fists, who kept all except themselves in line with the laws they created."

"What is the assignment?"

"To assess the situation, search for possible involvement by Cayetes or his empire and report our findings to Kooper without anyone being alerted to our presence," Justis shook his wings. "Look—another jumper."

"When will they learn that these waters are deep and the current too strong to swim?" Gurnil shook his head as Justis leapt over the rail and snapped his wings open; he was determined to rescue another foolish tourist from the water below.

∼

Vogeffa II

Quin

Curious stares met us as we rode into the village of Hay. All the faces I saw were similar—most had never had formal education. Few could read the Vogeffan language. Four generations without an official government, as poor as it was, had taken a toll on the planet's inhabitants.

It made me think of Fyris, and the damage Tamblin had done in less than a generation. Somewhere, on a planet known as Harifa Edus, Amlis, Rodrik and Fyris' survivors lived. I hadn't thought of them since my arrival on Vogeffa II.

I'd never seen their new world; I'd trusted Queen Lissa and Kaldill when they said it was suitable. I also wondered what Amlis had done in the way of sending children to school to begin learning for the first time.

Although most residents of Hay couldn't read, there was one area in which they hadn't suffered. They were shrewd bargainers, and the evidence of their trade with Gungl was everywhere. They'd sold their meats, vegetables and fruits to those in the city for things they didn't have or couldn't manufacture themselves. Until now, too, they'd been safe from predation.

That troubled me. I'd begun to think that Cayetes may have planned this all along—to empty the city of useful bodies while the small villages outside Gungl thrived. I saw few that weren't healthy and flourishing.

With the meeting in Gungl, he'd revealed his plans to take what he'd allowed to grow all along—healthy bodies. It worried me that we were about to tell them what we knew; they didn't have any reason to believe or trust us.

That was until the strange boy and his father stepped from a house near the center of town. The man was the local leader and the boy was his son. The boy blinked at me with white eyes—there were no pupils. He was physically blind; that meant he saw everything else—or nearly so. He frowned at me; he couldn't tell what I was and that puzzled him.

"Lafe, stop here," I said, patting my horse's shoulder and asking him to stop as well.

"Father, the horses trust her," the boy lifted his face to his father's.

"Welcome," the boy's father said. "Randl told me someone would come."

My second meal that day was much better than my first—I had eggs, bread and cheese while Lafe told Randl's father, Brandl, what we knew. Randl nodded as Lafe spoke—the boy was a clairvoyant—a powerful one.

His mother, unsurprisingly, was an abnormal from Gungl. She was also dead—of an unusual wasting disease when Randl was barely two years of age. Somehow, the talent she'd had was inherited—and strengthened—by her son.

Terrett sat beside me, eating and listening carefully while Lafe and

Brandl spoke. I worried that anywhere these people went, they still wouldn't be safe from Cayetes' Storm. They weren't prepared to stand and fight, either—they had no weapons, no training and little time to prepare for the battle that would come should they choose to fight.

"There are sixteen other villages," Brandl told Lafe. "All scattered. Not much beyond that—the lands become low and marshy past that point. Except for sea plants, nothing grows in that water—it's too salty."

He was right—Vogeffa II was mostly marsh, with only a few high points of land dotting its surface. Gungl was the largest city on the highest ground. Everything around it was lower, sloping toward the sea, which covered ninety-eight percent of the planet's surface.

"Father, we have little time. I see Cayetes' army coming in three days," Randl said. "That will only give us time to reach Reed."

"Reed is next to the farthest village, before the land becomes too marshy to farm," Brandl said. "Once we reach that point, we may be trapped and unable to get away."

"I feel we should go anyway," Randl's voice was low.

"Lafe, there may be a way," I said. "Perhaps we should take all we find with us toward Reed, and then see whether someone will respond."

"Are you sure?"

"Yes." I clamped wings against my back—Queen Lissa might be angry with me when I sent mindspeech, but I felt she'd hear me anyway. My revenge against Cayetes could wait—surely I could slip away sometime and make him pay for what he'd done.

Le-Ath Veronis

"I want you to go immediately," Kooper nodded to Justis, Berel and Kaldill. "We're getting unusual vibes from Vogeffa II, and we're worried that Vogeffa I may now be infected with the poison. There is still a thriving population on II, but I want feet on the ground and reliable reports," he added.

"Likely it won't take long—Gungl is populated with thieves and cutthroats. I'm concerned about the outlying areas. Send reports if any are worth saving. Lissa has her eye on the northern end of New Fyris—there's plenty of room for new farming communities there. The werewolves are begging for more meat and grain, and New Fyris can't supply all that's needed because the population still hasn't grown enough."

"It will take time for them to fully recover from what Fyris and Siriaa did to them," Kaldill said. "New blood is a very good idea and one I'd have suggested myself. Fyris was stagnant and inbred before its people were pulled away from Siriaa."

"Lissa said you'd see the sense in this," Kooper nodded. "Are you sure you want to go?" Kooper leveled a gaze on Berel.

"I am very sure," Berel shrugged.

"Very well. Kaldill, if you need assistance," Kooper turned back to the Elf King.

"I'll let you know immediately," Kaldill smiled. "This will give me purpose, which is a very good thing," he added.

~

Vogeffa II

Hay

"Randl kept us prepared," Brandl confessed. "We have food and supplies set aside, and our horses and wagons ready. It isn't far, but we'll have to collect the others on the way. I can send runners out and have them join us there," he added.

"Grassy won't come," Randl breathed a ragged sigh.

"Always stubborn," Brandl shook his head.

"Are they on the way to Reed?" Lafe asked.

"Yes—half a day's ride," Brandl confirmed. "Headman Widder is too stubborn. Doesn't think we're in any danger."

"We don't have any guarantee they'll hit here first," I said before I thought.

Randl swung his head in the direction of my voice as he

considered my words. He shivered. "She's right," he began. "I wasn't thinking that way. I assumed they'd travel in a straight line from Gungl."

"You know now they won't come on foot or horseback, don't you?" I asked. I was reading him just as easily as I could anyone. His gift was hampered on occasion by his limited experience—as well as his environment.

"What about those from Gungl?" Lafe turned to me and asked.

"They'll allow that army to take the first few villages. Rather than risk the rest of the population, they'll send airchoppers to get them before they have time to run. Remember, they're looking to take healthy bodies. Everybody else dies. It may be that they'll kill those from Gungl at the last, just for the fun of it."

What do you have planned? Terrett asked.

Getting all of them in one place; it'll be easier to move them if we do that, I replied.

You're thinking of contacting Queen Lissa, aren't you?

Yes. I hope you don't mind.

Why should I? I was happy the short time I spent on Avendor. She didn't punish me for being owned by criminals, and many would have.

She wouldn't, I said. *She's so much better than that.*

I wouldn't believe that if it came from anyone else. You made sure I was treated with respect instead of like a slave.

Because you're just as good as anyone else, I pointed out. *Better than most,* I added with a small smile.

He bumped his shoulder against mine and smiled back.

There was a question I wanted answered, too. I knew, just by reading Terrett, that most of his kind could do what Kaldill and others could do—fold space. He knew that, but didn't know why he couldn't. I had suspicions as to why that was, but didn't want to voice my speculations. He'd been hurt badly enough by his mother already.

Pulling away from that thought, I leaned my head on Terrett's shoulder. We had people to save and little time in which to do it.

Le-Ath Veronis

"Vogeffa II is mostly water and marshland," Kaldill said as he presented the dimensional map to Justis and Berel. "Here is where Gungl is located, on the highest ground. Here," he pointed to another portion of the map not far from the capital city, "is where the farms are. The land is high enough to grow crops and raise animals. Beyond this point," he turned his hand sideways to indicate a demarcation farther south, "is where the marshland begins. The land is too spongy and the water turns salty past that."

"The farmlands are where we'll do our research?" Berel asked.

"Yes. That's all Lissa and Kooper want from us—to study the people and determine whether any are worthy of moving. They are worried about that part of the population, therefore, we will go."

"Did they receive word of some threat or danger?" Justis asked.

"In a way. Lissa and Kooper were visited by a Shining One, who'd received a vague message from the Three."

"I wish I understood what you just said," Justis grumbled.

"Not to worry—I understand it," Kaldill smiled at Justis. "We have a job to do. My plan is to leave tomorrow at sixteen bells. That will place us on Vogeffa II an hour after sunrise. A good time to start, I believe. Kooper says the people there are used to the unusual, so you won't have to hide your wings this time—or hold back from flying."

~

Vogeffa II

Quin

Hay was organized and on the road quickly. I worried about the villages farther south, though, and how long it might take them to do the same. Whatever Randl and Brandl had done to prepare the population was working, however, as the second and third places we stopped were ready to go in a short amount of time.

I couldn't shake the feeling that something was watching, however, and Randl was clearly upset. He and his father dropped back to ride next to Terrett and me. Lafe rode at the front, both blades strapped firmly to his back.

"Something knows," Randl whispered softly.

"I feel the same," I agreed.

Can you call people—like you can call animals? Terrett asked.

"Huh?" I swung around to stare at Terrett.

"They're coming," Randl wailed.

For the first time, I sent a call—for humanoids.

Le-Ath Veronis

Lissa

I knew something was wrong, although I fought through the shock of hearing Quin's voice in my mind. She sounded terrified.

Without hesitation, I shouted mentally at Kaldill; he, Berel and Justis had left moments earlier. I should have known that Conner's warning, in her guise as a Shining One, was more urgent than I thought.

Kaldill, if you need me, I added to the message, but it was a moot suggestion—Vogeffa II was under attack. I folded space, shouting for my Falchani twins as I did so.

Vogeffa II

Quin

We heard the whine of the faster air vehicles first, with the chop-chop whirring of the airchoppers next. I was terrified, while some of the animals broke away from their herders and ran.

I didn't blame them—I wanted to run, too.

Anything to get away from the gunships Cayetes had sent after us. Lafe shouted at everyone to get down as the weapons of every ship fired in our direction. A dual line of bullets rained across the ground, heading straight for us.

Half the people around us screamed. For a moment, I felt weightless, before I recognized the sensation; Queen Lissa—and her power—had arrived.

~

New Fyris
Lissa

"Kaldill?" I approached him carefully. He, Berel and Justis stood in a knot, gazing at the crowd of people and animals they'd pulled away from the marshy lands just before the seas of Vogeffa II began.

Drake and Drew, my twin Falchani mates, escorted me as we walked toward the Elf King. I'd made the mistake of sending him swift information—not only to get as many people away from Vogeffa II as he could, but that Quin had alerted me to their danger.

"We have to find out why she hasn't contacted us before," I held up a hand. "There has to be a reason."

Kaldill is always so calm. Even tempered. There was an expression on his face I'd never seen before. *Daragar*, I sent, *we may need you.*

That's when Kaldill threw back his head and bellowed. Yes, I understood the word—*why* was shouted in the elvish language as he dropped to his knees.

Daragar appeared nearby, but he also looked stricken.

If my sister hadn't arrived to do what she could, I'm not sure I could have done anything at all. It took a tremendous exertion of the power of Love to calm everyone down well enough to speak and behave in a rational manner.

CHAPTER 3

New Fyris
    Quin

The people of Vogeffa II blinked and stared; animals wandered or ran—all of them were terrified on some level. We'd landed in a new place, scattered in the same way we'd been lifted away from Vogeffa II. Fields stretching as far as we could see surrounded us.

Somehow, too, my call hadn't been interrupted.

In only minutes, people from other villages began to arrive. Altogether, it took the better part of two days for all to arrive, but eventually they did.

I wasn't there to see it, although it made it easier for those who greeted the displaced farming population of Vogeffa II. They understood the danger they'd been in, but had no idea how they'd been pulled away from that danger.

I wanted to weep for any innocent lives remaining on Vogeffa II—they'd likely be cut to pieces by Vardil Cayetes' flying army, once he learned his quarry had escaped.

New Fyris
  Lissa

"What do you mean, she's only been there for a few months?" At least Kaldill was calmer, now.

"We've been studying the problem," Breanne sighed. I hadn't seen my sister in several years, yet here she was, attempting to sort a conundrum we hadn't known existed.

"What problem is that?" Berel worked to keep his voice calm.

"The Orb problem," Bree explained. "Quin is connected to the Orb, in ways I can't begin to describe. For whatever reason, it flung her five years into the future. We've had to search continuously just to find her, and then carefully put things in place just to keep her alive and protected. That's why LaFranza was there, with the mute Sirenali. Five years have passed for you—you've lived them. For Quin, only a few months have gone by and some of you—well, she thinks you're dead."

"Where is the Orb now?" Kaldill's voice was soft. Deadly.

"Kaldill, if we destroy the Orb, we'll destroy Quin with it. Now do you begin to understand?"

Kaldill cursed. Daragar, who hadn't spoken, placed a calming hand on Kaldill's shoulder.

"Whatever and however Liron planned all this, I think his intention was to protect Siriaa and its people. When Cayetes fired his weapon at Siriaa, the Orb reacted. I believe it's sending Quin on a suicide mission to take him down, now. If we attempt to circumvent that directive, it may appear and fling her into the future again. We had a hard enough time dealing with this the first time. I don't want to work that hard to thwart the Orb a second time."

"So the Orb is still working to obey a dead god's commands?" Daragar spoke for the first time.

"It looks that way. Unless we find a way to disconnect her from that thing, we may never be able to protect her properly."

"What do we do in the meantime?" I asked.

"First, we have to find her. Second, I have to do a similar attachment to anyone who wants to stay with her—it means you'll be connected to her as she's connected to the Orb, but the difference will be that I can perform a disconnect if it's desired. Quin has no choice, until we can figure this mess out."

"You mean that if she's flung somewhere by that infernal Orb, then we'll be flung with her?" Kaldill asked. I was surprised he hadn't punctuated his words with more cursing.

"That's what I mean. It won't alter your power; it'll only ensure that you travel with her, wherever the Orb takes her."

"Mighty Heart," Daragar inclined his head, "I believe we will accept that assignment."

"Everyone here agrees?" Bree studied each of them.

"Yes," Justis hissed.

"All right. Let's go find her."

New Fyris

Quin

At least the ones who'd come to greet the new arrivals came in a more conventional manner—driving up in solar vehicles. They brought food and water in larger vehicles behind them. Lafe and Terrett stood beside me as Brandl, with Randl standing beside his father, spoke with the interpreters.

Randl had already assured his father that these people only wished to help, and I was grateful for his perception and guidance.

"Quin?" Lafe took my arm and pulled me away from the crowd. It was the first time he'd used my real name when speaking to me.

"What is it?" I asked, looking up at him.

"Wherever you go, Terrett and I will be with you," he said. "I will demand it."

"What do you mean?" I asked, as Terrett nodded his agreement.

"It means he'll go with you," Queen Lissa said behind me.

I whirled to see her, discovering others at her back. Blinking back immediate tears, I stared in disbelief at Justis and Berel.

~

Lissa

Justis had her in his arms quickly, with Berel and the others right behind. Quin sobbed against Justis' shoulder—I understood, then, that she really had believed him dead.

"I told you," Breanne placed an arm around my shoulders.

"I missed you," I sighed, slipping an arm around her waist.

"We've been doing cleanup. You wouldn't believe how many booby-traps those idiots left behind, just waiting for somebody to trip over them and set an apocalypse in motion."

"Speaking of an apocalypse, what are we going to do about those creatures—the ones poisoning everything?" I asked.

"We have to get Quin disconnected from that Orb, first," she said. "Then we'll work on that problem."

"If you say so," I shook my head. "All we can do is put a bandage on it for now."

"I know. You'll have to trust us on this."

"All right."

"I'm going to change her eye and wing color, too—temporarily. LaFranza is correct—she'll stand out less with brown eyes, black wings and hair. This way, he won't have to keep dyeing them."

"That's a shame," I mumbled.

"It won't be forever. Just while she's still connected to the Orb."

"I understood that the Orb couldn't travel beyond Avii Castle," I said.

"That was on Siriaa. It can go anywhere it wants—now that Siriaa no longer exists."

"That's frightening."

"To me, too."

~

Quin

Eventually, when I couldn't stop crying, Daragar stepped in, lifted me from Justis' arms and began his soothing hum. I was asleep quickly.

~

Lissa

"I can take you back to Le-Ath Veronis," I said. "But I can't guarantee the Orb will allow you to stay there."

"I think we understand that, now," Kaldill shook his head. While Quin slept peacefully in Daragar's arms, Breanne had performed the link with each of them, LaFranza and Terrett included, because they refused to be separated from Quin.

"I'm hoping it'll give her time to rest before it shows up again," I said. "Is everybody ready? I'll take you to my palace and find beds. I hope you get to use them."

~

Vogeffa I

Vardil cursed, still. Everything in his suite was destroyed already. Even his warlocks cowered, and that was unusual. If anyone other than Bleek had brought the news, they'd have been killed—at Vardil's command.

The four-armed giant stood near the door, his stance stoic, all four arms crossed over his massive chest. It had taken all his skill to deliver a killing blow to LaFranza, and he'd been rewarded by Cayetes himself for that act.

In truth, Cayetes was afraid of Bleek. Bleek wanted to smile at the thought, but held back; Vardil was still too upset to see any humor in the situation.

The fact that every farmer, wagon and animal had suddenly disappeared was unusual in the extreme. Bleek had images of the disappearance—every gunship was equipped with vid-recorders.

Vardil had even witnessed the disappearance firsthand, as he'd watched a live feed from the lead ships. He merely couldn't believe it, or understand how it had happened. He'd been cursing for half a click about it, too.

"Find out where they went," Vardil said. Bleek kept his face expressionless as Cayetes uttered the first coherent words since the mass disappearance. "I want them back and the ones responsible for this outrage killed."

"As you command," Bleek dipped his head and turned to leave. He'd had enough of Cayetes for the moment, and hoped his search took him far away from Vogeffa I. He had no desire to stay on a dying world. If Cayetes had any sense, he'd leave now. Bodies could be found elsewhere.

Once the poison infiltrated your system, no matter how strong you were, you'd die. Not everyone had Cayetes' resources to move into a clean body once that happened. He'd seen Cayetes' continual dependence on new flesh and had no desire to be caught up in that unstable vortex. The poison and Cayetes weren't the only reasons Bleek had for getting away, either. He had no desire to discuss that with anyone; it would make him vulnerable.

"Get everything ready to move. Immediately," Vardil shouted.

"Get information," Bleek snarled at his First Lieutenant after shutting Cayetes' suite door behind him. "Find out who just increased their population by several thousand farmers."

"Yes, Commander Bleek."

Le-Ath Veronis

Quin

"Time to eat."

I knew that voice. It merely belonged to someone older, now.

I blinked my eyes open while Berel's image swam into focus. A wide grin split his face when he saw I was awake.

"Berel," I lifted a hand.

"I'm here, love," he took my hand and kissed it.

"Let me touch your face," I pulled my hand away from his. "You look so handsome." I ran fingers down his cheek. "So much like your father. How is he?"

"Father is fine. He was overjoyed to hear you're alive. Come, now. Dinner is waiting."

My stomach rumbled at his words. My most recent meal, after all, had been on Vogeffa II. "I'll get up," I said. Berel helped.

"Sit here," Kaldill smiled and beckoned for me to sit between him and Justis. Berel took the seat next to Kaldill's, while Terrett and Lafe sat on Justis' other side.

I'm sorry, I apologized mentally to Kaldill. I knew he'd suffered at my absence.

You're here now. My heart is singing, he replied. *Eat. You look too thin.*

I ate while the others talked around me—LaFranza was more than happy to find other Falchani at the table. I understood that he was meeting very old friends there, and he hadn't expected that. They spoke in his native language, telling stories of Lafe's experiences as a warrior and tattoo artist on Falchan in the distant past.

I wasn't the only one brought forward in time in an attempt to thwart Cayetes and his Storm. Terrett, too, had experienced much the same as I.

I'm glad you're here, I sent to him.

Leaning in so I could see, he gave me a smile and a wink.

"Quin, we've changed your wing and hair color so LaFranza won't have to dye it," Lissa said. "It's temporary—when we get this Cayetes mess sorted, it'll be changed back."

"That's fine." I rustled my feathers. I'd noticed that they looked much like Justis' feathers, now. At least I understood the reason for it.

"My love, it will be all right," Justis placed a hand on the back of my neck. "Black wings aren't so terrible."

"Why would I think that?" I asked. "Your wings are beautiful." He surprised me by leaning in to kiss me.

"I almost died," Lafe said, covering the hush that had fallen when

Justis kissed me. "I had no idea Quin could bring me back from a mortal wound."

"Quin has brought all of us back, I think," Kaldill replied. Terrett nodded emphatically. It made me giggle.

❦

Lissa

"Terrett, I understand you have mindspeech," I said. I'd sent for him after dinner; we'd met in my arboretum at the top level of the palace.

I do, he agreed. *Quin pointed it out.*

That's what I wished to speak with you about, I said. *Are you sure you want to be connected like the others? I can return you to Avendor if you want.*

I will stay with Quin, he said. *I love her, and I've never loved anyone, before. I am loyal to LaFranza, too—he treats me as a brother instead of a mute imbecile.*

The others are prepared to accept you as such, too. I merely wanted to confirm your feelings on the matter.

Quin said you were so much better than I could imagine, he said. *She was right. None other would ask for my opinion or place value on my feelings, except for her.*

Then you've been hanging out with the wrong people, I said and smiled.

Most certainly I have, Lady, he returned with a grin.

❦

Quin

"Any idea where on Vogeffa I the bastard's hiding?" Kooper Griff sat across from me in Queen Lissa's library.

"Not exactly, and I believe he intends to move—that's what I saw in his servant—the one who came to Gungl to convince the residents to attack the outlying villages," I replied. "I imagine the disappearances of his quarry will facilitate a faster move. It'll be difficult for any of your men to find him, because he's constantly switching bodies."

"I knew that already," Kooper dropped his gaze and stared at his hands for a moment. "That's why I never sent anybody there, although we suspected as much. Who the hell is going to recognize him, now?"

"I will," I shrugged.

"Yes. I heard that, too."

"I dislike the idea of you getting close enough to recognize him," Justis said.

"She—we—may have no choice in the matter," Kaldill scolded lightly.

"Ah. Well, she will have us with her, then. The bastard should prepare to die, should she point him out."

"He has a warlock with him—never forget that," Kaldill said. "The warlock is keeping the bastard alive by transferences."

"Any warlock willing to do that will have no qualms about killing any one of you." Lissa walked in, accompanied by her warlock mate and their son, the King of Karathia. He it was who spoke, as he would know as well as anyone what warlocks might accomplish. Karathia was filled with warlocks and witches.

"King Warlock," I stood and inclined my head to him. "Queen Lissa."

"How the hell does she know these things?" Rylend, King of Karathia, asked with a smile. "Hello, Quin. My mother speaks highly of you."

"What? Nothing for me?" Erland, Rylend's father, teased.

"Mighty warlock," I nodded to him. "May your spells never fail."

Erland stopped in his tracks. "Bugger me," he sighed. "My father used to say that."

"Quinnie Bee," Lissa said, "I have it on good authority that your official age is twenty. Here's your Alliance ID, showing you're a citizen of Le-Ath Veronis, in good standing and entitled to those things afforded to all citizens of this world."

She handed a small envelope to me. I frowned—I knew what it contained—a tiny chip that would identify me on any Alliance world.

"It will not harm you," Daragar said, reaching out to take the envelope. "I shall place it."

"I've placed a special spell on it—it'll only be found on Alliance worlds," Erland grinned. "Everywhere else, nobody will even know."

"You're not telling me everything," I said.

"True," he laughed. "Does that upset you?"

"No. I understand you only want to protect us." He, Lissa and Kooper could find me anywhere, with the small chip that Daragar employed power to place under the skin of my wrist. There was no pain—my Larentii saw to that. I hugged him afterward, which he enjoyed.

Our conversation continued after that. Lissa sat on a nearby sofa, between her warlock mate and her son. I understood their reasons for being there—we'd have to find Cayetes' warlocks, just as we had to find Cayetes. He had an army of loyal soldiers and servants about him, and that could take time.

At least nobody attempted to dissuade me from looking for Cayetes. Somehow, they understood that this was my mission. Fortunately, Kaldill and the others intended to go with me. I was grateful, as they had more experience at these things than I did. After all, I'd never set out to intentionally harm anyone before.

Cayetes, however, was an abomination. In order to save others, he had to be destroyed. "You've already started training her?" Justis pointed his question to Lafe.

"Yes—mostly self-defense; we haven't had much time."

"I was worthless the first moon-turn," I mumbled. "I thought you were dead. Berel, too."

"Back to business," Lissa interrupted. Justis was ready to rise and move everyone else aside to get to me. "Kooper and I wish to arm all of you—in a way that will make it easier to protect yourselves. I want to give mindspeech to those who don't have it, too. That means you, Berel, and you, LaFranza."

"I'll have mindspeech?" Berel's voice held reverence.

"I can give you that, at the very least," Lissa smiled at him. "I think Dragon and Crane will have something for our master swordsman, there. Terrett, I'll have something special for you, too. I expect you to use it wisely."

Terrett nodded respectfully to Lissa, his appreciation shining in his eyes. In all his life, nobody had ever given thought to him. He'd been a mute convenience and disregarded most of the time.

"Our Sirenali will ensure that none will find our party by scrying or using power," Kaldill nodded. "That in itself will be a welcome asset."

"You," she turned to Berel, "Kooper and I have this for you." She held out her hands, in which a carved, wooden case appeared. "Inside is a ranos pistol. Only you may handle it. It will identify with you and only fire for you. Anyone else it will destroy. Do you understand?"

"I do. I've done my research," Berel's lips curled in a small smile. I understood, then, that Berel had trained with Lissa's troops and knew hand-to-hand combat and how to fire weapons. He'd been busy for the past five years.

"I'm sending one more with you," Lissa said. "Yanzi?" she called out.

Another appeared in her library, employing the ability to fold space as Kaldill and Daragar could do. My breath caught.

They called him a reptanoid. He was so much more than that. A smile spread slowly across his face as he studied me. I smiled back—I couldn't help myself.

"I wish to go, Grandmother."

Someone else had come.

"Bel?" Rylend, King of Karathia, stood immediately. Bel, the new arrival, was his son and only child.

"Father, you said yourself that I am an accomplished warlock. Who better to send to recognize the work of other warlocks?"

"Honey?" Lissa stood and held out her hand.

Bel Erland Morphis, Prince-heir of Karathia, was in his mid-thirties, but I could see that he chafed at the protectiveness of his father and grandmother. I worried about him, too—his life was very precious.

For many reasons.

"If you go, you will only be an equal, not a prince," Erland, his grandfather, wisely pointed out.

"I know that. I look forward to it," Bel replied, giving his grandfather a slight nod. "I don't really need someone to clean my clothes and pick up after me. I know how to do that for myself. I can cook, too—Mom made sure of that."

His mother was Reah, and he was here with her blessing. He looked more like his father and grandfather than his mother or grandmother, though.

"Quin?" Lissa turned her eyes on me.

"You want the truth?" I asked.

"Yes."

"He should come," I sighed. "He will be in no more danger than the rest of us."

"I watch," Yanzi grinned, causing Bel to laugh. They knew one another—very well.

Gurnil, Ordin, Dena, Wolter, Orik and Deeds wish to see you, Justis sent. I understood that he'd notified Jurris of my survival. I also understood that Jurris wanted to see me, too, but Justis wished to keep me away from Avii Castle, in case the Orb might be lurking there.

All of them—that I could read, at least, were worried about the Orb. Something blocked all the information from reaching me, however. I couldn't explain that and resolved to ask about it later.

Will they come here? I sent mindspeech back to Justis.

They are coming, he closed his eyes slowly to acknowledge my sending.

I want time alone with you—and the others, I said. *I missed you so much.* That admission made me want to weep, but I forced tears back—Kooper was still speaking.

"Since you will have mindspeech, I expect to be contacted if you find Cayetes. He's turned into a bigger monster than his brother ever dreamed of being."

"He has a mercenary army," Lafe reminded him. "Bleek almost took my arm off."

"Bleek has four arms and four swords," I said, defending Lafe.

"Cayetes has a Blevakian?" Lissa asked.

Terrett nodded—he'd seen other Blevakians, it appeared. I wasn't surprised—he'd seen plenty of criminals during his enslavement.

"They usually don't get involved in someone else's war," Kooper observed. "They have enough of their own to fight."

"You think he may have been coerced?" Lissa asked.

"No idea. I've never heard of him before," Kooper replied.

"I've never seen him, so I can't tell you anything else," I said. "If that changes, I'll let you know."

Kooper didn't keep us long after that; when we walked out of the library, I found Dena and the others waiting for me. Dena wrapped her arms around me and wept, she was so happy.

Kaldill insisted that we resume our reunion inside his suite, which wasn't far from mine, as it turned out. Gurnil was bursting to tell me about the new information he'd gathered for the library; he'd studied constantly since his arrival on Le-Ath Veronis and was now well-versed on the Reth and Campiaan Alliances. Ordin was overjoyed that he'd been allowed to study with some of the best physicians in the capital city and had learned much, including Alliance common—both written and spoken.

Dena, Wolter, Orik and Deeds ran the tour boats for Jurris, receiving a generous salary for doing so. I didn't say it, but Jurris was so much better, now that Halthea was gone. He doted on his son, too; I learned that from Justis.

Still, Jurris worried that his son might not have red wings when he turned nine. That shouldn't matter, but royalty was royalty, no matter where you might find yourself.

"I hear from Amlis and Rodrik, now and then," Berel said quietly when he was able to get a seat next to mine. "They're doing well. Rodrik's wife is pregnant with their second child."

"I know she's happy about that," I sighed.

"She is. Do you wish to see them, sometime?"

"Maybe. I'll consider it. You understand that we have *history*, as Terrett is fond of saying."

"I'm astounded that Terrett had mindspeech all this time and none of his captors had any idea."

"I'm grateful they were never able to exploit him further than they did," I replied. "You'll have mindspeech too—soon, if I understood Queen Lissa correctly."

"I look forward to it." Berel's smile illuminated his face. I looked forward to private conversations with him, too.

Too soon, those from Avii Castle had to leave. Perhaps it was just as well; I was nearly asleep on Berel's shoulder by that time.

"Quin?" Justis lifted me away. My arms draped around his neck. He was just as strong as ever as he carried me away from Kaldill's suite. I wasn't surprised to learn that not only Justis would spend the night in my suite, but Terrett and Yanzi, who'd become fast friends, would also stay there. At least they had the other bedrooms inside my suite, although I wouldn't have minded if Terrett had let me sleep with my head on his shoulder.

That didn't happen—I was left alone in my bed. A part of me was glad—it stopped my worry that someone might demand a coupling, when I was concerned about my inexperience in the matter.

Terrett

I was never taught to read or write when I was young—I'd learned those things with difficulty later in my life by teaching myself. When the shining woman and Queen Lissa visited me early the following morning, I had no idea what they might offer.

It left me stunned, that gift, and I promised both that I would only use it if there were no other choice. I learned valuable things at the end of that meeting, too—and those things only made me more determined to protect Quin's life with my own.

Quin

When I opened my eyes the next morning, I blinked sleepily at Yanzi's other form. He was a lion snake shapeshifter; his large, triangular head rested on the edge of the bed, where he blinked at me as if he were happy to see me wake.

"Sir Yanzi," I reached out to stroke the top of his head. I could see he took pleasure from my touch—he closed his eyes, begging silently for more.

"Want breakfast?" I asked, sitting up and swinging my legs over the side of the bed, taking care not to disturb him.

Breakfast—yes, he informed me in mindspeech. I watched as he dropped his head to the floor and snaked away, heading toward the door.

"I'm not dressed yet," I pointed out.

You fine, he said. *Come. I feed.*

Feeling somewhat self-conscious by walking through the royal wing of Queen Lissa's palace in what she called pajama bottoms and a backless top, I shook my wings to unkink feathers and followed Yanzi to the kitchen.

"She want oatmeal," Yanzi directed the moment he became humanoid inside the kitchen. "Milk. Fruit."

He settled beside me at a table, where we were served breakfast. He had sausage and eggs while I ate a slice of the most wonderful fruit I'd ever eaten.

"Gishi fruit. From Avendor. Eat," Yanzi coaxed. He didn't have to convince me—I ate all the fruit first, before dipping into the oatmeal. It was flavored with maple syrup and brown sugar; I hadn't had such luxury in months.

"There you are," Justis' shoulders sagged in relief when he found us at the breakfast table.

"You could have sent mindspeech," I pointed out before placing another spoonful of oatmeal in my mouth and chewing.

Terrett, who peeked around Justis' wings, offered a cheeky grin before stepping around Justis and heading for the chair next to mine.

Did you sleep well? I asked him while we ate.

Very well, he agreed. *Although I might have slept easier with your head on my shoulder.*

At least there were no tree roots poking your back, I teased mentally.

True, he agreed.

Berel was the next to join us at the breakfast table, followed by Lafe, Kaldill and Bel.

"Good morning, my love," Kaldill leaned down to kiss me. I'd been kissed more in the past day and a half than ever before.

It was nice.

Kaldill's kiss made me want more of his kisses. My eyes followed him as he took a seat across the table, next to Lafe.

"I have it on good authority that a large compound is now vacant on Vogeffa I," Queen Lissa walked in. She was dressed casually, but I still felt self-conscious in my sleep clothes.

"So the bastard has gotten away," Lafe grumbled while thumping his mug of strong tea on the table.

"We'll find him," I said, attempting to pull Lafe away from a darkening mood.

"You can count on that," Kaldill agreed.

"We haven't trained in two days," Lafe schooled his features. My breath caught—I hoped he wasn't one of those who looked to take his anger out on someone else.

"Quin, come with me. Now." Lafe rose from the table. I wasn't dressed for training. I wasn't sure he realized that and I was afraid to decipher what lay behind his expressionless eyes.

Frightened, I followed Lafe as he stalked from the kitchen. We were halfway down the hall leading to the royal wing when he stopped and turned. I stopped two paces behind him, suddenly terrified.

"Quin, when a sursee agrees to teach a student, there can be no personal relationship. Every sursee understands this. Once the training is over, that rule no longer applies. I merely wanted to tell you that for me, this training period will almost be unbearable. Go back to the table before I forget myself and soothe that look of fear from your pretty face."

He whirled and strode away swiftly.

Swallowing with difficulty, I did as he asked and walked back to the kitchen. I believe Terrett was the only one to notice that my hand shook when I lifted my glass of juice to finish it.

Lissa

"I feel like we're waiting for a time bomb to go off," I said as I straightened the coronet on my head that I wore to Council meetings. It was lighter and I could forget it while working my way through proposed legislation.

Merrill had arrived to attend the meeting with me; he nodded silently as he watched me settle the thin, jeweled band over my hair. "Kiarra says that taking Quin to Avendor and leaving her at SouthStar may alleviate the Orb's hold on her, but that probably means she could never leave there again."

"I've thought of that, too," I agreed while slipping earrings on. "Kee's right; I think we should only consider that in an emergency."

"We're prepared to help, should the need arise."

"I appreciate that—I have no idea what Cayetes has in his arsenal, other than a warlock strong enough to perform a transference and probably a Sirenali or two to keep him hidden. Let's face it—none of us could pinpoint his location; we could only act on our suspicions where that asshole is concerned. My shield around the palace is likely keeping the Orb at bay for the moment, but when Quin steps outside," I shook my head.

"Are the others making their preparations?"

"I've asked them to. Kaldill passed the message along. Berel now has mindspeech and a ranos pistol; LaFranza has spelled blades made by Grey House and Terrett has been taken care of."

"Kiarra sent something for Justis."

"Huh?" I turned on my dressing bench to look up at Merrill.

"This." He *Pulled* a box to his hand and gave it to me.

Inside, two items nestled side-by-side—a ring and a cuff. Both were carved to match. Each bore three faceted Tiralian crystals.

"Protection spells?" I blinked at Merrill.

"The best," he agreed. "Each crystal is spelled to activate separately. He's protected for six attacks, should he need it. Ashe made the suggestion."

"Then Justis will need these," I sighed, closing the lid. "Let's find him before we have to go to this infernal meeting."

CHAPTER 4

uin

"We believe the Orb sent you to Vogeffa II because Cayetes' Storm was there the night you dropped out of the sky on Lafe's head," Berel explained.

"So it understood that I wanted revenge for Siriaa?" I asked.

"In a way," Kaldill shrugged. I could see he held something back, but I couldn't get past an unusual fog to see what that could be.

At least I was showered and dressed while we had our meeting in Queen Lissa's arboretum. It was beautiful there, with lamps positioned throughout to provide a substitute for sunlight.

No sunlight fell on the half of Le-Ath Veronis where the capital city lay—the planet rotated on its side, leaving half in total or near-darkness. The planet was perfect for vampires, most of whom couldn't step into sunlight unless they wished to die from it.

I sat on a comfortable swing, with Justis' right arm and wing draped around me. Berel sat on the floor nearby, with the others scattered about us. My eyes often wandered to Lafe, but each time, I hastily dropped my gaze and turned away.

Likely, he regretted saying what he had. We had a training session scheduled after our meeting, which would last until lunchtime. Justis would attend, as he was well-versed in training troops. I imagined all of them would come to watch, and that in itself served to embarrass me.

What's wrong? Terrett's voice sounded in my mind.

Nothing.

Quin, I have been alive long enough to know that when a woman says nothing is wrong, then something is very wrong.

I brushed a tear off my cheek that insisted on falling and turned my head away.

The training session was just as bad as I imagined—perhaps worse. To my eternal shame, when Lafe tossed me onto the mat after I failed to move away from his grasp, I burst into tears, stopping the entire debacle.

Yes, all of them had come to observe.

That made it so much worse.

"There's no crying in training sessions." Someone new had come. "I'm taking over," he announced. "I'll go with you and the others, too," he added, extending a hand to help me up.

I blinked tears away to bring his face into focus. He was dressed in black from neck to boots, had black hair and a crooked grin lighting dark eyes. "Salidar DeLuca," he said, pulling me to my feet. "Lafe has agreed to allow me to take over your training. I warn you, I don't train slackers."

"Or criers, I imagine," I mumbled dryly as I stood unsteadily and wiped my face on a sleeve.

"I've never trained anyone with wings, before," he said, ignoring my statement. "We'll make that work to your advantage."

"Sal was trained by the best," Lafe said. "I'm sorry, Quin. I thought we could work through this. I should have known better. From now on, it'll be you and Sal in training, with no observers unless you give permission."

"Thank you," I whispered, hanging my head in embarrassment. I should have been able to ignore the upset, as he said. I couldn't, and that made me feel weak.

"You don't get to insult yourself—that's my job," Salidar informed me, plucking the thoughts from my head. "Today's session is over. Tomorrow, you answer to me."

"Yes, Sursee," I mumbled.

"Hold back for now—she's upset," Kaldill advised.

"I fucked this up," Lafe rubbed his forehead. "I shouldn't have said anything."

"I'm glad Salidar volunteered—you didn't have to ask," Kaldill nodded. "The rest of us made it worse by coming to watch."

"Quin doesn't like to make mistakes—all her life she's seen what to do in others' faces. This, though—it's muscle training. That's only gained by practice," Berel offered.

"You'd know—you've spent the last five years training with Lissa's Falchani," Kaldill sighed.

"It's not just that she doesn't like making mistakes," Justis said. "She doesn't like disappointing anyone she cares for. She saw every learning mistake she made with you as a disappointment to you, too."

"That's not—that's wrong," Lafe breathed. "I wish she could see the mistakes I made when I was learning. She always gives her best, and I can't say the same thing about myself when I was taught."

"Then you should say that to her—when she's willing to talk to us again," Justis suggested. "I think Daragar is the only one who wasn't there, and I'm not sure she'd speak to him, either."

"Telling Quin that you cared for her unsettled her, then you followed with a training session where all observing appeared judgmental to her. I heard my name, therefore, I am here," Daragar said after his sudden arrival.

"We made that same determination—afterward," Justis observed.

"We feel like asses for it, too," Kaldill added.

Quin

I'd hidden in the arboretum, in a corner surrounded by ferns and palms. Wiping the occasional tear away, I hoped I wouldn't be found.

Queen Lissa found me anyway.

"Honey," she lowered herself to the floor beside me, "Nobody expects you to be perfect. A sursee only asks you to learn from him. He knows mistakes will be made. He's training your muscle memory, just as he's training your mental one." She draped an arm around my shoulders and pulled me close to kiss my forehead.

They were all watching, I employed mindspeech; I didn't want the Queen to hear the tremble in my voice.

"I know," she whispered. "They didn't mean to upset you. They only wanted to be as close to you as they could get—remember, several of them have been away from you for five years. They'll take any sort of closeness they can get. They weren't looking for your mistakes; they were looking at the woman who stole their hearts."

"I still feel embarrassed."

"I know. Why don't you come with me? I can have lunch sent to your room."

"I'm not very hungry."

"I understand. You'll need your strength, though, if Sal takes over your training. He was trained by Caylon Black, the best swordsman Falchan ever produced."

"He already told me there's no crying in training," I mumbled. Lissa laughed at my statement.

Yanzi arrived in snake form to share my lunch. I fed him off my plate, until he shook his head and informed me through mindspeech that I wasn't taking enough for myself.

Terrett stole into my suite shortly after. When I finished eating, he and I sat against the headboard of the bed, where he allowed me to lean my head on his shoulder. Yanzi coiled himself at the foot of the bed and fell asleep.

Terrett

Daragar appeared not long after Quin fell asleep on my shoulder. He settled a warm blanket over her, offered a smile and disappeared. Yanzi raised his head minutely before settling down again—he wasn't worried about the Larentii. I understood then that anyone who thought to bring harm to Quin would have to deal with him.

I understand completely, brother, I sent to him.

We stand together, he agreed and drifted to sleep again.

Zephili

"This will hide us well until we find a way onto Vic'Law," Magul explained. "The farming operation is in place and the employees know their jobs. It'll only take the removal of a few managers, then replacing them with some of ours to make it completely legitimate."

"Where will the bodies come from?" Vardil demanded. "I have two left, and I'd reject them if there were any other choice." Vardil studied the spacious plantation house Magul had purchased for him with a critical eye. Zephili, an Alliance world, wouldn't have been his choice either, but as long as he could pass his presence off legitimately, he didn't care.

Provided the bodies he needed could be acquired easily.

"Mar'Dun isn't far, isn't Alliance and the jungles are filled with indigents. They look much like the inhabitants here, Lord Cayetes. Your warlocks have already developed an identity for you—you were born here and worked your way up to the ownership of a very successful nanna plantation."

"When will the first bodies arrive to complete my disguise?" Vardil complained.

"In less than a day. Be patient, this plan is perfection. Neither world is beset by the poison; that has already been determined."

"Any word from Bleek?"

"Not yet—he has several locations to visit. Never fear, those responsible will be dealt with harshly."

"Did he take the boy?"

"Yes—you know he won't leave any star system without the stasis coffin. He knows only your warlocks can remove the boy, and that won't happen until a cure is found for the disease."

"Convenient to have a Blevakian under your control and leading your army, eh?" Vardil smiled for the first time in days.

"Bleek is the most effective general I've ever seen."

"We'll have his undying gratitude and continued service if we find a cure for the boy."

"I know. The warlock tells me he is constantly searching for that very thing—when he has free time," Magul dipped his head to Vardil.

"Is it always this humid here?" Vardil complained, turning Magul's attention away from Bleek and his son. Vardil knew the truth about the boy; Bleek, Magul and the others believed the lies they'd been told. Vardil had reason to keep it that way.

"My Lord, the moment you change to a Mar'Dun body, you will be acclimated," Magul claimed.

"Then I look forward to that. Make it soon, Magul."

"It will be as you say, my Lord."

❧

Quin

My training with Sursee Salidar began the following day, after breakfast. "Hit your attacker across the eyes with your feathers—it may effectively blind them for a moment or two. That is long enough to deliver a blow or fly away."

By the end of the session, I could aim the ends of my primary feathers to strike an attacker in the eyes. Salidar wore protective glasses for the exercise, so he wouldn't be injured.

I was grateful it was only the two of us in training—no others had come to watch. I was also grateful that he didn't belittle me when I failed to deliver a proper blow; perhaps sureness and confidence would come as I perfected my skills.

When the session was over, I bowed to him as was proper, and thanked him for his instruction.

I hadn't wept once, and I was grateful for that.

"How it go?" Yanzi grinned at me when I arrived in our suite.

"It was all right," I shrugged. "He didn't yell."

"Glad," he nodded. "Need bath now?"

"Yes." My answer was short and emphatic.

"Queen send clothes—you have much to wear," his grin widened. "Terrett in closet, looking at yours and his."

"Terrett has new clothes?" I was more excited for him, I think.

"Yes. Much. Get clean. Then you see."

Terrett was dressed casually in new clothing when we left our suite for lunch. He looked quite fine and I told him so. I received a smile and a swift hug for my observances.

Terrett and I weren't the only ones with something new to wear—Justis wore a ring and wrist cuff I'd never seen before. I blinked for a moment while information soaked into my mind—both items were spelled to protect him.

I was grateful to those who'd supplied that protection. I had no idea what we might face in our hunt for Cayetes; therefore, any protection offered I would gladly accept.

Salidar, Kooper Griff and several others joined us at the Queen's table. Kooper had information from several agents, all of whom supplied possible sightings or evidence of Cayetes.

"He can't have been in all those places—those span star systems and several are within an Alliance—either Campiaan or Reth," Salidar pointed out. "He hasn't been seen on an Alliance world in decades. He sends his flunkies to do the dirty work on Alliance worlds."

"He has warlocks at his disposal," Queen Lissa observed. "Although you're right about some of these—he'd have to bend time to appear there on the dates given."

"At least we know that's out of the question," Bel said. "A warlock can do a lot, but bending time has never been one of our given talents."

"You don't know how happy I am about that," Lissa smiled at her grandson. He grinned back at her.

"This is the one I'm worried about," Kooper said, pointing at a dot on the vid-map hovering over the table. "Bodies have been disappearing regularly."

"Where?" Lissa asked.

"Vic'Law," Kooper replied. "It started recently, and coincides with Cayetes' disappearance on Vogeffa I."

"Perhaps you should make arrangements, then," Lissa stood and moved around the table. Kooper tapped his comp-vid to enlarge the hovering image. "Vic'Law applied to join the Campiaan Alliance six years ago. Their application was rejected."

"A good sign that they're harboring the criminal element. Perhaps one of Cayetes' friends offered to conceal him."

"I suppose that's possible," Lissa agreed. "Whatever the reason, I can't get a lock on what's going on. That spells Sirenali involvement to me. No offense, Terrett."

Terrett shook his head, telling her silently that he'd not taken offense. He knew as well as anyone what might be accomplished by a Sirenali—employed or enslaved—by a criminal.

"I can be ready to go in an hour," Kaldill said. "Kooper, do you have a place for us to stay?"

"I can sort something out," Kooper nodded. "If you're ready to leave in two hours, I think I can have accommodations for you by then."

We'd received our marching orders, as Queen Lissa put it. I hoped Vic'Law was more hospitable than Gungl had been.

~

Lissa

"I hope we're circumventing the Orb, here," I said. I couldn't help pacing, although Karzac asked me to sit beside him on the end of my bed.

"Whether you are or not, I'm sure it will make its presence known eventually."

"Yeah." I sat beside him, then. He accommodated my unspoken request and pulled me close. "We haven't told them everything yet—in case the Orb shows up and tosses them elsewhere the moment they get to Vic'Law. Kooper says it'll only muddy the water if they memorize what must immediately be forgotten. Bel says he'll keep us informed," I said, settling my head on Karzac's shoulder.

"He will," Karzac soothed. "As will Kaldill."

"Kaldill isn't my grandson," I mumbled.

"I know. We can only do as much as we can do," he stroked a thumb gently across my cheek. "Bel has much of his grandmother in him. He will find his way."

"Erland says the same."

"Erland is wise. Come, they are preparing to leave. We will see them off."

Quin

Daragar would transport us—he'd already offered. It didn't matter how much we wanted to take—he would bring all of it.

Several of the Queen's comesuli packed everything for Terrett and me; therefore, we had little to do except fret while we waited.

Yanzi and Berel pulled us to the arboretum, where we found Kaldill, Justis, Lafe and Bel. Berel took my hand and led me to the glass surrounding the arboretum, then pointed out Casino City in the distance. I squinted to find other landmarks he described in the constant darkness surrounding the palace.

"I wish to see Avii Castle when we return," I said. I knew it lay in deep waters on the light half of the planet, and Dena had explained how they'd added shutters to every window, so they could close off the constant sunlight when necessary. The castle's residents found it easier to sleep that way.

"I'll make sure of it," Berel agreed. "The waters are rougher there, but that doesn't keep curious tourists away—many travel to Le-Ath Veronis just to see the castle, when they used to come in droves to gamble in Casino City."

"Either way, it's on everyone's list to see while they're here," Justis joined us at the window. "I always worry that Jurris will open the castle for tours, too, which will upset everything. The troops are distracted enough as it is."

"Justis and his troops pull thrill seekers from the water regularly. They jump off the boats, trying to swim to the castle, hoping they'll get a peek inside. They're dumped back on the boats, instead."

"I think they like getting hauled in by a winged soldier," Kaldill said. "Lendill lets me know when the social sites blow up with another vid—everybody on the tour boat records the rescues."

"Are you in vids?" I turned to Justis.

"More than I want to be," he grumbled. I laughed.

"It is time," Daragar said behind us. "I have already transported all your things to the designated site. Director Griff has outlined a reason for your presence on Vic'Law. You will find that information waiting for you there."

Forcing down sudden fear, I turned to face Daragar. *I will be with you often*, he reassured me.

I love you, I replied.

And I you.

With that, we were transported from Le-Ath Veronis.

"This isn't what I expected," Berel whispered as we looked about us. We found ourselves inside a small palace, with more than enough space and bedrooms for everyone.

"Kooper says we're running from the ASD," Salidar said, holding up a comp-vid. Somehow, he'd arrived with us, although he hadn't been in the Arboretum when the rest of us were moved.

"We're criminals? That didn't take long," Bel joked.

"Wealthy criminals," Kaldill observed. "We need a few servants to make this look real."

"You will be hiring," Kooper appeared to make the announcement. "I've placed agents inside the city—you'll hire them from the applicant pool."

"They know how to cook and clean?" Kaldill lifted an eyebrow.

"In addition to carrying weapons and handling them expertly," Kooper nodded. "I've laid the groundwork—you're drug smugglers that the ASD has finally caught up with, precipitating your removal from Le-Ath Veronis. You're wanted by the Queen, now."

"It appears drug smuggling is quite lucrative," Justis grimaced.

"You're wealthy—wealthy enough to live here for years without lifting a finger," Kooper agreed. "There's one other thing."

"I'll tell them," Kaldill said. "Except for Quin, Terrett and Justis, who weren't included in the initial requests, I've adjusted everyone else's appearance to match those on the application sent by the original criminals. To anyone else who sees the rest of you, you'll look different. You'll still be the same—to yourselves and the rest of us, but the outside world will see something different. Those images will also match the ones distributed by the ASD, who are now actively hunting us—according to their records."

"Those images are on the comp-vid Salidar has," Kooper said. "Study the images so you'll recognize them. Vic'Law allows for an extra six people to travel with those submitting the application; those six generally are wives, concubines or lovers. Quin, Terrett and Justis are the only three added to the original application."

"They will not see me as Larentii," Daragar supplied. "My humanoid disguise is included in those images."

This was becoming far more complicated than I'd expected. I wondered why they'd waited to tell us this, but shrugged it off. My mission was to find Vardil Cayetes and destroy him. I hoped it wouldn't take long to do so.

We'd arrived in the Vic'Law city of Der'Vek during the night, therefore, I didn't get to see the extensive grounds surrounding our palace until the following morning. Daragar and Kaldill had set perimeter shields so nobody could get inside without their permission while we slept.

I'd slept badly—the bed was fine enough, but the strangeness of the place unsettled me. Terrett and Yanzi hadn't fared much better—both were in the kitchen when I wandered in. I was offered tea and eggs. I accepted both.

"Der'Vek has six millions," Yanzi informed me while raking scrambled eggs onto my plate. "Will find fruit later," he promised.

"Big city, then," I nodded. "The eggs are wonderful," I chewed a mouthful.

"Reah teach," he grinned.

Sal says that people are disappearing from the poorer sections of Der'Vek, Terrett sent mindspeech to Yanzi and me. *We must find an excuse to go there.*

"That easy," Yanzi shrugged. "Claim missing kinsman. Ask questions. See what we find."

"Not bad," Justis joined us, taking a seat at the wide table. "We can say he had some reason to go there, then disappeared."

"We're working on it," Salidar arrived and set a mug on the table. He'd already had tea—that was evident.

"I've spoken with Kooper," he said. "After training," he turned to give me a stiff nod, "we'll venture into the city. It may take a day or two to officially lose an imaginary member of our party, but it'll be easy after that."

I discovered what Sal had been doing after rising so early; he'd turned a small ballroom into his dojo. That's what he called it, anyway. The wall decorations and lighting fixtures clashed with the canvas-padded floor, the racks of weights and wooden practice swords, but he refused to notice or apologize.

The main thing I carried away from my first lesson on Vic'Law was this; *move faster, punch harder.*

Der'Vek reminded me of my first sight of Kondar—tall, glass-clad buildings towered over shorter neighbors, leaving them in shadow during parts of the day. With six million inhabitants, it shouldn't be a surprise to see such a modern, sprawling city.

"There are strict laws, here," Berel informed me as our hovercar carried us along. "Littering is punished by a harsh beating, as are several other, somewhat minor infractions."

"I don't think I want to know what the more serious punishments are," I said, although I'd already seen it in his face.

Public beatings were handed out by a brutal constabulary. Berel's research on Vic'Law suggested that the criminals who ran the planet were very particular about what their residents could and couldn't do. Perhaps they took pleasure in another's pain—Yevil certainly had, and he was among the worst I'd ever seen.

As I hadn't met any of these yet, I couldn't say what their eyes and faces might reveal. The thought made me shudder.

"Are you cold?" Berel asked after witnessing my shiver.

"No. I was thinking about Vic'Law's criminal overseers."

The day was fine, sunny and cold—late fall had come to Der'Vek. Rain and storms were predicted later in the eight-day, but today was a good one to explore the city.

Newer streets were wide enough for eight lanes of hovercars; older streets were narrower and barely able to handle the passage of two going in opposite directions. Streets were clear of any type of debris; disposal recyclers were spaced evenly along the pedestrian sections.

"Almost everyone works for the government in some way, and as you know, the government is made up of criminals. Everything is mostly owned by the government, and housing is provided, according to your job," Salidar said. "We're here in place of the real criminals who had to apply to move here—Kooper and his agents shut down their operation on Le-Ath Veronis not long ago."

"I wouldn't be surprised to get a visit from the landlord, so to speak, and yes, we had to pay for the privilege of living where we do," Kaldill said. "Only a few are allowed to own land or the homes and businesses built on it—we're included in that lucky few."

"So the ones we're impersonating had to pass a strict eligibility test?" I asked.

"Yes," Kaldill smiled at me. "Very strict. The amount of money at our disposal was a rather large factor."

"What about the poorer sections, then?" I went on. "Do they work?"

"Most of them do, but they do physical labor. Many are disabled—as you can imagine, there are no government programs to take care of them if they are injured and can't work. They're often shuffled off to the slums in the hopes that they'll die. Sometimes those who live there take pity on them and share their food and housing. Some families are able to do the same; usually that means a better standard of living, although no food allowances are given for the disabled ones. Families have to stretch everything to feed another hungry mouth."

"Most of them die," Berel muttered. "It's the way things are, here."

"Reproduction is held to a minimum—the government doesn't want overpopulation," Sal explained. "They measure the deaths against allowed births. Mandatory sterilization is often their answer."

"This is a terrible place," I whispered, hugging myself as I studied the modern, overly clean city outside the hovercar's windows.

"Gungl had some sort of freedom," Lafe offered. "After you discount Cayetes' involvement."

"How did you get information on the disappearances?" Berel asked. "If Cayetes is here, I doubt the government, such as it is, would report it."

"Kooper and Teeg have agents here," Sal explained. "They live and work among the population. In effect, they're residents. We'll be hiring a few of them to work for us."

"I wish we could hire some of those disabled ones," I sighed. "I think I could make them better."

"My dear, you'd have to hide them from now on if you did that—the government has them micro-chipped and identified as disabled." Kaldill wore an expression of pity for those who couldn't be helped.

We can't fix everything, Justis sent.

We can try, I returned. He responded by rubbing his forehead.

"Where do the shops get their wares—are there factories?" Berel asked.

"Yes—owned by criminals, just as the businesses are. Prices are too high, as you might imagine," Sal clarified.

"Don't worry," Kaldill said. "Daragar and I will see to it that we are well-supplied during our stay. Our new employees will gather our allowances from the appropriate local places, but what we lack will be brought in."

"What about the criminals—do they bring supplies in, too?" I asked.

"Yes. They have ships that transport whatever they want," Sal answered. "They merely think that nobody else is entitled to those things."

"People live like slaves," Yanzi observed. I agreed with him, as I'd dealt with much the same thing most of my life.

"How will we hire the right ones, then, if the government has so much control?" I asked.

"That's one of the things our money purchases for us—our choice in domestic servants," Kaldill replied. "Names and images will be supplied—we will make appropriate selections."

I'd stopped looking at the city before we made our way back to our new home—I was no longer curious about any part of it—it was a shining surface, concealing a terrible disease.

CHAPTER 5

Quin

"Here are the images and work experience for those available," Kaldill set a comp-vid before me at breakfast the following morning. I found myself hoping Sal would have mercy on me during training—I hadn't slept well for the second night in a row.

Kaldill pointed out the ones who were hidden agents—Kooper had given that information to him. Out of the twenty or so agents, he and I chose fifteen. His arms were around me while we made our choices; I appreciated his care and concern.

Sal was not sympathetic.

"The enemy won't care that you've not had enough sleep," he informed me, his voice terse and unrelenting. "They'll merely badger you while they beat you senseless or kill you outright."

I hadn't complained of a lack of sleep—he could see the dark circles beneath my eyes for himself. Too many times, I failed to block his blows during that session and ended up limping out of the dojo.

At least he hadn't insulted me while he taught; that would have been too much, I think.

"I don't want anything," I grumbled when Terrett found me

soaking in the hot water of the indoor spa at lunchtime. "My ribs are almost too sore to breathe."

At least I'd found a swimsuit among my things, although it had been torture to pull it over an aching body before climbing into the spa.

I'll bring a sandwich, he said and walked away. Minutes later, he returned with Berel, Yanzi and a plate of food.

Yanzi turned to lion snake immediately and dropped into the water beside me. "Do you mind if we get in, too?" Berel asked.

"Of course not," I said without thinking. He and Terrett removed their clothing and climbed in with me. I should have been embarrassed.

I wasn't.

Justis merely lifted an eyebrow when he found us in the spa—I ate my sandwich while Yanzi, Terrett and Berel enjoyed the bubbling hot water.

I want that, too, Justis informed me silently. *Just the two of us,* he added before walking away.

"I haven't seen anything like this since leaving Fyris behind," I said. Berel, Daragar, Kaldill, Justis and I surveyed the building behind our small palace—this was where the servants were expected to stay when they weren't working.

"We will make improvements," Daragar declared. I'd seen what he was capable of doing—he and Kaldill both—while on Siriaa. The building, with cracked floors, no walls between beds and few comforts, was transformed that afternoon.

Walls appeared, with doors to afford privacy. A communal kitchen was built, with new appliances added. New tile replaced old on the floors, with a nice rug in each bedroom. Six bathrooms with extra toilets and shower stalls were added, to accommodate the residents when they arrived.

Last of all, Daragar provided uniforms for each servant—I suppose

Kaldill had given him information on each. They would dress in black, with silver trim. It reminded me greatly of what Lissa's palace employees wore. We would have no poorly dressed servants—not only were they ASD agents, but deserved whatever comforts we could give them.

"We'll do the interviews tomorrow—I asked for forty to be sent," Kaldill stated. It would be unwise to appear to pick and choose what we'd end up with; someone was likely watching every move we made.

Kaldill felt the same; we understood that somewhere, eyes were upon us as we settled into our new surroundings.

Freighter Killshot
  Bleek

"Commander Bleek, these farmers immigrated from an infected world." My First Lieutenant set a comp-vid before me.

"Verified?"

"Yes. They only got out of quarantine an eight-day ago—Pykris wouldn't allow them on the planet until they passed their physicals and were determined free of the poison."

"Where from?" I pushed the comp-vid back in Whip's direction.

"Gryphis," Whip shrugged. "I verified the transport myself."

I cursed. So far, this was the best lead we'd found. "Keep looking," I growled. "They have to be somewhere. I heard from Cayetes this morning. He has something special planned for any world found harboring Vogeffa II's refugees."

"I understand." Whip dropped his gaze. Cayetes always had something special planned for those he considered betrayers. Without further comment, he lifted the comp-vid and walked out of my temporary office aboard the freighter.

Quin

At least we went through stretching patterns the following day during training. I'd slept better the night before—Daragar had seen to it by placing a healing sleep. I suspected he'd eased my bruises, too, but didn't want to point that out to Salidar in case he decided to do a repeat of the previous day.

"When you complete your hand-fighting lessons, we'll start with wooden blades," Sal informed me when the session was over. "You're doing well so far—don't disappoint me."

"It is never my intention to disappoint you, Sursee," I dipped my head respectfully.

He chuckled while I walked away.

~

"She passed the test," Salidar took a seat beside Lafe at the small kitchen table and accepted a cup of tea from Terrett. "Most trainees complain when we force them to work after a sleepless night. Quin didn't say a word."

"Do you have any idea of the hardships that girl endured while growing up?" Justis thumped an empty mug on the table before taking his seat. "Those imbeciles in Fyris cut her wings off every spring. She never said a word then, either."

"I hadn't heard that," Salidar sighed. "I won't let it interfere with her training, but that's good information to know. How painful is that?"

Justis snorted his answer.

Tea? Terrett offered.

"Thank you," Justis nodded.

~

Quin

I found Lafe, Sal, Justis and Terrett talking in the kitchen when I arrived there for lunch. "Where are Yanzi and the others?" I asked during a lull in the conversation. They were discussing sparring with swords when I walked in; Justis wanted Lafe to teach him two-blade fighting.

"They're bringing food for lunch, then we'll meet the applicants in the reception area," Sal answered.

"Food," Berel announced as he, Kaldill and Bel appeared. Boxes and bags appeared with them; I caught the scent of apples immediately.

Terrett and I worked with Bel and Berel to put everything away; Lafe, Justis and Salidar set about making sandwiches.

"Cheese sandwich, my love," Justis handed a plate to me. "With crisps and a pickle spear."

"Thank you." I stood on tiptoe to give him a kiss. He hid his surprise well and deepened the kiss for a moment before pulling away and smiling at me. I'd made the first move this time—before, he or one of the others did.

With my cheeks flaming, I scurried toward the table, more than grateful that nobody laughed.

The interviews that afternoon were thorough; Kaldill, Justis and Sal asked the questions while I sat in a corner of the room, watching and listening.

Everything went according to plan, except for the next to last interview.

Kaldill, we have to hire her, I sent.

She's not one of our agents, he began. *We don't have a spot for her.*

She can help in the kitchen, I said.

Why do you wish to hire her? It could reveal us to the enemy.

I understand. I still want to hire her.

She can clean rooms, Sal suggested. It surprised me that he was taking up my cause. *She can stay in the house—there's a small room at the back,* he added. *That will keep her away from the others.*

I'll ask Lissa to place compulsion, Kaldill offered a mental sigh. *So she can't carry tales.*

She wouldn't anyway, but whatever makes you comfortable, I replied.

"You—are you prepared to clean and carry?" Kaldill asked the girl.

"I will do whatever you require." Her eyes were lowered—she hadn't looked at Kaldill during the entire interview.

"Cleaning will be enough," Kaldill said. "You will work for us."

"Thank you, Lord," she mumbled and shuffled toward the side of the room where our new employees waited.

She was the last of our hires—we now had sixteen servants, fifteen of whom were undercover ASD agents.

"They call me Jayna," she mumbled when I asked her name. I already knew that, but I wanted to make her comfortable. I couldn't tell her what I already knew about her—it would frighten her terribly.

"Do you like that name?" I asked.

"It's fine."

"Jayna, this is your room," I led her to the door at the back of our palace. "It's small, but it has its own bathroom. We'll have uniforms for you soon."

Jayna was little more than seventeen and had already led a drudge's life. That wasn't all she'd been exposed to, however. I was determined to correct that.

"This is mine—all of it?" Her eyes widened as she looked at me for the first time. She was pretty, with deep-blue eyes set in an oval face framed by dark-brown hair. She needed a haircut and a shower, but that could be easily arranged.

"It's yours," I said. "Soap and shampoo are already in the bathroom if you'd like to clean up and get comfortable. You don't have to work until tomorrow."

"Quinnie Bee," Lissa's hands dropped onto my shoulders as she appeared and smiled at Jayna. "Jayna, you will not be able to talk about anyone in this household, do you understand?" Jayna blinked and nodded as the Queen's compulsion settled over her.

"Better safe than sorry," Lissa hugged me. "You'll forget I was ever here," she added. Jayna nodded a second time.

"Thank you," I whispered to empty air.

Queen Lissa was already gone.

"You have wings," Jayna took a step backward. It was then I realized that Kaldill had shielded my wings—and probably Justis' too —from those who'd come for the interviews.

"I can't believe there are Avii here," one of our agent-cooks declared when I came to the kitchen for breakfast the following morning. "I'm Mell," she held out a hand to me. I took it, as was polite.

Justis had already arrived and wasn't thrilled with the sudden attention he was getting. *She's already had her hands on my feathers,* Justis grumbled. I could see he wasn't pleased that she'd touched him without asking permission.

"No touch without permission," Yanzi said as Mell's hand reached out to finger one of my wings. "Same with anybody. I not touch you unless you want," he added.

"Oh. Sorry." Mell went back to the stove. I released the breath I'd held when she reached for me.

"You were informed last night," the head cook scolded.

"Don't worry—most people are fascinated by wings," I sighed, taking the chair Justis pulled out beside his. "I hope you understand how unsettling it can be when everyone wants to touch."

"I never thought of that. I'm sorry," Mell apologized.

"Eggs are good," Justis nodded at Mell, who'd cooked them.

She smiled, which served to defuse the situation.

"We're having a meeting with all the agents after training and lunch," Sal informed me. "We'll get what information they have and go from there. We may be going into the slums tonight, depending on what we hear."

"All right," I nodded.

"Defensive posture," he snapped. My hands were up and ready before I even thought about it.

~

"He teaches you to protect yourself?" Jayna asked as I shrugged out of my training whites.

"Yes. I wish I were as good as he is, but that takes time," I sighed. "I'd like to avoid the bruises, too, but Lafe says that's a fool's dream when you're training or fighting."

"I wish I could learn those things," she mumbled, her eyes downcast.

"I'll ask, then, if that's what you want."

"I'm afraid I'll get you in trouble." She still didn't lift her gaze to me.

"I won't be in trouble. I'll ask," I insisted. I understood, too, why she would ask.

"Do you know how to read or write?" I continued. I knew the answer, but this was a polite way of getting information.

"No."

"Would you like to learn?"

"Who would teach me?" she snorted.

"Berel is a scholar," I shrugged. "He and I together can probably teach you."

"I would like more than anything to be able to read books," she whispered, her eyes shining. "You know most are outlawed here— some see them as a waste of time."

I wanted to weep at her explanation. Vic'Law, for me, had become a much larger version of Fyris. I wondered at those who ran it—at how short-sighted they were. Yevil and Tamblin had destroyed Fyris in a short amount of time. I resolved to sit with Berel and research Vic'Law's criminal overseers.

"We will teach you two hours each day," I promised. "You will have your evenings to read and study."

"Is this a dream?" she asked, her voice soft and timid. Her eyes met mine, begging me silently to say it wasn't a lie.

"It isn't a lie, Jayna. Learning isn't easy, but it is worth every moment."

~

"These are ones we know have been taken," Pellen, the lead agent, set a comp-vid before Kaldill. Sal and Justis sat on either side of Kaldill, with the rest of us scattered throughout Kaldill's suite.

"Quin?" Kaldill turned to me and beckoned.

"What can the girl do?" Pellen huffed.

"More than you know," Justis growled. I walked toward Kaldill and accepted the comp-vid. Five images were shown—three female, two male. The females were all pretty girls in their mid to late teens. The males were slightly older and in prime physical shape.

"I don't believe they're missing for the reasons we think," I said. Part of the reason I'd understood after seeing Jayna. Another part of the reason was hidden from me, but I was getting used to foggy roadblocks to needed information.

"What do you know?" Kaldill asked. I was resolved not to say anything about Jayna when I explained that someone was choosing the young, handsome and beautiful from the slums to sell as sex slaves.

"What the fuck?" Pellen cursed.

"You just described many crime families on Vic'Law," Jeslin, the head cook, observed. Mell, standing beside him, nodded her agreement. "Most are tied to multiple crimes—the sex slave trade is a lucrative one, so this doesn't surprise me. This could be any crime family on Vic'Law."

"Quin will know when she sees them," Kaldill said.

"We must wait for them to approach us," Pellen inserted smoothly. "That is the way of this world."

What the hell is Cayetes up to—if this is Cayetes. You think he's following in his brother's footsteps and merely selling older children? Bel silently asked.

It would appear that way, Sal replied. "I intend to go to the slums tonight," he said aloud.

"I'm going with him," Lafe agreed.

"Then Terrett and I will go," I said. "To hide you from those who have wizards or warlocks in their employ."

"You're not going without me," Justis said, giving me a pointed look.

"I go," Yanzi declared.

"I guess we're all going," Kaldill sighed.

This is where one of the girls lived, Sal informed us as we landed on the roof of a poorly constructed two-story building. Little more than a dormitory, the structure was crowded on three sides by others just like it.

When was she taken? Bel asked.

A week ago, Sal replied. *Her family is devastated.*

How you know this? Yanzi spoke next.

I was here two days ago—as wolf. I saw and heard a lot. They didn't see me—I know better than that.

I here last night—as snake, Yanzi responded. *I hear things, too. Some families afraid to report loss—they lose food allowance.*

This is so fucked up, Bel said.

Are we going to talk to them? Kaldill asked. *Or just stand on their roof and discuss it all night?*

We will speak with them, Daragar appeared. *I will ensure that they do not remember us afterward.*

I always suspected that Larentii had their own version of compulsion, Kaldill grinned.

We do not employ it often, Daragar sounded as if he were offended.

Let's go—it's cold up here, Berel said.

It was cold—even though we were warmly dressed, the wind had risen, chilling exposed skin. A bleak, early winter had arrived in Der'Vek.

~

"Who are you?" The man couldn't have been more than forty, but the work he did beneath the streets of Der'Vek had served to age him past his years. His anger at his lot in life, coupled with the disappearance of his daughter, made him angrier than usual.

"We are looking for one of ours," Kaldill replied smoothly. "A young girl—a daughter. We are searching for her. We hope you can give us information on your daughter's disappearance. In return, we will also look for her."

At first, the man appeared confused as he stood in the doorway, blocking the weak light from inside with his bulk. "Come in," he turned and walked back in the house, expecting us to follow.

"We don't know," the wife wiped tears away. "She worked in one of the shops in the city, selling sweets to those who can afford them. An eight-day ago, she never came home. We've asked those who live on the edge of our area—they didn't see her walk past, as she usually does."

"How did she come by that job?" Sal asked.

"They only take the pretty ones to work in the shops," the man grumbled. "Reetha was pretty. Like her mother."

"Our experience is much the same," Kaldill agreed. "Pretty—and now missing."

"Constables say they're looking into it, but nothing ever gets done when it involves one of ours," the man said. "They only come to take the bodies away when we die."

"We know this," Lafe nodded.

I watched Justis—he stood in a corner of the badly furnished apartment, his eyes hooded, arms crossed tightly over his chest. Once again, Kaldill had hidden our wings, else we'd never have been allowed inside the house.

"You should keep that one hidden," the wife pointed at me. "Whoever is doing this would certainly consider her."

"We are watchful," Kaldill said as I forced myself not to shiver.

"I wish we'd taken the rumors more seriously," the wife said. "I don't think we'll ever see Reetha again."

"We'll go," Kaldill said softly as the man rose to comfort his wife, who'd started weeping.

All of us were somber as we left Reetha's parents to grieve behind us. Daragar stayed behind for a moment—he was ensuring that these didn't remember our visit.

Tomorrow, we visit the sweet shop, Sal said.

"How are they hiding information from us?" Bel asked. I could tell he'd used his warlock gift to search for clues, but hadn't found anything.

Terrett made a growl in his throat.

Another meeting was held, once we arrived at our palace after visiting Reetha's parents. The agents were included, as they were before. Only Jayna wasn't present—she was sleeping already.

"They wouldn't," I turned to Terrett in alarm.

He laced my fingers in his and shook his head—he couldn't say for sure, either, but on at least one occasion, a Sirenali child had been sold to hide criminal activity.

"What are you talking about?" Pellen demanded.

"Terrett's race," Sal said. "He has a special talent for hiding activity from the powerful, so he was sold as a child to criminals, who cut out his tongue to prevent him from speaking."

"That's barbaric," Mell declared.

"We worry that more of his race may be here," Kaldill said. "Possibly held against their will and used for the same purpose—to hide criminal activity."

"Why would the sweet shop be hidden?" Jeslin pointed his question toward Sal.

"That's what we need to find out—it may be the place where targets are marked and taken. If so, then a Sirenali's presence would be more than justified."

"I know this is the capital city, but what about other cities?" I asked.

"There are others, but this is where the crime families make their homes," Pellen replied. He raked a hand through dark hair peppered with silver—he was eldest of the agents present and it showed. "All the manufacturing is done elsewhere—they don't want the stink of their factories to spoil the air in Der'Vek. Farming is done between cities, most of it near the equator so crops may be grown year-round."

"All ASD agents on the planet are here in Der'Vek," Jeslin added. "To watch the crime families."

"Who runs the other cities?" I asked. Someone had to, and I couldn't imagine they'd turn that task over to the normal population.

"Brothers and sisters, sons and daughters, nieces and nephews," Pellen shrugged. "They're being groomed to take over here, should the need arise."

"It's government by a council of criminals," Mell offered. "They call themselves the Grand Coalition. Each member has an equal vote, which is as close to a democracy as they'll ever get."

"Will we be a part of that?" I asked.

"We have to live here three years and then be invited to join the lowest tier. They'll watch us between now and then," Kaldill explained.

This is confusingly fucked, Terrett informed me. I'd never heard him use profanity before, but he was correct.

You're right, I agreed. *I think there's more going on than they suspect, and we haven't gotten any real information, yet.*

Only living in one city equates to wearing blinders, Terrett returned. *They have no idea what's going on. This is where the criminals live. Their work goes on elsewhere.*

I think the same.

I know this—I've lived among them most of my life, Terrett snorted. *I know how they think, their often twisted idea of pleasure, their greed—all of it.*

I wish I could fold space, I replied. *You and I would do our own investigation.*

We must convince them, Terrett said. *I do not wish to place you in danger. Promise me that you will never go out alone. That will frighten me more than I have ever been.*

I'll try, I closed my eyes for a moment. Terrett couldn't hide his concern—it soaked from his skin into mine as he gripped my hand tighter. Before I realized it, my head was on his shoulder and I was huddling into his warmth.

I didn't mean to scare you, he soothed. His hand disentangled from mine and his arms went around me. I felt embarrassed that the others were watching, but I closed my eyes tightly and struggled to ignore them.

My love, is everything all right? Kaldill asked gently.

I scared myself, mostly, I replied. If I'd spoken aloud, my voice would have trembled.

"We will take this up again tomorrow," Sal announced and ushered the agents out of Kaldill's suite.

"Quinnie?" Yanzi reached Terrett and me first.

"I'm all right," I croaked, pulling away from Terrett's shoulder.

We worry that there is more going on than the agents think, Terrett sent blanket mindspeech.

"Terrett knows criminals—he's been forced to live among them most of his life," I mumbled. "That's why we think that Der'Vek isn't the only problem."

"Don't shit where you eat," Bel Erland nodded his head. "That's one of Gran's phrases, but it fits."

"You think that missing people is only scratching the surface?" Lafe asked. He didn't sound skeptical—he sounded convinced.

"Yes," I said. Suddenly, I felt weary. It was quite late and breakfast and another training session were scheduled early in the morning.

"We still need to visit the sweet shop," Sal said. He was right—it was a place to start and all we had at the moment.

"It will be a hard winter," Daragar announced as he materialized. His words sounded prophetic to me. I dipped my chin to acknowledge his truth.

Zephili

"Any word from Bleek?" Vardil examined his new body in the mirror.

His assistant, Dorgus, shook his head. "Nothing today, my Lord," he replied. "You look quite fine, Lord Vardil. You can walk down the streets of any of Zephili's cities and be admired."

"You think so?" Vardil preened a bit before the mirror.

"Most certainly. May I interest you in a late meal? Transferences can be draining, or so Deris claims."

"A meal sounds quite appealing. Dress me and have food delivered to my suite."

"As you require, my Lord."

"Dorgus, do you think there's a way to keep this body—or at least this look?" Vardil was back to preening. "This is the finest, handsomest body I've ever had."

"I'll look into it, my Lord."

~

Bleek

Barc was six when the disease came. That was nearly eight sun-turns ago. The disease ravaged his body for two sun-turns before he was placed in stasis—it would have killed him, otherwise. In stasis, he still looks eight. If he were wakened, he would have only an eight-year-old's memories.

So much has happened since he was placed in stasis and locked in a spelled glass coffin by Deris and his sister, Daris. At times, I worry that I will die, leaving Barc to this fate forever—lying still within a glass coffin, waiting to be awakened with power so he might breath his last breaths alone and unloved.

My soul belongs to Vardil Cayetes. Not only in payment for keeping my son alive; the deeds I've performed in service to Cayetes ensures that his grip on me—and my fate—remains tight.

I no longer recognize the Blevakian in the mirror; I have traveled so far from what I was. I only see a murderer, now. Someone my child would not be proud of.

I have no choice, I keep telling myself before turning back to Cayetes' latest demand. I had three more worlds to examine. Three more newly arrived communities of farmers to research.

I had an idea what Cayetes planned for the world found guilty of taking what he thought was his—but that had caused so much trouble the first time, I wondered that he was considering the same again.

"Not my concern," I muttered to myself.

"Did you say something, Commander?" Whip asked.

"No, Whip, just thinking aloud."

Quin

My breakfast was a fruit omelet with juice; my training session included Jayna, which surprised me. I hadn't had time to ask Sal about her training, thinking that perhaps Lafe would train her if I asked.

Instead, Sal had invited her and she'd been overjoyed to accept.

That's when I learned that for my training, another Sursee would join us every day. Caylon Black arrived, offered Sal a brief nod and proceeded to take over my training.

"Defensive position," Sursee Caylon barked and I immediately complied. He came at me, peppering me with blows.

I was able to block most of them.

"Thank you, Sursee," I bowed low to him when the lesson was over.

"Tomorrow," he replied, dipping his chin slightly in reply.

"I told you she was learning quickly, Caylon," Sal grinned and offered Caylon a cup of Falchani black tea.

"Faster than I imagined," Caylon nodded. "That will work well for her, since her bones are more fragile than most humanoids. In a few weeks, I'll ask Torevik to come, just to see how she reacts to a much taller opponent."

"Caylon, I hope you don't mind staying," Kaldill arrived in the kitchen, interrupting his and Sal's conversation. "We've received an invitation to stay with the Churg family—for the next month."

CHAPTER 6

Quin

"The Churg family?" My confusion must have been evident—Justis pulled me against him as the news was given to us.

"I thought they'd drop by unannounced and take a look, then leave," Sal said. "I never considered that we'd be invited to spend time with them."

"It's a command, disguised as an invitation," Bel said. "On their turf. Their servants, too, unless we wish to take a personal servant. Quin, you can take Jayna if you want; you'll be known in that household as Quin BlackWing."

"When are we expected?" Lafe asked.

"Tomorrow. They're sending vehicles so we'll pack tonight, after we visit the sweet shop."

"I think only a few should go to the shop," Sal said. "Quin, Terrett, Yanzi and I."

"Wait," Justis held up a hand.

"No, he's right," Kaldill nodded. "Only a few. It won't do for all of us to crowd in."

"Then I'll wait in the car," Justis huffed, pulling me tighter against his chest.

"I'll wait with you," Caylon nodded. "Pellen can drive us."

~

More than an hour later, Pellen parked the car near the sweet shop. I'd expected the business to be small.

It was far from small.

"This is owned by one of the minor families—second tier," Pellen explained as I gaped at the building that took up a city block. "There's a bakery, a chocolate-making section and a candies section, with an attached restaurant and shop."

"The poor section we visited can't afford this, can they?" Justis said.

"No," Pellen replied. "But their sons and daughters work here, as you've likely guessed. The prettier ones. Uniforms are provided, of course—they can't afford that, either. The higher-skilled workers are given better allowances to spend as they like. Those from the slums in low-skilled positions can't hope for something this nice."

I recalled a time when I'd never tasted sweets—they were reserved for better and higher born. Justis' face was grim as he turned his gaze briefly on me. I clamped my wings tighter to my back, distressed by the memory of my past.

"You not worry," Yanzi pushed a stray lock of hair behind my ear. I missed my lighter hair at times such as these. He'd never seen the real colors of it.

"Come," Sal nodded to Terrett, Yanzi and me. We climbed out of the car and walked across the street.

A bell rang over the shop door when we walked inside. I'd been to Niff's in Casino City, once, where sweets crowded behind glass displays, each type competing with its neighbor to draw a customer's gaze.

This shop rivaled that image. Someone walked in behind us and went straight to the counter.

"These are for Master Barstle," the clerk lifted boxes from behind the counter. I watched as Sal and Yanzi went perfectly still for a moment, before turning my attention to the boxes in question.

Yanzi and Sal learned what they knew by scent; I learned it with my gift.

I just didn't have a name for it, yet.

Yanzi and Sal, though—they knew.

I also knew that nothing else in the shop contained what those boxes contained. Our mystery had just deepened, and I had no idea what to do about it.

"May I help you?" The clerk—a pretty girl of perhaps sixteen, asked after the first customer left the shop with the boxes he'd been given.

"We'd like a table in the restaurant, please," Sal said, his voice smooth and a smile lighting his face.

"Of course. I'll call for someone to take you in."

A young man arrived moments after she called; he led us through a wide doorway and into the restaurant, which specialized in sandwiches, soups and the sweets produced onsite.

Order dessert, Sal instructed. *Yanzi, the restrooms are nearby. Do you think you can change and look around without being noticed? If not, I'll come back later with Caylon.*

I can, Yanzi agreed. *Eat slow. I be back.*

"He'll have the redberry cake," Sal ordered for Yanzi. I had a chocolate fudge cake with vanilla ice cream, while Terrett ordered a slice of caramel swirl cake.

It's all right—the food, I said, when it was set in front of us. Yanzi still wasn't back, but our waiter didn't say anything.

Yanzi was back before we finished and ate swiftly, demolishing his dessert in very little time. Mine was good, but what I'd gotten at Niff's was better.

Sal paid, producing a small, gold coin to hand to the waiter.

He smiled and went to put the money away while we gathered coats and hats. "Come again," the clerk in the shop said as we walked out the door.

Sal didn't say anything until we were in the car and moving away from the shop. "What the bloody, fucking hell is drakus seed doing on Vic'Law?" he cursed.

~

"We had no idea," Pellen said. I wondered whether our scheduled visit with the Churg Family would put a crimp in our investigation.

We hadn't heard everything yet, however.

"I see what hiding those at shop," Yanzi volunteered. "I made, not born," he began. "Sirenali at shop—also made, not born. He look—he look like Terrett, when Terrett change."

It was my turn to grip Terrett's hand—he was growling low in his throat again. "How old?" Kaldill asked, voicing my question aloud.

"Half-grown," Yanzi described the Sirenali. "Not speak."

"Probably can't," Justis huffed. "This is impossible. How many do you think they can make?"

"If this first batch—all same age," Yanzi shrugged. "That how it was for me; they make many. Sell. Kill some, too."

"I thought drakus seed—and all the plants were destroyed," Pellen insisted.

"Hmmph," Yanzi snorted. Terrett nodded once at Yanzi.

"We should inform Kooper," Kaldill suggested.

I watched Pellen's face—he'd missed this and felt he was responsible. While drakus seed hadn't been seen during his lifetime, he knew the history of it. He imagined that Kooper would accost him for missing the information, too. After all, if the drug were in the hands of the criminals on Vic'Law, then it could be transported elsewhere.

Sal, Justis and Pellen went to find Caylon the moment we arrived at our palace; I found Berel waiting for me. "Quin, we have a class to teach, then we have to pack," Berel took my hand.

"Yes," I sighed. "Let's find Jayna."

~

The Churg-owned hovercars arrived after breakfast the following morning. We were transported into the hills overlooking most of Der'Vek, which culminated in a view of one of Vic'Law's oceans.

"Don't forget, you're with us," I reassured Jayna, although I felt queasy at the prospect of living with a crime family, whose sole purpose in inviting us was to place us under the closest of scrutiny.

Pellen accompanied us as Kaldill's personal servant; Mell, Jayna and Jeslin would fetch and carry for everyone else. The rest of the staff stayed behind at our palace.

We saw the Churg family holdings from the air—it looked like a small city, with numerous buildings, pools and gardens surrounding an enormous palace.

Eventually, the car settled on the stone patio at the back of the palace. Another car, carrying our bags, landed behind us.

Two men waited for us at the foot of white marble steps. "Welcome to the Churg estate," one of them said, sweeping out his hand in a grand gesture. "Master Churg invites you to join him for dinner tonight at eight bells. Nerr will take you to your quarters, and provide any assistance you may need to settle in."

I was hoping we'd have a separate place to stay, Justis' mental voice was dry.

Already I hate this, Terrett informed me.

This fucked, Yanzi declared.

"Extend our gratitude to Master Churg for his invitation; we look forward to dining with him this evening," Kaldill responded. This was the Elf King, who could outclass anyone with style and grace. I didn't miss the hardness in his eyes, however. Churg would be under our scrutiny, just as we were under his.

Jayna and Mell were given a room to share, as were Pellen and Jeslin near the suites in our wing of the palace. I was grateful none of the Churg family was quartered nearby—so far, we hadn't seen any of them.

The palace was so huge, it really wasn't a surprise that we'd only seen servants. Clothing I'd never thought to wear hung inside the closet adjoining my bath; the suite I'd been given was larger than the one I had at our mansion in Der'Vek.

Churg servants had been instructed not to speak to us unless we asked a direct question, but the two who unpacked my things couldn't help staring at my wings. With my gift, I understood that they were bursting with curiosity, and I imagined that Justis was receiving similar treatment inside his suite, which lay across the hall.

"Quin?" Justis appeared in my doorway, as if he'd been called. Likely it was to escape the scrutiny of the servants.

Where is Kaldill? I asked.

"Come down the hall with me," Justis held out a hand. I moved toward him and allowed his hand to grasp mine. His hand and fingers were warm and reassuring as they enveloped mine.

Both servants inside my suite sighed as we left—I heard the sound easily as Justis and I walked away.

Kaldill wouldn't shield our wings from those who owned and ran Vic'Law; our race and photographs had been included in the final application. Berel joined us as we walked along the hall; Yanzi and Terrett caught up with us as well.

We found Kaldill, Sal, Lafe, Bel and Caylon inside Kaldill's suite. "I've asked for lunch to be delivered here," Kaldill informed us. As the designated head of our family, Kaldill received the largest suite, just as he'd done at our palace.

"I have a sound shield set up," Bel said. "We can talk without anyone listening."

"Quin, if you detect anything about Cayetes in anyone in this household, send mindspeech immediately," Sal said. "It's in our best interest to find him, as you know."

I understood that—Cayetes was my priority as well, but I couldn't help thinking that other, more pressing matters had taken precedence. I also couldn't explain it—not to anyone—in a reasonable way. Terrett might understand, but I wasn't sure about the others.

The drug we'd discovered at the sweet shop troubled my mind just as much as the disappearances, and the fact we weren't searching other cities concerned me greatly. I wasn't in charge, however, and wasn't likely to be. I studied Salidar DeLuca as he outlined a plan in case we discovered Cayetes' whereabouts. I also wondered how (and when) he'd taken charge of this operation.

Caylon's presence, too, felt just the same—that he was Sal's superior in this and his word could be the final one on any decisions made.

Kooper Griff, Bel Erland's voice drifted into my head. *He made these decisions. Nobody here has enough field experience to take charge.*

How did you know? I returned. He'd read my thoughts, somehow.

I could see you, shifting your gaze from Sal to Caylon, he replied. *I've spent too much time reading Dad's subjects in court. I know what those glances and puzzled expressions mean.*

Then you are an adept, I responded. *Nobody else has a clue.*

I saw his smile—a genuine one—for the first time since we'd arrived on Vic'Law. It was worth the wait; he bore a strong resemblance to his grandfather, Erland. *Perhaps,* I thought to myself, *I'd have another ally, should I make my request to hunt elsewhere.*

Just ask, Lady, he nodded slightly. *I am at your service.*

"Your reading lessons will be in Quin's suite; this is where you will learn from Sursee Salidar," Caylon led Jayna through our temporary dojo. Already, wooden practice blades and weights hung on a wall, while the floor was covered with the inevitable canvas mat.

I'd already seen the room earlier; Jayna, who'd been settling into her shared room with Mell, had just gotten free to visit with me. Caylon found both of us and now led the tour through our training room.

"I'm afraid," she whispered when Caylon stopped for a moment.

"Don't be. It is our decision whether we will train our servants or not," Caylon said softly. "Come to me or Salidar if anyone troubles you about it."

"Yes, Sursee Caylon." She dropped her eyes.

"Sursee Caylon, I'd like to ask Kaldill to provide a disguise for her while she's here," I said.

Caylon blinked dark eyes at me for a moment before nodding. "I'll see to it," he agreed. "Come. We will pay Master Kaldill a visit."

~

"Easily done," Kaldill said the moment I asked. Jayna, who was quite confused by this time, could only stare at Kaldill in shock as he changed her appearance. After all, she felt nothing, and to us, she appeared the same. To anyone else, she would be quite plain, tall and sturdily built. The perfect candidate in Churg's eyes to train to protect us.

"This is what you look like to anyone outside our family," Kaldill handed her a small mirror. "To us, you are yourself and appear no different."

"How is this possible?" Jayna breathed.

"Ah. Since you cannot carry tales, then perhaps you should know that some elves wander outside their lands—when necessity demands," Kaldill smiled.

"Elves are real?" Jayna's eyes grew quite large. "There's real magic?"

"Real power, and yes, elves are real—just as winged people are real."

"I've only heard stories," Jayna mumbled, her eyes dropping again.

"You'll be reading the truth soon enough," I put an arm around her. "Berel and I will teach you."

"Where will the books come from?"

"Don't worry about the books," Berel smiled at her. "We'll find what you need."

~

I was dressed well enough and flanked by Justis and Terrett when we walked into the grand dining hall of the Churg estate. My stomach wanted to rebel at the thought of having dinner with known criminals.

That turned out to be the easiest part.

"Father, I want wings," Birtes Churg's fifteen-year-old daughter demanded the moment she caught sight of Justis and me.

"Zela, these are our guests," Birtes smiled at his eldest daughter. "We will ask where their wings came from, and then I shall find some for you."

"I want wings, too," a six-year-old said in a high voice.

"My dear, you shall have them," Birtes said, leaning down and kissing six-year-old Rela on the forehead.

"She always gets her way," Zela fumed as Rela clapped her hands and beamed at her father. These were spoiled children who'd developed a rivalry, each attempting to get something the other didn't have.

May the gods be merciful, Terrett muttered inside my head. I could see that he'd dealt with the spoiled children of wealthy criminals before.

Does he have other children? Justis asked.

An older son, who is working in Puntia, I replied. I'd seen that in Birtes—his son was much older than his daughters were—by design. Birtes didn't want the younger ones to struggle against his eldest, so there was twenty years difference between Nardes, his son, and Zela, his second-born.

Puntia is a manufacturing city north and east of here, Berel offered. *It isn't the largest one, however—Mundia is the largest manufacturing city. It is run by the Juffa clan, the biggest and wealthiest crime family.*

"Please, sit," Birtes invited. Both his daughters insisted on sitting between Justis and me. Rela's small hands were all over my feathers during dinner, with no polite orders from her parents to stop.

Justis silently fumed as Zela ran her hands down his wings on several occasions. They'd never been taught manners or consideration for others, that was obvious. Zela—well, she was fortunate that Justis found her contemptible. Any other man that she touched that way would take it as an invitation for sex.

I was grateful the girls were sent to bed after dinner, while the rest of us were invited for an after-dinner drink in another room. I knew the question was coming, I just wasn't sure how to answer.

"The information concerning our winged companions is in the final paperwork we submitted," Kaldill explained patiently for the second time. "They are born with the predisposition to grow wings—the only race to do so. They manifest in the child's ninth year."

"I will demand that Juffa send copies of the paperwork," Birtes muttered. He was angry that he couldn't get wings for his daughters that were exactly like Justis' and mine.

"There are mechanical wings that can be grafted, but they require a delicate operation," Caylon inserted smoothly. "When your daughters are fully grown, the operation can be performed. For now, their bones are still growing and no reputable physician will perform the graft, as it could damage their bodies."

"This is untenable," Birtes grumbled.

He doesn't want to say no to his children, I sent to Justis. I wished at that point that Kaldill had hidden our wings from the Churg family.

He is weak, Justis replied.

Justis was correct—Birtes inherited his position from his father. He had no problem allowing his son and employees to see to his interests in the world of crime on Vic'Law. What did it matter to him if people died through the use of poorly manufactured weapons that his factories produced?

He'd cut corners—that was easy enough for me to see. His weapons were affordable to non-Alliance armies, who kept buying, even when many of their members died from using the weapons in question.

I sent the information I'd seen in Birtes to Justis and Caylon; I knew they'd pass it to Kooper Griff.

Birtes was fit enough, but only because he had regular medical treatments to keep his weight under control. He was vain—anyone could see that in the way he dressed. His four wives were beautiful; that was all he cared about—that they were pretty enough to be seen with him.

We had to spend a month with him.

I could see that none of our party was looking forward to any part of that month.

~

New Fyris

"Where is she, then?" Amlis asked as he and Torevik Rath were served wine in Amlis' study. He'd learned in the past two days that Quin was alive.

"On a non-Alliance world, searching for the criminal who destroyed Siriaa," Tory explained. "It's complicated, too, and I'm not allowed to say more than that."

"I know she probably doesn't want it, but I'd like to see her," Amlis stood and strode toward the window overlooking the castle courtyard.

"Perhaps when this assignment is finished," Tory shrugged.

"I'll extend an invitation," Amlis said. "She will be welcome in New Fyris anytime."

"How are the new arrivals fitting in?" Tory asked, changing the subject.

"Very well. Brandl has been appointed Chancellor of New Vogeffa; he attends Council meetings and carries four votes with him. His son, Randl, well, I've asked that he be allowed to serve here in the palace. The boy is an actual seer, and I can't say how valuable that would be to me. We have some of ours working with the volunteers your mother sent, teaching them how to use the farming equipment. They seem to be dealing with the changes well enough."

"They're probably happy that the laws of the Alliance protect them, now," Tory offered. "So they decided to call their land New Vogeffa?"

"Yes—the name was recently submitted for approval to the Grand Alliance Council. We expect to hear from them in a month, regarding approval. As for the Alliance laws, Brandl is very intrigued about them —we're teaching him and the others to read and write, by the way. Who is with Quin—to protect her?"

"Several, including the Falchani blade master who taught me. She is as safe as we can keep her, given the circumstances."

"I'm glad," Amlis sighed. "Will you keep me informed as to her progress? I realize that Siriaa was dying because of the poison, but still it is a blow that it no longer exists."

"It was your home. I'd feel the same way about Le-Ath Veronis. It's where I grew up and I'd be furious if someone destroyed it."

~

Zephili

"Lord Cayetes, did you call?" Dorgus spoke softly—the hour was early, before dawn reached the plantation.

"I had a dream. The same one for the third night," Vardil complained.

"My Lord, it was but a dream," Dorgus began.

"No. This one is different. In each dream, a glowing sphere hangs over my bed. It tells me I am marked for death. This time, I shouted at it. I demanded to know who was invading my sleep to tell me such lies. It responded," Vardil threw covers back and dropped his legs over the side of his bed before standing.

"What did it say?" Dorgus asked, lifting Vardil's robe from a chair and holding it out so Vardil could slip into it.

"It said *I am Liron, and I have commanded your death*," Vardil whispered in bewilderment.

~

Vic'Law

Quin

Ignore them, Caylon sent mindspeech. Jayna and I had an audience —Zela and Rela, with their nanny and companions, arrived to watch our lessons the following morning. Jayna did ignore them—mostly in self-defense. She may have had a fit of terrors if she hadn't. In my opinion, Sal was working miracles with her, keeping her engaged and her mind far from the audience we couldn't turn away.

Caylon set about doing the same; I had to concentrate on the blows he delivered so I could block them, which kept my mind on the lesson.

I had no idea that Caylon working shirtless would draw a tremendous amount of attention—but I should have known better. The onlookers didn't know whether to stare at the tattoos he wore of black panthers or at my wings—which I employed often to block blows.

Before long, I realized that Caylon had removed his shirt deliberately—to draw some of the attention away from me. By the end of our session, four household guards had also slipped in. I could see in their faces that they were interested in getting tattoos, now.

I wondered if Lafe would keep his skills to himself—after all, he'd done Caylon's tattoos. I knew that he'd begrudged many tattoos he'd done while in Gungl—before, the tattoos he'd done had been deserved by the Falchani warriors he'd inked.

"The demonstration is now over," Caylon nodded to all our observers. "Anyone who comes from now on will be expected to train. When Salidar and I train, we do not train shirkers or the curious. Our students will be serious or they will not be our students. I suggest you seek other training if that is the case."

I saw a widening of eyes—neither daughter nor the caregivers who'd come wanted to be pummeled—Caylon had given them a demonstration of what would happen when a student failed to block his blows. He'd thrown me to the mat four times, and I knew I'd have bruises from those falls.

When Jayna and I walked out of the dojo, Lafe and Justis walked in. Lafe would teach Justis two-blade fighting.

"Thank you, Sursee Caylon," I bowed to him before walking out the door. He nodded to me. Jayna did the same for Sal.

"Ugly, that one," a guard muttered at Jayna's back. I saw her smile; she was happy with her disguise.

Zephili

"I received word from Bleek," Magul reported to Vardil. "Three more worlds have been examined; the ones you seek weren't on any of them." Magul studied Vardil after delivering the news—he'd never seen Vardil so haggard, even wearing a body that needed replacement.

Dorgus said Vardil wasn't sleeping; Magul could see the evidence for himself. "I have another assignment," Vardil growled.

"Of course, my Lord," Magul offered a respectful nod.

"I want you to search for anyone named Liron and report your findings to me. I warn you, I may require deaths, should you find any bearing that name."

"With pleasure, my Lord."

Vic'Law

Quin

"We're not prisoners, although we should inform our host whenever we go on an outing," Kaldill said. Pellen poured tea for him as we had lunch in his suite—Berel, Yanzi, Terrett and I.

Bel Erland had decided to train with Justis and Lafe, while Sal and Caylon had chosen to have lunch delivered to a table in the garden.

"Where were you thinking of going?" I asked.

"To the high-end shops near the ocean—where the wealthy families buy. The shops are owned by their contemporaries, as you may imagine."

"I search for drakus seed there," Yanzi nodded. "I smell; Quin see."

"We're invited to a ball at the Juffa estate next eight-day," Kaldill sighed. "We must be properly dressed and on alert—this will be a part of their test," he added.

"What about Justis and the others?" Berel asked.

"They'll make a separate shopping trip," Kaldill shrugged. "It will provide us with an excellent opportunity to look for Cayetes' involvement, plus anything else Director Griff should know. He was quite unhappy with the news that drakus seed is being grown somewhere—perhaps here. All his agents are now on high alert, including those we left at the house in Der'Vek."

That worried me immediately. "Will they be investigating while we're here?" I asked.

"I believe that's what they've been told to do." I watched as Kaldill set his teacup down, the cup making a tiny, chinking sound as it settled on the saucer. At that moment, I wished Kooper Griff hadn't ordered our new servants to do investigative work while we were forced to stay with the Churgs. I couldn't imagine that anything good would come from either of those things.

"You worried," Yanzi turned to me.

"Yes. We're going to lose some and face possible exposure." I also felt ill—what I'd eaten had suddenly turned sour in my stomach.

"Three of ours have been killed," Caylon appeared inside Kaldill's suite.

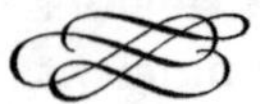

CHAPTER 7

Quin

Until that moment, I'd only suspected that Caylon could fold space. My suspicions had been proven correct, but were accompanied by terrible news.

"Where? How?" Berel was already on his feet, his hands clenched as if he were preparing for war.

"A few blocks from the sweet shop," Caylon growled. I could see him struggling to hold back his anger—he wanted to find those responsible immediately.

My wings were clamped tightly to my back—I'd known the moment Kaldill told us about the investigations that something was wrong. Terrett gripped my hand. I turned toward him. *We'll sort this out,* he promised.

"We have to go shopping as planned," Kaldill said. Once again, his eyes had become hard. I pitied anyone who thought to cross the Elf King when he looked like that.

"We've already alerted Kooper," Caylon blew out a breath. "Stay safe." He disappeared as quickly as he'd arrived.

Mindspeech only when discussing the investigation, Kaldill cautioned as the hovercar, driven by Pellen, dropped us off at a large shop. The curved shore of Der'Vek's Western Bay was lined with shops, small and large.

Pellen knew which shop held the best clothing and had taken us there. He was silent as he drove—he'd lost three under his command and felt responsible for their deaths.

"We'll call when we're ready to go," Berel told him. Pellen nodded and steered the vehicle away.

Terrett, I feel queasy, I confessed as we walked toward the entrance.

I know. We'll get through this.

What's wrong? Berel asked.

She doesn't feel good, Terrett responded.

My dear, we must act natural, no matter what happens, Kaldill said. Yanzi opened the door for us; we walked inside. Moments later, guards sent by the Juffa family arrived to arrest all of us.

We have to attempt to salvage this operation, Caylon sent to us the moment we were shoved into a large cell where he, Sal, Lafe, Bel and Justis waited. *Deny any knowledge of the activities of newly hired servants.*

That would be easy enough to do—I'd only learned about it just as they were being killed.

One by one, we were pulled away from our cell and questioned. I wasn't surprised to see that I was left until last—in their minds, the only female among the males would know the least. The others had been taken elsewhere—they didn't return to the cell. They'd gotten nothing from them; I knew that just by looking at the guard.

I knew many other things as the guard who'd come to collect me led me into a small room nearby, where Drood Juffa waited.

Drood, middle-aged and patriarch of the Juffa family, had come to do his own questioning. Like Birtes Churg, he'd inherited his family holdings from his father. Where he and Churg differed, however, was that Drood was smarter, harder and somewhat fairer than Churg would ever be.

"Leave us alone," Drood waved a hand at the guard, who left the room, shutting the door behind him.

"Please, sit," Drood pointed toward a nearby chair. He'd chosen to stand while he interrogated me—it was meant to make me feel small and vulnerable. I gripped the chair arms when I sat to hide my inner terror.

"Now, what can you tell me about the three servants who died?" He began. "I will know if you lie."

I wanted to laugh—he was passable at best at telling a lie from the truth. "Nothing," I said. "I'd only seen those three once—as they were being hired. We left them behind to take care of our property. As you can see, they ignored our orders the moment we were out of sight."

"Come now, you must be able to tell me something," he coaxed.

"Your guard outside is plotting against you," I said. "He is taking money from Xilva to sell you out. He expects a higher position and Xilva's niece in exchange."

Drood Juffa went completely still for a moment, staring at me in near-disbelief before pulling a communicator from a pocket and barking orders into it. An hour later, the guard outside the door was dead, other guards surrounded Drood to keep him safe and my life as an advisor to the wealthiest criminal on Vic'Law began.

Le-Ath Veronis

Lissa

"She started a turf war?" I shook my head at Kooper.

"Not started—no. It was already beginning, but Drood Juffa wasn't aware that one of his guards had been paid to assassinate him. Quin pointed that out. Kaldill says she sees Drood as more honorable than Xilva, and suspects one of the Xilvas is behind the drakus seed."

"Did she see anything about Cayetes in Drood?"

"Kaldill says that Drood knows of Cayetes—but doesn't have any dealings with him and doesn't know where he is."

"Do you think Xilva knows where he is?"

"It's possible. I'm becoming very concerned about the cloned Sirenali that seem to be everywhere on Vic'Law. Employing a wizard or warlock is worthless to look into the doings of your enemy if he hides his actions behind a pet Sirenali."

"I'm more concerned about drakus seed," I pointed out.

"I'm worried that Cayetes and the drakus seed may be connected."

"We'll have to let Quin get this information for us—as long as she's on Vic'Law, we know that's where the Orb wants her."

"At least Drood is keeping the others at his compound—to make Quin happy."

"So much for performing a search in secret, huh?"

Quin

At least we had our own, very large house on the Juffa estate, and there were no whining children asking for wings—Drood kept his family in the main palace. I hadn't seen any of them, yet.

So far, I'd been summoned to his study once—to give advice on business deals.

He was testing me.

"Quin, Drood's bodyguard is here," Caylon announced during Jayna's reading lesson on the third night.

Be careful, Quinnie, Berel sent as I stood. Jayna looked up at me with worried eyes, silently begging me to do the same.

Caylon escorted me to the reception area of the house, where the guard waited. At least this one was loyal to the Juffa family, even if he saw no use in me or any other female.

"I'll come with her," Caylon informed the guard, who nodded curtly and stalked toward the door.

Nice, Caylon grumbled mentally as we followed the broad-shouldered guard out of the house.

~

Zephili

"My Lord," Dorgus approached Vardil cautiously.

"What is it?" Vardil's dreams still contained the floating light at times, although medication from his personal physician sometimes prevented him from recalling it. Still, he was on edge, worried every night that he'd be visited by the infernal thing again.

"I may have found a solution for you—to keep a likeness you choose for yourself," Dorgus smiled. He'd worked on the problem quite hard, after all, and wanted Vardil's approval of his efforts.

"What is it?" Vardil barely sounded interested.

"I found," Dorgus' smile widened, "a very rare thing. Mind you, I had to pay a large sum for it and promised it wouldn't fall into the wrong hands, but I've managed to procure a container of the outlawed Lyristolyi drug."

Vardil was on his feet immediately, blinking at Dorgus in hopeful surprise.

~

Quin

"What about this one?" Drood handed a sheaf of papers to me. The papers contained information on a medicine being developed in the Campiaan Alliance to combat an unusual infection—the disease was a mutation of a very old bacterium, which in effect became pneumonitis at first, and then drowned the victim when their lungs filled with fluid because there wasn't any drug available to destroy the infection.

"Don't invest in this one—it will seem promising at first, before side effects appear later. Another drug is being developed, which will be much better and won't end up killing anyone."

"Do you have information on the other drug?"

"Do you have a list of drug manufacturers?" I countered.

"Here." Another sheaf of papers was shoved across his desk. I leafed through them before pulling out the proper one and handing it back.

"Your life may depend upon the accuracy of this information," Drood's eyebrows drew together as he frowned at the information on the paper.

"I understand that, Master Juffa," I replied.

"How long—before the other drug is proven faulty?"

"It may take a year, Master Juffa."

"So this is something of a long-term investment?"

"You'll reap the benefits in two years."

"I fail to understand how you came to be here on this world," Drood lowered the paper and stared at me.

"That is easy enough to explain," I said. "Vardil Cayetes destroyed my home world. I managed to see his intentions and save the inhabitants. However, he managed to spread the poison infecting Siriaa across the universe, as I'm sure you're aware."

"My question still stands," Drood said.

"Then you must understand that it is my intention to destroy Cayetes," I shrugged. "I am following his trail, wherever it leads. I've noticed you do not have any of the pet Sirenali that many are keeping throughout Der'Vek."

"Sirenali?" He'd never heard that word before.

"There is one at the sweet shop," I said. "I saw it when we went there not long ago."

Quin, Caylon voiced a warning in my head.

He doesn't know about them, I said. *Second tier families are circling like carrion eaters. He has no knowledge of the drakus seed, either, and wouldn't allow it if he knew.*

"Why are you telling me this?" Drood snapped. "This could connect you to those three who were killed near there."

"I understand that," I said. "But I worry for you, Master Juffa. Cayetes was allowed to set up a compound on Vogeffa I. In short order, he took control of that world. Recently, he has left it behind because the poison infected it. I don't believe he is here, yet, but that doesn't mean his eye isn't on Vic'Law."

Drood cursed before standing and stalking away from his desk. A wide window was his destination, where he looked upon the lawns surrounding his palace and cursed again.

I detected the unease and suspicion rolling off him as he gazed out the window, considering desperate measures to maintain his grasp on Vic'Law. I knew then that the decisions he made from that point forward would determine his fate—and the fate of those around him.

"What about the bodies missing here?" Caylon demanded, once we were dismissed by Drood and back inside Kaldill's suite. He'd asked Sal, Kaldill and Justis to come before he began to interrogate me. He saw my words to Drood Juffa as a betrayal. I wanted to tell him that Drood could be the one thing standing between Vic'Law as it was and a direct takeover by Cayetes.

"I told you what I thought about the disappearances. Someone here is funneling them away. Cayetes may be involved, but we need to look here for the one or ones cooperating with him to take the victims away."

"Do you believe that those responsible here may have direct contact with Cayetes?"

"No idea—and I won't know until I see them," I admitted. I couldn't help hugging myself—Caylon thought I'd done wrong. That never failed to frighten me—I'd been struck too many times in my past for real or imagined errors.

"It's done," Kaldill snapped. "Never forget we can leave if we want," he added. Kaldill's eyes were hard and narrowed as they grazed Caylon's face.

"*You* can leave," I pointed out as my voice and body trembled. "I can't. I have to see this through."

"There—are you happy now?" Justis growled at Caylon. "All you've done is scare her to death."

"That wasn't my intention," Caylon huffed and stalked out of Kaldill's suite. Kaldill must have sent mindspeech—Berel, Yanzi, Bel Erland and Terrett arrived to pull me away. Truly, all I wanted was to hide somewhere until my trembling subsided.

Instead, I was ushered into the spa—without a swimsuit this time. The others dropped their clothing and climbed in with me.

"My love?" A gentle kiss was laid against my forehead. I couldn't recall getting in bed with Justis, but Bel Erland had employed his warlock talents to bring in a bottle of something that tasted faintly of berries while we sat in bubbling water the night before. Everything else was a blur after that.

I didn't want to wake. I wanted the numbing effect of the alcohol I'd consumed the night before to keep doing its work. It didn't. Instead, I had a sour taste in my mouth as I drew in a deep breath and snuggled farther into Justis' embrace.

"My love, we must rise and go to breakfast, or you'll be late for your training session. Sursee Caylon will not be pleased if you are late."

"Fuck Sursee Caylon." I was surprised to hear those words drop from my lips. I hadn't even opened my eyes, yet.

"No. You will not fuck Sursee Caylon. I demand the honor of loving you."

Weak sunlight burned across my brain when my eyes flew open. Justis' nose was nearly touching mine. I blinked to bring his face into focus. A corner of his mouth curved into a wry smile.

"I'm afraid," I buried my head against his shoulder.

"I know," he soothed, a hand stroking gently down my side to rest on my hip. "I think I can talk you through this if you'll let me—when the time is right. Come now, you need to clean your teeth before going to breakfast. You smell like a winery."

It was my turn to smile.

~

I worried that Caylon would take his anger out on me during our time in his newest dojo.

He didn't. The training session was no different from any other, except that I had a pounding headache throughout most of it. As he'd said before, an enemy wouldn't care that I had a headache from drinking too much the night before. I wasn't about to complain about it, either. My lips were pressed tightly together as I forced myself to block blows.

Before we were done, Drood and his personal bodyguard arrived to watch. My headache forced me to concentrate on Caylon's teaching instead of our audience. Jayna, who trained with Sal across the room, was also under scrutiny but didn't care. Jayna's disguise had worked wonders for her—she no longer worried that she'd be ogled for the wrong reasons.

One look at Drood's face before I left to take a shower told me that Caylon was better than anyone in his employ at hand fighting. I wasn't surprised, either. Caylon was an elite warrior, who'd only met his match once.

Sal was also better than anyone Drood could bring against him. I had a feeling Justis and Lafe would also hold their own against anything Drood could throw at them. Drood was beginning to realize that.

He was also beginning to realize he might need an army against the growing threat of rebellion by those in the Second Tier. After all, there were six families in the First Tier and twenty in the Second. Third tier contained hundreds of families, but they hadn't begun the plot to destroy Drood Juffa. Drood's dark thoughts troubled me; the criminal in him was showing more and more.

I think we'll be summoned to a meeting after lunch, I informed Kaldill in mindspeech as I walked the hall toward my suite. *The ball is coming and Drood wishes to be ready in case he's attacked.*

Then we should have a meeting at lunch, Kaldill replied. *To discuss what we should do when Drood asks us to protect him.*

"Churg doesn't know anything," I said. "He'd be ineffective anyway."

"True—he is weak. He allows his son to make most of the family decisions, now," Caylon agreed. I blinked at him—his face was as inscrutable as it usually was, but on this matter, he agreed with me.

"What did you see about the Xilva family in Juffa's guard before he was killed?" Justis asked.

"He didn't know much—he was being paid and he imagined that he'd have a legitimate position in the Xilva family if he married into it."

"Do you believe they'd follow through and allow him to marry into the family?" Berel asked.

"I don't know. He believed it, so that's all I saw. Without seeing someone involved from the Xilvas, I can't say for sure."

"You have to understand that most of the crime families aren't native to Vic'Law," Sal observed. "The guard was from here. I find it highly unlikely that he'd be offered a place in the family."

"My question is this—if Cayetes is behind the Second Tier rebellion against the First Tier, what do they hope to gain from this?" Bel Erland spoke up.

He'd hit upon the question I wanted answered. Would those Cayetes had chosen take over everyone in the First Tier? Had he promised them that? In my wildest imaginings, I couldn't see a master criminal like Cayetes offering anything unless he were in charge, somehow. That meant he was lying to them. He'd take Vic'Law in his fist and crush it, reshaping it into something he wanted.

Second Tier stood to lose everything if they'd made a deal with that devil. Therefore, other questions popped into my head. Where was Cayetes now? Vic'Law was the only candidate Kooper had found where people had regularly come up missing, and I doubted that Cayetes had arrived on Vic'Law, yet.

Perhaps the ones doing the kidnapping on Vic'Law had a close relationship with Cayetes and had allied with him for the promise of money, elevation in status or another, unknown reason. I'd know if I saw the ones involved, but so far, that hadn't happened. As for Cayetes, somewhere, perhaps far away, people were disappearing and nobody had noticed.

"Here's the crux of the situation—do we agree to stand with Juffa or not," Caylon said.

"I say yes—for now," I responded immediately.

"Tell me why," Caylon shot back.

"Because he wants membership in the Campiaan Alliance," I said. "And in the past, he was willing to do what was necessary to get it." I didn't add that recently, Drood Juffa didn't bother to hide his darker side. If he strayed farther down that path, my mind would change about helping him.

Caylon, his dark eyes enigmatic and his face expressionless, studied me for several moments before nodding. "Very well," he agreed. "We stand with Drood Juffa—for now."

The expected meeting with Drood happened shortly after lunch; all of us were asked to follow two of his guards into his study, where extra chairs had been placed so we could sit. Even Jayna, Pellen, Jeslin and Mell were asked to come.

"I hear rumblings from time to time," Drood began. I studied him as he hesitated. He wasn't a handsome man, but he had a presence about him that drew others. On any other world, he'd be a successful politician. I imagined that if he were to study with Edden Charkisul, he could learn everything he needed or wanted to know in a short amount of time. For now, he was only concerned with keeping Vic'Law and his life intact.

"Through the years, I've had six attempts on my life," Drood continued. "Before, I never had reason to distrust any of my guards or servants—they are paid well enough not to carry tales or plot against me. That changed recently." His eyes turned to me.

"I've investigated the guard—I'm sure you understand he was killed after admitting he'd been paid to assassinate me. His connection to the Xilva family has been verified, although they lied to him about his marrying into the family."

My chin dropped in a half-nod—we'd suspected as much.

"Xilva is unaware that we know these things," Drood said. "He is the unofficial head of the Second Tier; it doesn't surprise me that he'd attempt a coup. If I find he's had dealings with Cayetes," he stopped for a moment before shaking his head.

I knew he'd kill the entire family. I didn't think they all deserved death and resolved to bargain for some of those lives.

My love, allow us to take care of that situation, Bel Erland inserted gently in my mind. Again, he was using the gift he had to read others.

I wanted to let my shoulders sag in relief, but I didn't—that would send a signal to Drood that I preferred he didn't have. I was also beginning to understand that Bel Erland was a diplomat of the highest order, like his father and grandfather before him. I imagined that his ability to read others was something of a gift, however, and somewhat akin to what I held.

"I can accelerate your acceptance into the Second Tier, and perhaps pave your way into the First if I find any of them have a hand in this," Drood said, "if you agree to stand with me and act in the defense of my family and me should it become necessary."

"We have some stipulations," Kaldill began.

"I expected as much. Tell me." Drood steepled his fingers and waited for Kaldill to explain.

"We will only deliver a death if it is deserved."

"I agree," Drood nodded.

"We chose our servants carefully. I'd prefer to question them if they commit infraction in the future, rather than hearing they were killed outright for wandering into the wrong areas."

"Those deaths were dealt by Cardino guards," Drood

acknowledged. "The information was passed to me, which, as you know, resulted in your arrests."

"We're well aware," Kaldill responded, his words dry. "Nevertheless, those were our servants, not his. I understand there was no questioning—only shooting."

"That is my understanding as well," Drood agreed. "Shall I bring in the Cardino son responsible for the raid?"

"I'd like to see him," I volunteered.

"Why?"

"To make note of whether he wishes you dead," I shrugged.

"Your wish, my command," Drood said and stood abruptly. "Come, we will sort this first, and then you will give me an answer."

~

Wyyld II

Lissa

"This is what's left of the ranos cannon that blasted Siriaa to atoms," Kooper led me into the locked area of a weapons warehouse. "We've checked it for the poison creatures—and didn't find anything."

"When you send your troops after something, they get serious," I said, walking toward the burned, twisted pile of metal in the center of a concrete floor.

"Hit with laser rockets," Kooper shrugged. "Didn't see us coming, I guess." He smiled then, making me realize he'd shielded the attack ship himself. I didn't care; nobody needed to worry that a ship carrying a working ranos cannon might be close enough to destroy their planet.

"We've gone over it with our best equipment, and there are no markings, fingerprints or anything else to identify the manufacturer." Kooper was angry about that, I could tell. "Metal is up to Alliance standards, so it could be had almost anywhere. The computer brain was atomized, so there's nothing to examine."

I knew what he wasn't saying—we'd both gone *Looking* for the source, and hadn't found anything. Sirenali involvement was becoming a terrible curse. I blamed plenty of dead gods for resurrecting that race and setting it free to roam. According to Caylon, too, there were cloned Sirenali on Vic'Law, which presented another set of problems.

"I don't really like supporting one criminal against another," Kooper huffed, bringing us back to a heated debate we'd already had before arriving on Wyyld II.

"It's the only solution we have," I pointed out. "Juffa is the path to all the others, and if some of them are allied with Cayetes, we need to know who and we need to know now."

"I understand that," Kooper grumped. "I just don't like that Bel has been shoved into that—he has no experience in this sort of thing."

He'd hit the sore spot with me and he knew it—Bel Erland. While Erland wasn't saying it, he was now worried that Bel was in such close proximity to the criminal who ran everything on Vic'Law.

He and I imagined that Bel would stay hidden unless they needed a warlock's talents for something. I silently cursed the Orb in all this—I felt it was in control and none of us had a clue about its intentions concerning Vic'Law.

"Caylon cursed the entire time he explained this fiasco to me," Kooper attempted to direct me away from the subject of Bel Erland. "Quin practically handed Juffa their whole reason for being on the planet to begin with."

"I know. I worry about that, too. Now tell me—why are we here again?"

"Because Cayetes is still out there, and we stole from him."

"Stole what?" At first I didn't understand. Then it hit me. We'd taken bodies away from him—bodies he intended for himself when I transferred farmers from Vogeffa II.

"He doesn't like that," Kooper said. "It's all right for him to kill or steal from everybody else, but do it to him and you're an enemy until he can make you dead."

"You think he may be building another one of these?" I jerked my head toward the remains of a ranos cannon.

"We found nothing on Vogeffa I that could manufacture that,"

Kooper stared at the twisted metal before shaking his head. "That means Cayetes had it built elsewhere. We have to find where it came from before he aims it at Le-Ath Veronis or New Vogeffa."

"He has no way to trace this back to me," I began.

"Where did the Avii survivors end up?" Kooper demanded. "Who's Acting Regent and watching over Harifa Edus because New Fyris is there? It's only a matter of time before he determines the truth. While you can shield Le-Ath Veronis if he fires on it, I worry greatly about Harifa Edus."

"We need to find that bastard," I hissed. For the first time in a very long time, my fangs descended and Kooper stared at my red eyes in alarm.

~

Vic'Law

Terrett

I keep telling myself that I can only do as much as I am able. My heart squeezes, however, when I consider where we are and Quin's involvement. Juffa sees us as a private army. If he had our willing cooperation, he had no idea what kind of army he would actually have.

Likely—that would be more power than he ever dreamed of holding. In this, too, I couldn't decipher what Quin was thinking, or whether she was merely a puppet to the Orb's whims at this point.

I worried about her. I worried about the others, too. In the past, I never cared what happened to the criminals who owned me. I was a silent tool for them to use as they saw fit. Juffa might be better than most I'd seen, but he was still a criminal. His willingness to kill anyone who stood in his way attested to that.

We'd still not seen others of his family. Quin appeared to be unconcerned about that. Again, I worried about the Orb's involvement. It tainted everything and I wanted it to loosen its hold on Quin.

I think we all wanted that. I could tell Kaldill wasn't happy; I felt the same. What terrified me most was this, however; that we'd be forced to disconnect the bond between Quin and us, and let her go. It was obvious to almost everyone that she'd chosen a path of destruction with the criminal element of Vic'Law.

If I could find Cayetes for her, I'd do it. He wouldn't live long, either, if I had anything to say in the matter.

"Brother," Lafe sat beside me. I'd taken a bench outside our house on the Juffa estate. I nodded to acknowledge Lafe's presence. "Know anything about what Quin's up to?" he asked softly.

I worry that she may be committing suicide, I replied.

"While we're stuck in the middle of a maelstrom," he agreed. "What do you think we ought to do about it?"

I think we should sharpen our blades, I said.

CHAPTER 8

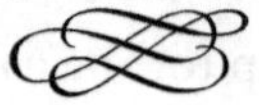

*B*el Erland

"Come after me harder than that—you'll only make your opponent mad with that kind of thrust," Salidar snapped.

He'd agreed to teach me knife fighting. I thought I was getting good at it.

I was wrong.

Gran always said Sal had ninja skills, whatever that meant and whatever a ninja was. I was beginning to realize that you never saw a ninja coming; Sal was so fast, he was mostly a blur.

At least I held a knife in each hand, now. He wielded one. Even armed with two blades, I couldn't get close to him. "What would you do," he began, as if he were making casual conversation while I flashed my knives at him as fast as I could. "What *could* you do," he amended with a grin, "if I really were an enemy you faced right now?"

"I'd slow him down with power," I snapped, breathing hard with my efforts to touch him with dull practice knives. "Then stab the daylights out of him."

"Why haven't you tried that?"

"Because that would be cheating."

"You think your enemy is going to hold back from cheating?" Sal

110

managed to lift an eyebrow as I swung at him again. He stepped neatly away from my intended slash and banged me on the back of my neck. He'd just shown me that he could take my head with little effort and a seven-inch blade.

I stared at him, heaving loud breaths from the effort of fighting with him. I thought I was in better shape than that. After two eight-days of working out with Sal, I knew my stamina needed improvement.

"I still won't cheat—with you," I said. "Anybody else better watch out."

"Good." Sal walked toward the wall, cleaned his practice blade and hung it on its pegs. I followed him, forcing my rubbery legs to work and lethargic arms to clean dull metal before hanging both blades beside his.

"Want water?" I asked.

"Sure."

I *Pulled* in two sealed bottles and offered him one. He grinned and accepted.

Quin

I hadn't used my wings to fly in days. Justis rode the wind beside me as we glided over the Juffa estate. I could see Juffa as he walked out a door far below us—a servant had likely informed him that his winged allies were flying above his grounds.

From my vantage point, he was small. I knew him anyway. Had he thought our wings just for show? He knew better, now. He shaded his eyes from the sun bearing down as he watched us wheel and head in another direction.

Justis was taking me through the beginning exercises his troops did—of following their commander. I stayed on Justis' left, my right wing only a few hand-widths away from his. I glided when he did, so he could check on the distance between us.

He appeared satisfied—using my wings to fight had improved my control in the air. That's when we saw Drood Juffa waving at us, then motioning us down. Justis didn't like it, but we complied.

"I thought your wings were ornamental," Drood said as a servant poured tea for us inside his study. "This is quite the surprise."

"Our race grows wings in our ninth year," Justis explained. After all, that information was now on any Alliance comp-vid.

"Fascinating. From where I stood, I could hear nothing."

"Birds make little noise," Justis shrugged.

"The drones employed by the families make a familiar whine," Drood began. "I have sensors set up to detect their approach—by sound and movement."

"We can't hide ourselves," Justis said.

"Ah, but perhaps I can."

"What do you mean?" I asked.

"One of my manufacturing concerns is working on developing a fine shield. You make the noise a bird makes, which can't be detected on the ground. My shield will conceal you well enough that anyone will think it a nightbird after prey if they hear anything at all. I've managed to steal the plans for these shields from the ASD." Drood sounded proud of himself.

I understood that he'd committed murder to get them, too. That could change my plans for him in the long term, but I shoved that thought aside for the moment.

"You want us to spy for you?" Justis asked, his voice cold and hard.

"Perhaps—if I deem it necessary," Drood shrugged.

"Our agreement states that we won't murder anyone for you, unless *we* deem it necessary," Justis reminded him.

"Yes, of course. I may wish to know what is going on in other places, that's all. The general population have no weapons—only the constabulary. My peers and those in the Second Tier are armed quite well. I need to know if any are building a larger arsenal than is necessary."

"The ball is two days away," I said.

"I know. That's why I want to give you a map so you can go out tonight."

~

I didn't need a map, but handing Drood Juffa proof of a larger-than-necessary arsenal on other estates was more than dangerous.

The map was delivered to us two hours later, with names printed on corresponding estates. "Which ones, love?" Justis asked while peering over my shoulder.

"We only have to go to this one," I stabbed a finger on the Cardino estate.

"They're the ones who killed our three agents without asking questions," Pellen said.

"Which family does Master Barstle belong to?" I asked.

"He is Kynn Cardino's youngest brother," Pellen replied.

"I need to see him—and his brother," I muttered, staring at the map. Barstle could be allied with the Xilvas, and together they could be leading the charge against Juffa. The Cardino estate was just as large as the Juffa estate, but it was surrounded on all sides by what looked to be a forest.

"Do you think Kynn isn't aware of his younger brother's addiction to drakus seed?" Kaldill asked.

"I can't say that he's the one addicted, but something is making my brain itch whenever I consider his connection to it," I replied.

"This spells coup to me—perhaps the Second Tier and all the younger ones in First Tier are weary of bowing to their elders or the higher-placed," Caylon said.

"I agree," Lafe nodded to Caylon.

"My concern," Sal said, "is that someone, somewhere, is luring the coup-minded in with drakus seed. We know how addictive that shit is. They may not. Either way, they'll kill to get it if their supply is cut off. If they don't die from it, first."

Something niggled my brain, making it itch again at the mention of the drug and its addictive qualities, but I couldn't muddle through that mystery, yet. Perhaps it would reveal itself soon, as I was beginning to tire of the mounting questions on Vic'Law, to which we had very few answers.

"We shield. I not trust shield of Juffa," Yanzi stated flatly.

"That may get us in trouble," Sal said. "Juffa may think his version infallible, when it may be next to worthless, should our shield be employed."

"I have these," Justis held up his hand to display the ring and cuff he wore.

"We may have to rely on that, but what about Quin?" Kaldill asked. "You may not be able to shield her every moment."

"Then we'll protect Quin and allow Justis' spelled stones to work for him. If he's shot at and the stones fire to counter the attack, that will tell us how effective Juffa's shield experiments have been," Caylon agreed.

"Do you have black leathers?" Sal asked, his dark gaze settling on me.

"No, Sursee."

"You won't wear them in the dojo; you're not qualified yet. You'll wear them now to hide yourself," Caylon joined in. "With Kaldill's help, I think we can come up with something before your flight to the Cardino estate."

"Thank you," I dipped my head to acknowledge the gift.

The black shirt and jacket I wore had a large cutout in the back to accommodate my wings and wouldn't restrict movement. Like many of my shirts, they fastened below my wings. Justis took care of those snaps and zippers for me—he was dressed similarly in black leathers, also supplied by Caylon and Kaldill.

The leather pants and boots fit perfectly; the boots were light enough so they wouldn't be a burden in the air, but sturdy enough if I had to run in them. I could tell Justis liked his boots very much—for the same reasons.

Where our outfits differed was this—his had a wide strap and buckle holding his scabbard against a leg—he would carry his blade with him in case he were forced to fight on the ground.

He also had a pistol tucked into an inside jacket pocket—in case the sword wasn't enough.

I had no weapons, as I hadn't trained with them yet. I only had my knowledge of hand fighting. I hoped I wouldn't need it.

Justis' steps were light and soundless as he walked out of our house. I followed him, hoping I'd be just as soundless and even less of a burden to him. He ran across the stones of the courtyard before snapping his wings out and taking flight. I copied his movements, hoping not to make a mistake.

Terrett

"She harmed, I kill," Yanzi settled onto a seat beside me—I'd chosen a chair near the fireplace inside the small library; it was next to Kaldill's suite and had seen little use before our arrival. I'd chosen it as my place to wait for Quin and Justis' return. Yanzi had found me there —for the same reason.

I will kill beside you, brother, I agreed.

"I was hoping to find someone here to share this with," Kaldill arrived, holding up a bottle of wine.

"Not Elf vintage?" Yanzi frowned.

"Not this time—I think you'd like to be awake if we're called upon to help," Kaldill replied.

"That why I ask," Yanzi leaned back in his chair with a sigh. Kaldill poured three glasses of wine and handed one to Yanzi and me before sipping from his. The wine was Refizani—I recognized it easily. Often, during my unwilling stay with Marid of Belancour, I'd drowned myself in wine. After all, it didn't matter whether I was asleep or awake—my Sirenali talent for hiding my questionable associates from anyone with power worked no matter what.

Lifting my glass to Kaldill to compliment his choice, I sipped more wine and considered the danger Quin might be in, shield or not.

Before long, the others wandered in. Kaldill used his talents to *Pull* in more wine. We sat around the fireplace, sipping wine and buried in our worries. Daragar arrived last and waved off a glass of wine—he'd never tasted it. Larentii didn't eat or drink to my knowledge, although that knowledge was quite limited.

Lafe had settled on the floor not far from my chair, cross-legged with black hair braided down his back. He'd told me once that if someone offered to unbraid a Falchani's hair, they were asking for sex. My hair was short so I couldn't braid it. That didn't keep me from wanting to sleep with Quin—in the traditional, lover's way.

I'd seen her before her wings, hair and eyes were changed. She was beautiful either way, although the black wings and hair lent a mysterious air to her graceful movements. Her training with Salidar and Caylon had only improved upon what she had naturally.

Fuck, I sighed mentally.

"I hear that," Yanzi agreed.

Jayna and Mell were ushered into the library moments later, both held by Juffa's guards while Juffa stalked in behind them. "I want to change the terms of our agreement," Drood hissed. "If they find a cache of weapons, I wish to send a message to Cardino by killing any guards there. If you want these two to live," he said, nodding toward the two women, "then I sincerely hope you have a way to get messages to your winged companions."

Quin

All my life, my talent for finding things has been both blessing and curse. The arsenal Drood wanted us to find was in a building on the Cardino estate, surrounded by dense forest.

The structure was also heavily guarded. Every door and window into the building (there were two of each) was also locked and alarmed.

Two armed guards stood at each entrance, too, as if they were waiting for us to arrive.

Justis thought the same. *Do you think someone warned them?* He sent mindspeech.

I don't know, I replied. *I won't, either, until I see it in one of them.*

I say we leave now, Justis huffed. *We don't need to risk our lives just to get visual evidence.*

I was ready to agree with him when mindspeech came from Kaldill. Drood had waited until we were away to change the rules and ensure that we complied with his wishes.

Drood is holding Mell and Jayna at gunpoint, Kaldill reported. *He says if you and Justis fail to kill the guards and bring back evidence, they will die. Daragar says that we can save both, but it will reveal us to Juffa and our cover will no longer be effective. What do you wish to do, my love?*

Drood Juffa had just crossed a line with me. Any plans I had for the future of Vic'Law would certainly not include him. He'd been so close—I shut down that train of thought.

We will comply, I told Kaldill.

Quin, Justis joined the conversation. He was far from pleased with my decision.

Stay back, Justis. I trust the shield Kaldill provided. Let me draw all the guards out of the building. I believe the Orb will appear if I'm threatened. While they fire at me, sneak inside, get the evidence and then fly for the Juffa estate. It is my hope the Orb will intervene. Either way, I will be behind you quickly.

Will your shield hold? Justis demanded of Kaldill.

A ranos pistol couldn't crack it, he snapped, sounding offended.

Very well. I could tell Justis still didn't like my hastily formed plan. Truly, it was all I had, while he had no alternative to offer.

Then go, Justis growled. *Draw their attention away. I'll do my part. Just —don't risk your life for me, all right?*

If your life isn't worth the risk, then I don't know whose is, I replied.

He and I had circled over the building that housed the weapons while we'd employed mindspeech—with Kaldill and each other. Our wings had been all but silent while we flew and glided above the target. Taking a deep breath, I folded my wings and dived for the ground below, only opening them to slow my descent before I touched down.

A small clearing, yards away from the main door, was my

destination—I dropped soundlessly upon half-frozen ground. Since Justis and I had taken flight, the chill in the air made me more appreciative of the leathers Caylon and Kaldill provided.

Gripping leather in my hand and drawing my collar up, I strode toward the door, making as much noise as possible. The crunch of fallen leaves helped, but still the guards were slow. Regardless, the two outside the door leveled their weapons at me eventually, while one of them sent a message via headset to the others inside the large building.

"Put your hands up and stay where you are," the other guard demanded, pointing his weapon at me.

"No," I said, taking another, shaky step toward the guards. Yes, I was trembling from head to heel, but I had to get all of them out of the building. When the first shot was fired, ricocheting off my protective shield with a heart-stopping whine, the Orb appeared. It blasted such a blinding light that guards poured out of the building to see what was attacking them.

I knew the moment they were all outside, firing at me as if their bullets and laser pistols might make a difference. They couldn't see me —the Orb made sure they were all firing blindly.

The lucky shots didn't get through the shield, but that didn't mean it was peaceful and calm behind it.

In fact, it was anything but. I admit to cowering whenever a bullet cracked close to my head. The noise of weapons firing was so loud, too, that they failed to hear my whimpering. I could feel the anger, fear and malevolence radiating off all of them—they wanted me dead. They'd been instructed to make any attacker or spy dead. Their lives and their drakus seed addiction saw to that.

I'm out, I have what we came for, Justis informed me.

I was glad, and if he'd gotten away cleanly, I would have been more than happy. That didn't happen.

One of the guards happened to look upward. A sliver of moon was blocked momentarily. He took aim and fired at the shadow.

The Orb, still shining brightly, stayed with me.

Justis, on the other hand, was now being fired upon. I watched as one of his spelled stones bloomed in the sky. Then another.

When the fifth one bloomed, I screamed.

He only had six.

You know what to do, the Orb informed me with a haughty voice.

I didn't want to.

Justis' sixth stone bloomed. He was vulnerable and the shield Drood supplied was worthless.

Lowering my gaze to the men who wanted to bring Justis down, I sent out my call. Not to creatures of the night, or any other thing visible to the naked eye.

I called to what was already inside them.

The drakus seed.

It rose at my command, and forty-seven of Barstle Cardino's handpicked guards dropped dead.

I wanted to weep.

My eyes were dry as I hugged myself; the leather I'd dressed in creaking around me in the sudden silence as I surveyed the damage I'd done. Forty-seven bodies lay on cold ground; they'd dropped where they stood. In the distance, I could hear the noise of hovercars and running feet. The Cardino estate had finally wakened.

Quin? I heard Justis' mental voice as the Orb disappeared.

I'm coming, I breathed into his mind. Taking a shaky, running leap, I left the ground and flew toward Justis.

I could find him, after all.

Terrett

They were on their way back, although a message from Justis sounded garbled. He said Quin flew beside him, but she hadn't spoken during the trip back. There was something else—they'd left dead behind them, and Justis hadn't known how that was accomplished.

He sounded shaken, so I waited silently for them to appear and explain things.

Drood Juffa and two of his guards were also inside the library; the guards held Mell and Jayna at gunpoint until Quin and Justis returned.

I knew Quin would be angry that Juffa had done that—she and Justis had undertaken this assignment in good faith.

Juffa showed all of us how undeserving he was.

He stood, though, when Justis stalked through the door, Quin almost stepping on his heels, she was so close behind.

The small comp-vid Justis carried was shoved into Drood's hands. I could tell Justis was half a finger's width away from strangling Drood. All his protection jewels were now dark—he'd been very close to death.

"Your shield is worthless," Justis growled before turning, lifting Quin in his arms and walking out of the library.

Bel Erland

Kaldill practically shoved Drood Juffa out our door, once Jayna and Mell were released. We wouldn't make that mistake again—all of ours would be protected from now on, if I had to see to it myself.

It was a foot race after that to get to Justis' suite, where he'd taken Quin.

I'd never seen anyone so terrified before—she'd looked like a ghost as she followed Justis into the library.

Kaldill had instructed the rest of us to hold back, in case our movement placed Jayna and Mell in even more danger.

I think if Drood had returned that night, he'd have been killed—vindictively and from several directions.

Inside Justis' suite, we found him sitting on the bed, his arms and wings wrapped around Quin as she shuddered in his embrace.

What happened? Caylon asked.

Forty-seven dead, if I counted correctly, Justis replied.

How?

Quin did it, I think, with help from the Orb.

Did you see it?

I recorded it—it's on that infernal thing I handed to Juffa.

May the gods be merciful, Lafe sighed.

Quin

If it hadn't been for Justis and Daragar, I might not have made it through the night. By the morning, after Juffa had watched Justis' recording several times, he'd sent an army against the Cardino family.

All of them were dead except Barstle, who'd somehow escaped.

I was done with Drood Juffa. He'd failed a test and wasn't worth worrying about any longer. If the others wanted to kill him and feed his body to voracious ants, I wouldn't lift a finger to help him.

Too, I hadn't explained to the others what I'd done the night before. They thought it was the Orb. It wasn't. It only reminded me of what I'd suspected for a while. I hoped I'd come to terms with that someday; for now, I felt horrible at the thought.

I knew I'd rather feel guilt and shame, however, than to suffer through Justis' loss a second time. I'd spent the night in his bed while he held me, and Daragar sat in a corner, humming me back to sleep whenever I woke.

Terrett

No lessons were held the following morning, and Quin and Justis didn't arrive in the kitchen to eat until almost lunchtime. I think all of us who waited there breathed a relieved sigh—she looked rumpled but walked steadily beside Justis.

Kaldill had already gotten a message from somewhere. He was informed that another ring and cuff would be supplied for Justis, in exchange for the ones that were now emptied of their spells.

Oatmeal? I sent to Quin as Justis seated her at the table.

Fruit? She asked. *With oatmeal?*

"She wants fruit and oatmeal," Sal informed Jeslin, who set to work making food for her and Justis.

~

Quin

Mell and Jayna had been served breakfast inside their suite; Pellen had arranged for more of his agents to be brought in to guard their door. Both women had been outside when grabbed the night before—they were disposing of the garbage in the recycler when captured by Drood's guards.

I didn't have enough profanity in my vocabulary to accurately describe Drood or his guards. Jayna and Mell had fought back, but when weapons were pulled, they'd been forced to stop. Jayna had cracked ribs and Mell had a black eye and facial bruises as a result.

I intended to heal those things after I finished eating. I didn't have to see those things personally—I'd already seen them in Bel Erland's gaze.

~

"I'm so glad you're safe," Jayna whispered when I sat on the edge of her bed. It hurt for her to draw breath after the damage to her ribs.

"I'm here to fix that," I said, laying a hand on her left side. "Don't worry, it won't hurt at all."

Jayna was speechless afterward—she'd seen me glow with healing power as the pain in her ribs disappeared. I then turned to Mell, who sat in a corner chair, also speechless with wonder. When I finished healing her face, most of the bruises and all the pain were gone.

"Quin is talented," Bel Erland smiled and explained as I walked wearily for the door.

"I can see that," Mell dropped her gaze.

"Juffa is at the front door," Sal poked his head inside the room. "He wants to speak with you."

"Really?" My question was flat and filled with sarcasm. I followed

Sal; Bel Erland, Justis, Caylon and Kaldill followed me. I kept my steps firm and long as I walked the length of the house to get to the front door where Drood Juffa waited.

"I want to know how," he began the moment I stopped before him.

"Fuck you," I snapped and slammed the door in his face.

"My shields are up," Kaldill announced.

"As are mine," Daragar appeared beside me.

A knock sounded on the door.

"Want me to open it?" Sal asked.

"Sure."

He opened the door with a flourish. I stood facing Drood and two of his guards. One aimed a pistol at me. Daragar held out a hand and released his particles before pulling himself to his full height and showing Drood that he was Larentii.

"The same thing will happen to you if you point your weapon at Quin," Daragar lifted an eyebrow as Drood Juffa gaped and his second guard took a step backward.

"You're a myth," Drood whispered.

"Larentii are not a myth; they seldom have reason to associate with criminals," Daragar said, his voice as close to a growl as I'd ever heard.

"I suppose you think elves are a myth, too," Kaldill crossed arms over his chest and glared at Drood.

"They are," Drood began as flowers bloomed at his feet, the stems and roots climbing through the stones on our doorstep. Roses formed in reds, yellows and pinks before a razor-sharp branch filled with thorns circled Drood's throat and tightened itself against his skin.

I watched with satisfaction as a trickle of blood stained the white collar of his shirt.

"I know you believe in warlocks," Bel Erland announced before turning the wood of the door to stone, then brick and then chocolate.

"Fuck me," Drood choked on his words.

"We do not serve you," Caylon said. "We will never serve you.

When you threatened ours last night, you made sure that we would never cooperate on your behalf again. You, sir, are on your own."

I was happy to be transported elsewhere; Drood's life would be worthless, come time for the ball.

~

Zephili

"We found two, Lord Cayetes. Brothers. Older. That will not matter, once the drug is administered," Dorgus informed Vardil. "The search took longer than I thought, but these brothers are both from Lyristolys. The drug is guaranteed to work on them."

"Do you have images—of these two in their younger years?" Vardil demanded. The time had arrived for a transference and his temper was short as a result. Dorgus and Deris waited in his bedroom with a new body; the hapless man from Mar'Dun was drugged enough to cooperate.

"Here, my Lord—both quite handsome. Twins, as you can see."

"Good—very good," Vardil examined the images. "How long after the drug before they will be ready?"

"You must understand that the drug is only half of it," Dorgus explained. "We must take blood from each—not so much at a time so they'll be weakened, but enough eventually so that you will be assured of new, identical bodies for many years to come."

"How long?"

"A month, perhaps. Two at most."

"Get on with it, then," Vardil snapped, waving Dorgus away. "I must go to Deris and Daris. This body chafes and dies about me."

CHAPTER 9

*Q*uin

"How does it feel to be an outlaw on an outlaw planet?" Bel teased as we sorted through our belongings. We now occupied a previously empty mansion outside the industrial city of Mundia.

The mansion was owned by the Juffa family. In my mind, Drood owed us—while he still lived, anyway. After his death, it wouldn't matter anyway. Sal had already advised Kooper Griff of our move— and the reasons for it.

He also let him know that Drood Juffa was behind the pirating of the plans for personal shields employed by the ASD. Drood's objective had been twofold—experiment for ways to get through the shields, then make replicas of them when needed.

We knew he'd not perfected the shield yet—Justis' life was saved by spelled stones. Justis now wore a new cuff and ring—someone was watching over him and I was grateful.

Someone else—perhaps Daragar—had gathered the rest of the ASD agents living in Der'Vek and brought them with us. Those who didn't know much were advised by Pellen, Jeslin and Mell after their arrival.

"The ball is tonight—what do you think will happen?" Bel Erland *Pulled* in a sweater and helped me into it, his hands warm and gentle as he adjusted the shawl collar. The house was slow to warm—winter had hit Mundia harder than it had Der'Vek, and the heat was off when we arrived at the empty mansion.

"Juffa will die. He has no idea how much opposition he has. The weapons were stored in that building on the Cardino estate, but most of the Second Tier had contributed to that arsenal, including the Xilvas."

"Juffa's family?"

"We can't save them," I mumbled, clamping my wings against my back.

"If he had any sense at all, he'd send his children away from the estate," Sal walked in, a cup of hot tea in his hands.

"We've already seen that he doesn't always have the best judgment," Lafe followed Sal into the dining hall, which doubled as a clearinghouse for all our belongings. Like Sal, Lafe's hands were wrapped around a cup of hot tea as he surveyed the piles of clothing and other items cluttering the floor. I knew which items belonged to whom—by employing my ability to find things.

"My love, are you cold?" Lafe asked.

My breath stopped and I didn't speak for a moment. He'd seen me pull the sweater more tightly around myself. I'd gone still because he'd declared his love.

"I am. A little," I admitted, forcing my lips to form words. "Bel Erland brought the sweater, but this place will take forever to warm up."

"The kitchen is warmer," Lafe held out a hand. I took it; I thought I hid the trembling well enough; I could tell by the grip of Lafe's fingers that he'd noticed anyway. "Come with me—you'll sit in the kitchen for a while. Your fingers are blue," he said with a slight grin.

Jayna, who worked beside Jeslin and Mell in the kitchen, made a cup of tea for me while I sat in the shelter of Lafe's arms.

You feel good here, Lafe informed me as I sipped tea and warmed my hands with the cup at the same time. With a sigh, I closed my eyes, relaxed and leaned back against Lafe's chest. *Even better,* I could hear the grin in his mental voice.

Bel Erland arrived to sit across from us and accepted a cup of tea from Mell. I smiled at him when my eyes opened to acknowledge his presence; he gave me a wink and a smile in return.

"Lafe?" I said.

"What, love?"

"Will you teach me how to braid my hair?"

"Of course I will."

Zephili

"Here is the update from Vic'Law," Magul handed a comp-vid to Vardil. "Everything went as planned, even with the destruction of the weapons cache held by the Cardino family. I worried after Juffa sent his troops to kill the Cardinos that we'd have a difficult time taking over during the ball. It turned out easier than we thought."

"All dead?" Vardil slid his finger down the screen to read the report.

"Every Juffa on the estate is now dead," Magul confirmed. "By your command."

"They think we're backing them," Vardil huffed before smiling. "Juffa was the largest obstacle in our path to Vic'Law. Soon, we will have all of it."

"I have something else," Magul said.

"What is that?"

"The only one I could find with the name Liron is a child—barely five turns in age."

"Kill him," Vardil shrugged.

"He is the crown prince of the Avii, who now reside on Le-Ath Veronis."

"The Avii who were supposed to be destroyed with Siriaa?" Vardil lifted an eyebrow.

"The same, my Lord."

"He would have reason for a vendetta when he comes of age, would he not?"

"I believe that to be true, my Lord."

"Kill him at your earliest convenience," Vardil waved a hand. "His parents, too, if he has any."

"I will see it done, Lord Cayetes."

"One more thing," Vardil tapped fingertips together, as if he were in deep thought.

"I am at your command," Magul dipped his head.

"See to it that our army is prepared to go—when the infighting is over on Vic'Law, I will have Bleek lead our troops in to destroy any who survive."

"As you command, Lord."

Le-Ath Veronis

Lissa

Six children. *Six orphans*, I reminded myself. Bel Erland sent them to me—he didn't want their blood on his or the others' hands.

I waited for Amara and Edan's arrival—they'd take them and find a good home for the lot of them.

Bel had only taken those under the age of fifteen—those older had been old enough to know what they were doing. These six were from Drood Juffa's youngest wives. They'd seen enough of the violence going on before Bel pulled them away to realize their parents were dead.

For now, several comesuli were caring for them while we waited. Amara would ensure that they were loved and cared for—she and Edan were more than adept at matching children with prospective parents.

I worried at what appeared to be happening on Vic'Law. My suspicions were raised that it was happening now—shortly after Cayetes' disappearance from Vogeffa I.

In addition, I'd learned recently from some of Kooper's agents that

Vogeffa II no longer held living humanoids—those from Gungl were either dead or conscripted into Cayetes' service.

If he intended to take Vic'Law eventually, he'd need a small army to accomplish it. If he had another ranos cannon at his disposal, it would only strengthen his position. Kooper and I still had no evidence as to where the cannon used to destroy Siriaa was manufactured; we continued to search with no results as yet.

"Lissa?" Amara's voice was low and soothing.

"Thank you for coming," I breathed as she held her arms open. I accepted her embrace gratefully. Besides my sister and Ashe, Amara was the only other I considered family.

My father—well, I hadn't spoken to him in years.

That didn't bother me at all. Bree and I—we'd written him out of our story. Ry saw him now and then, but their relationship was far from comfortable.

"You're thinking about Brenten, aren't you?" Amara stepped back and let me go.

"Yes," I hunched my shoulders.

"He has his own agenda and always will," she said. "Don't let him upset you any more than he already has."

"Good advice," I agreed, although the thought of him had already disturbed me more than I cared to admit. "Will you find a good home for these?" I nodded toward the children, all of whom were frightened.

"We will," she promised. "I'll make sure you know where they are."

"Thank you."

Vic'Law

Quin

"Bel?" I found him in the library, which he'd warmed with a wood fire in the fireplace and power he'd provided himself.

"Quinnie?" He shut the book he'd been holding—at least this

library was stuffed with books—unlike the other places I'd seen so far during my stay on Vic'Law.

"Thank you for those lives," I dropped my gaze. I'd known earlier that he'd rescued six children from the Juffa estate—before the coup claimed their lives. I'd seen it in his gaze, but chose not to bring it up in front of any of the others.

"Come sit with me," he patted the seat beside him. "It's warm in here."

"Thank you." I settled beside him; he draped an arm around me. Then, leaning in, he placed a kiss on my temple. "Gran already took care of them—they'll have a new home with somebody who loves them."

"Thank you." I drew my knees up and snuggled against him.

"Quin, I only have so much control with you," he warned. "I think almost everybody here is going crazy because they want you."

"I don't know what to do," I whispered. "Really. And how can I choose the first?" I blew out a breath and moved to stand.

"No, don't go," he pulled me back.

"I may have a solution," Daragar appeared. "But you must be in the proper mood, first."

"By proper mood, I think he means wanting sex badly enough to jump somebody," Bel grinned.

"How should I get in that mood?"

"Like this." Bel leaned in to kiss me. It was a kiss meant to make toes curl. Justis had come close to it at times, but he'd always held back.

Bel Erland wasn't holding back.

So beautiful, Terrett's voice sounded in my head.

I love you, from Justis. *More than anything*.

Whose fingers removed my blouse?

Heat suffused my body.

I have waited for you so long, Kaldill breathed against my ear.

Ai yevu—my only, Lafe sighed.

My love—from Yanzi.

My heart, Berel crooned.

Where was I? I felt as if I were floating. Another kiss scorched my body. Hands on my breasts—whose hands were they? Fingers caressed. Thumbed my nipples. I moaned.

My love, there will be no pain—this or anytime, Daragar sighed. *Your first time—as is fitting, will be energy sex with all your mates.*

The world exploded around me, my body writhed in ecstasy and I lost consciousness shortly after.

~

I woke tangled in black feathers.

They weren't mine—they belonged to Justis. I was in his bed. "Someday," he nuzzled my cheek before kissing me, "we will mate in the air."

"Will it be that good?" I asked, innocently.

"I don't know if anything will be that good," he smiled before kissing me again. "Kaldill told me about the pleasure of energy sex, but the reality was far better than the description."

"You knew? It was planned?" I attempted to move away from him.

"Shhh," he soothed, pulling me back. "Daragar said he was waiting for the right time. That happened an hour ago. You have been asleep since the climax."

"I was the only one to lose consciousness?"

"No, we all did for a while—we merely woke before you. Daragar asked Queen Lissa's Larentii mates to guard us while we were asleep."

"How did we end up in your bed?" I asked.

"You are very persistent," Justis tapped my nose. "Connegar and Reemagar sorted us into our beds, so we'd be comfortable. Waking on the hard floor in the library wasn't an option any of us would appreciate when we woke."

"True," I sighed and closed my eyes for a moment, savoring the warm comfort of Justis' wings. "Is that where everyone ended up—in the library?" I opened my eyes again and studied Justis' face.

"Yes. Daragar pulled all of us in. Somehow, we were floating—all of us coming in contact with you eventually. Before the climax."

"I thought I was dreaming," I said.

"No, love. It was no dream."

Terrett

Yanzi and I sat in the library—I think each of us wanted to savor the experience we'd had with Quin, courtesy of the Larentii. Yes, I'd had sex before—when I was ordered at times, or in stolen moments at others, but those were far in my past.

This—with Quin and a Larentii's help—nothing may ever come close to that again. "Churg dead, son kill," Yanzi sighed.

The war has begun? I asked.

"Fast," Yanzi agreed. "Nardes Churg, Barstle Cardino, allies."

The only Cardino who survived Juffa's attack? I asked.

"Yes."

Fighting for the control of Vic'Law and Juffa holdings, I snorted. I'd been part of several crime family holdings in the past—like a gold coin or piece of jewelry. Something valuable enough to keep alive, but little else. I'd been won and lost, just as Drood Juffa's things were now a point of contention among those who remained.

"He not threaten, he still be alive," Yanzi pointed out.

How long before the war comes here? I asked.

"Hmmph," Yanzi replied. "War already here. We just far enough away that we not see it, yet."

Quin

"They'll let the people starve while they shoot at each other," Lafe said, motioning for me to sit beside him for afternoon tea.

"Are things happening here already?" I asked while Lafe dumped honey in my tea and stirred before pushing the mug into my hand.

At least the house was warmer now—although I believed the Larentii had a hand in that. Daragar had gone to find a sunny place to feed; a winter storm had pushed gray clouds over Mundia, and snow was coming. He needed sunlight and rest after what he'd accomplished earlier.

It was also a terrible time for people to be hungry, and I knew well enough that most in the city were afraid to go to their jobs when the factories and other businesses were in danger of attack.

"Where are the warehouses—where food is stored?" I asked.

"Between here and Puntia, and they'll be under heavy guard—wars are often won and lost according to who holds the supplies."

"You think we need permission to go there?" Bel Erland grinned at me as he sat nearby. Again, we were in the library—the fire was still going and it was more than comfortable, now.

Terrett and Yanzi sat across from us, watching and listening as Lafe and I discussed the current state of affairs on Vic'Law.

"Juffa hold space station—until now," Yanzi broke in. "Fighting over that, now. Shipments lost or delayed, too."

"So they have outside help. Probably Cayetes," Caylon settled gracefully on the rug near the fireplace. Sal followed him in—I admired the way they could drop so carefully to the floor without spilling a drop of their tea.

I'll teach you, Caylon hid a smile.

Thank you, Sursee, I gave a slight nod.

"Where can we find information on the interrupted shipments?" Justis asked. "Is it possible to hijack those before they fall into Cayetes' hands?"

"I can hijack—but I have to know where they are," Bel Erland said.

"I can find anything," I shrugged. "Although Vardil Cayetes is hiding pretty well."

"Don't worry about that—we'll draw him to us," Kaldill said. "If we take what is his, he will be searching for us, never fear."

"Kaldill, do you suppose he's looking for what we took away from him on Vogeffa II?" I asked, my voice small and filled with worry. Kaldill's words had brought that back to me of a sudden, which concerned me greatly.

"It's possible," Sal answered my question. "I'll put Queen Lissa on alert."

"We know what Bleek is capable of," Lafe observed. "Tell everyone to be wary of that monster."

"You think Cayetes would send Bleek?" I turned toward Lafe.

"Bleek was commander of Cayetes' Storm. He always arrived with his troops to rape Gungl. I have no doubt that Bleek is in charge of this mission, if Cayetes wants those people back."

"He'll want them back—even if it's to kill them all," Caylon growled. "He is more than possessive, and intended to kill an entire planet filled with people to get to one man—Marid of Belancour. It's my guess he isn't taking responsibility for what the poison is doing to other worlds across the universe—by blasting Siriaa to bits and sending those terrible creatures everywhere."

Many criminal minds are warped, Terrett said, causing everyone to nod in agreement.

"We have to decide our first order of business," Sal pointed out. "Prioritize our goals and attempt to recreate the enemy's thoughts and plans."

"I believe the people of Vic'Law should come first—they'll starve or freeze in this winter if we don't do something," I said. "Juffa had all the power companies. Someone will want those and fast. It's sad that very little is solar powered on this world."

"There's very little money in what can be had for free," Kaldill said. "The families won't care that the population freezes to death while they fight over the power stations."

"To say nothing of those who may be killed in the crossfire as the families pick each other off," Berel offered dryly.

I suddenly felt as if we were on an island, besieged on all sides by an enemy whose only care was for himself.

~

Le-Ath Veronis
  Lissa

"Honey?" I stood in alarm the moment Bel Erland appeared in my private study.

"Everything's fine, Gran," he held up a hand as he grinned at me. I opened my arms; he came to give me a hug.

"What do you need, then?" I smiled as he pulled away.

"I need a pirate ship," he said and laughed.

Vic'Law

Quin

"I have this," Yanzi appeared as dinner was served that evening, Terrett right behind him.

"These are manifests," Caylon scrolled through the comp-vid Yanzi handed him.

Ships bound for here that are being diverted, Terrett informed us. *Where they're from, what they carry and when they ought to arrive. For the next two months.*

I could see that he and Yanzi had employed a bit of subterfuge to get what they had—I wasn't sure I wanted to know how much danger they'd been in to get it.

"Where did this come from?" Sal asked, peering over Caylon's shoulder.

"Juffa records at Juffa estate," Yanzi grinned. "Terrett hide us. I steal."

"You wily sidewinder," Sal breathed as he studied the information.

"Not sidewinder, but accept compliment," Yanzi chuckled.

"They have warlocks, don't they?" Kaldill asked.

"Many. Each family there," Yanzi agreed. "Having standoff. Barstle make claim for dead family. Others not like."

"How powerful?" Bel Erland arrived in the middle of our conversation.

"Hmmph. Best third level," Yanzi huffed.

"At least they're not pooling their abilities," Kaldill said. "They could be dangerous if they did that."

"They worry about getting paid. Not others," Yanzi said.

"Usually the way it is with outlaw warlocks," Bel Erland nodded. "What's for dinner? I'm starved."

You're fifth level, aren't you? I sent to Bel, who grinned as he helped himself to a pile of fried chicken.

Yeah. Wizards are backward—they work their way from fifth to first. Warlocks work from first to fifth. Don't get that argument started between a wizard and warlock in a bar. The bar usually ends up paying the price.

Did you do something like that?

Dad and Grampa made me fix it afterward, so yeah, I guess I did.

I snickered. Bel grinned.

There's something else, he said, employing power to place a roll and a pat of butter on my plate.

What's that? I asked.

You'll see it after dinner.

∾

"What the holy hell?" Sal walked around the command console on the bridge of a new starship.

"Here's the outside image," Bel said, holding out his hands and forming a picture with power.

The ship was built large enough to hold us, yet small enough to speed past most anything else that flew through star systems. It was black, like the night about us, except for the name and insignia on its sleek skin.

BlackWing was painted boldly in white on the sides, with a strange image of a skull and crossed bones shining beneath the name.

"A pirate ship?" Sal made a face at Bel.

"What better way to take Cayetes' shipments and piss him off at the same time? We'll be the criminal element he doesn't know about. He'll come after us. Isn't that the objective? Gran thought it was a good idea. Kooper knows already, so we can slip away from the ASD when we need to."

"Pirates?" I frowned at Bel.

"Quinnie, if there's a way to draw Vardil Cayetes away from whatever hole he's hiding in, this may be it. He'll be infuriated that we take what he intends for himself. We can keep the people of Vic'Law supplied with food and necessities behind everybody's back, too. If we equip some of the larger cities with solar power and hide it from the warring families, we may be able to keep the population alive while everybody else is trying to take over."

"I think it's a magnificent idea," Berel breathed as he studied the console. "Who's flying it?"

"High five," Bel Erland held up a hand. Berel slapped Bel's palm with his and grinned. A friendship was forming between them and I was glad. Both had diplomatic skills that would make most rulers envious.

"We need a captain who isn't connected to the rest of us," Kaldill suggested. "Someone trustworthy and above reproach, in case all of us are needed elsewhere."

"We will think on that," Caylon agreed. "Surely someone can be found quickly, before we steal our first cargo ship."

Avendor

"Bear, what do you have planned for the next six months or so?"

Bear Wright, a grizzly bear shapeshifter, blinked at Ashe Evans. When the Mighty Hand asked, it was usually a good idea to pay attention.

"Whatever you want me to do." Bear, whose feet were resting on a thick tree stump he'd pulled from the ground by himself, dropped his boots to the porch outside his front door and stood to stretch.

"You think you'd mind captaining a starship with Amos and Flossie Thompson? I think I heard them complain about not going anywhere recently."

"That sounds like a fine idea," Bear grinned. "When do we leave?"

Vic'Law

Quin

During the night, after I'd gone to bed (Terrett slept beside me, while Yanzi's snake was coiled at the foot of the bed), the explosion that destroyed Juffa's natural-gas plant in Mundia woke all of us.

Dressed only in pajamas and barefoot, I raced after Terrett and Yanzi, who ran toward the library.

Without natural gas, there would be no heat in Mundia. "We need to turn it off before the entire city burns," Caylon snapped the moment we arrived in the library.

He, Lafe and Sal already had blades strapped to their backs. I wasn't willing to let them leave me behind—I understood that people had been hurt in the blast. I blamed it on the Cardino/Churg alliance; I imagined their goal was to freeze or destroy anyone in Mundia who might still be loyal to Juffa. The others were already gathered in the library—those who were able had folded space to get there.

"Bel, I need a coat," I begged. I was ready to fly myself to the fire if the others wouldn't take me.

"I'll take you," Bel Erland gave me a curt nod while a warm coat appeared in his hands.

"I take," Yanzi declared. "You save power. May need," he informed Bel.

"I'm coming," Berel ran into the library. He'd dressed hastily, but at least he was dressed.

"I'll see you there," Kaldill nodded at me before he disappeared.

"Just get us there," Justis said, coming to stand beside me. Caylon, Sal and Lafe disappeared; Yanzi, who was powerful in his own right, ferried the rest of us.

The natural-gas power plant was one of the few things the workers refused to abandon after Juffa's death; it was vital to provide heat for Mundia. Roaring flames from burning gas licked the air while flakes of ash from the burning building swirled toward the clouds; I saw that first as Yanzi set us down outside the perimeter.

What made me angry was this—Barstle Cardino and Nardes Churg had ordered their bomb squad to keep the Mundia Fire Patrol away from the burning facility. They were content to kill anyone who approached; two lines of heavily armed men prevented anyone from getting close enough to fight the blaze.

Amid the roar of flames and the groan and crash of melting beams, I could hear the screams of the workers who'd survived, only to be ignored by those who'd bombed the facility in the beginning.

"I can seal it off to remove the fuel source," Bel Erland shouted.

"What about the survivors?" I shouted back. Heat rolled off the fire as another loud explosion rocked the ground; the winds blew fire and ash in our direction. The very air around us was stained orange and red as we struggled to keep our feet.

"It will only take a minute or two to kill the fire," Bel shouted back.

"What about those guards?" Berel yelled while flinging an arm toward the bombers who blocked access to the building. Their weapons were raised—they'd seen us and were prepared to fire.

"Easy enough," Kaldill joined the shouted conversation. Holding out a hand, he made each weapon disappear. The guards, thirty or more of them, stared in shock at empty hands for a moment before striding toward us.

They'd been paid—and instructed—to kill any who attacked them.

We were about to have a fight on our hands.

Justis took flight, arrowing downward after making a circle overhead. He grabbed the lead attacker with one hand while his wings beat a strong, steady rhythm. The men left behind shouted; the man screamed as Justis dropped him into the raging fire.

He'd done the proper thing—they were weaponless, now.

"I'm going," I shouted at Terrett.

Take me with you, he demanded. Before I could stop him, he was clinging to me like a sloth to a tree. Before I left the ground, Yanzi's snake was wrapped around both of us.

It wasn't the most graceful flying I'd ever done, but I carried them past the attackers and toward the nearest victim who needed my help.

CHAPTER 10

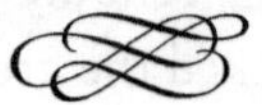

Terrett

By sunrise, I think the entire city of Mundia knew the name BlackWing. Yanzi and I helped Quin as much as we could while Caylon and the others destroyed a small army of bombers. Afterward, they turned their attention to finding victims and bringing them to Quin.

Caylon then led a search for those in the city who'd helped plot the destruction of the gas plant; most of those were related in some way to several crime families. Barstle Cardino's reach had grown quite long.

After Caylon's party dispatched the last of those responsible, he sent a message to Barstle Cardino on a communicator he'd taken from one of the plotters. I wish I'd been there to see Barstle Cardino bluster and call Caylon Black a liar, but I only heard about it afterward.

In essence, Caylon told Barstle to come and take the city back—if he could.

Quin, though—she'd worked through the night, saving anyone who remained alive after the explosion. Eyes opened in wonder as burned and blackened flesh became pink and whole again.

Wounds from the blast were eliminated—as if they'd never been.

For those we couldn't save, we promised a memorial. That would happen after Quin slept—she'd nearly dropped from exhaustion after healing so many.

The rest of us slept in shifts during the day—just to make sure someone was awake if there were an emergency. Thankfully, Mundia wasn't attacked again while we rested.

News came too, that we now had a captain and small crew on the *BlackWing*; the ship orbited Vic'Law while being shielded by someone aboard. I was anxious to see who'd be transporting us whenever we traveled on it—I wanted to make sure they respected Quin and the others.

Terrett? Quin's sleepy voice invaded my thoughts.

I'm coming, love, I replied.

Quin

Yanzi and Daragar fixed the pipes and equipment at the power plant, but we'll discuss bringing in solar panels after the memorial, Terrett helped me off the bed. I felt rumpled and dirty—someone had wiped soot and ash off me before placing me beneath the covers, but I couldn't get the smell of burned flesh and metal out of my nose.

"Do I have time for a shower?" I asked while Terrett searched beneath the bed for my house slippers.

Yes—I sent mindspeech to Kaldill—he says to hurry if you can—dinner is waiting and then the memorial.

"I'll hurry," I promised, although I only wanted to get clean and crawl back in bed. Terrett understood—he looked tired, too, so I did my best to make his job of herding me about as easy as I could.

Dinner was a hurried affair—sandwiches and soup. Terrett advised me to dress in the black leather; it was an appropriate color for mourning on Vic'Law.

A sea of people waited for us when we appeared and walked toward the circle of stones set up for the event. I could see Kaldill's hand in the area—flowers grew in the harshest of conditions about the stones.

Family members came forward to give the names of their dead and to tell the crowd about them. Several weren't old enough in my opinion to be working such a late shift at a power plant.

Juffa hadn't cared about any of them. I cared not that he was dead. In the beginning, I'd seen him as the most reasonable step toward capturing Vardil Cayetes. He'd proven himself faithless and worthless in a short amount of time.

After the lengthy memorial was over, several Mundians separated themselves from the others and approached us.

"We wish to know if you intend to replace Juffa," one of them said.

He was tall, with sparse brown hair and a look about him that bespoke a difficult life. He was also the eldest among those who came.

"We have no desire to replace that excrement," Kaldill huffed.

"Then why are you here?" he asked.

"Master Shim," I stepped forward, surprising him with the use of his name, "We have no desire to place ourselves over you, if that is what you mean. Drood Juffa was a callous man whose main concern was for himself and his family. It is my hope that we can assist Mundia in finding a better life for all its citizens."

"You're BlackWing. The one who saved so many," Shim breathed.

"I did as much as I could, although some were beyond my saving."

"We are grateful. Is there a time when we," he gestured at the others about him, "can meet with you and your companions, to discuss Mundia's future?"

"We will meet with you tomorrow," Caylon stepped forward and nodded at Shim. "Shall we come to you, or would you like us to transport you to our temporary home?"

"We will come to you," Shim agreed. "We know where you are—the tracking information at the plant indicated when energy was being used at one of the Juffa estates nearby."

"Then we will welcome you tomorrow, if you'd like to have dinner with us."

A time was agreed upon; we watched as they walked away, fading past surrounding buildings.

"For you," Kaldill snapped a rose from the flowers he'd grown and handed it to me.

"Thank you." I sniffed velvety petals—it smelled so sweet and innocent, compared to the stench of death and injury I'd been exposed to the night before.

"Quin?" Jayna came to me, carrying an extra shawl. She, Mell, Jeslin and Pellen had come with us—the rest stayed to guard the mansion.

"Wrap her up, she's shivering," Kaldill directed. I hadn't noticed; perhaps I was too weary and concerned to notice. I only wanted a warm bed and not to be wakened until morning.

If I'd read things properly, Mundia was now cut off from the rest of Vic'Law—Caylon's challenge to Barstle Cardino had seen to that. Mundia would need food and supplies from somewhere, only I was too tired to think everything through at the moment.

"Will we have a meeting to decide how to bring in food and supplies?" I asked as Jayna wrapped the shawl about me.

"We will—after you've rested," Kaldill assured me. "Don't let it disturb your sleep tonight, Deah-Mul."

Freighter Killshot
Bleek

The answer was so simple I cursed myself for not researching it at the beginning. Whip shoved a comp-vid into my free hand that morning. At first, I held onto it while tapping ship coordinates in with two hands and sipping tea from a cup held with a third.

When I finished drinking, I held the comp-vid before my eyes while two other hands continued tapping coordinates. Blevakians have four frontal lobes in their brains, after all, with a total of six. Other humanoids only had four. At times, I pitied them.

Then, I found what I searched for—an application from those who'd escaped Vogeffa II—they'd applied to the Grand Alliance

Council to name their new country New Vogeffa. I stared at a map of the proposed New Vogeffa, located on the northern end of a large continent on Harifa Edus. My cursing started then and didn't abate for many ticks. I cursed myself first, because I hadn't considered the idea, then I cursed Whip for his lack of insight. I cursed Cayetes, too, but in my own language, which Whip didn't understand.

"Give me time to change our course and coordinates," I growled when my cursing fit was over. "I'll inform Lord Cayetes of our discovery then."

"Of course, Commander Bleek." Whip backed away before turning and leaving Killshot's helm quickly, his footsteps clacking on the rub-metal mat for quite a distance. I understood he was heading directly for the freight-vator to inform the crew—and to inform Cayetes, too.

I'd known for some time that Whip was Cayetes' insurance against me. That every move was analyzed and reported. So far, nothing had alerted Cayetes that I was anything but loyal to him. This would be no different. Cayetes would expect me to head for the target first, so as not to waste time. He wanted this and wanted it badly.

My guess—because I also had spies in Cayetes employ—was that I'd be directed to haul the escapees away, then check each for a particular blood type. Only those fitting the appropriate profile would be kept. He'd expect me to destroy the others, simply because he was angry that they'd gotten away from him to start with.

Vardil was Hordace Cayetes' much younger brother, and during his childhood, he'd been spoiled by Hordace, who'd given Vardil anything he wanted.

Vardil hadn't changed his ways. He was still spoiled and used to getting his way. In my opinion, his mother should have drowned him in the birthing tub when he was born.

My hands flew over the tabs, setting new coordinates for Harifa Edus. At our best speed, we'd arrive the following day.

Zephili

"Bleek will inform you of our course change the moment he has the ship headed in the proper direction, Lord Cayetes," Whip spoke via comp-vid with Vardil.

"Harifa Edus, eh?" Vardil, ensconced in a fresh body, tapped a finger on his chin. "Isn't Harifa Edus where some of Siriaa's former population now resides?"

"That is what I discovered when searching for that world," Whip agreed. "They call their lands New Fyris."

"Very good. I'll have Bleek hold off for a day or two until I can move more freighters in—we'll take those from New Fyris, too. The crews will determine which bodies will be suitable for me in the future."

"What about the others?"

"Kill them," Vardil shrugged. "They should have been dead already."

"Will Magul be in charge of the extra ships?"

"No—he's on a private mission," Vardil snapped. Whip recoiled—this was obviously a private matter concerning a touchy subject. He resolved to find out as much as he could as a result.

"We're having problems with one of the Sirenali clones," Whip diverted Vardil's anger. "The ship's doctor thinks he's dying."

"Younger or older?" Vardil asked.

"Older—from the first set. The ones nearing twenty."

"Keep me advised—I'll have someone check the others from that set. If we have to replace them all, we will."

Whip nodded, although in his mind, they should never have sold Terrett—he was three centuries old and a real Sirenali. He'd understood his place, too. Whip also knew where Terrett had ended up—as a slave to Marid of Belancour. Probably dead, now—just as Marid was.

New Fyris

"False alarm," Rodrik waved a hand as he walked into Amlis' study. "Beatris is resting—the doctor says soon but not yet."

"The child is healthy?" Amlis asked, standing and stretching.

"Very," Rodrik grinned. "If he's anything like his older sister, he'll make his presence known the moment he can."

"Perhaps I should look for a wife, Rod," Amlis turned toward the window at his back and surveyed the courtyard and the city beyond.

"But you don't want to. I can see that much," Rodrik said softly.

"I believe I've burned my bridges, as Queen Lissa says."

"You're not the only one she'll never forgive. Remember that."

"I've been told that she may never be able to birth a child. That is another strike. Look for a suitable bride, Rodrik. One who will produce an heir for New Fyris."

"As you command, my Prince."

Le-Ath Veronis

Magul smiled and nodded at the agent checking his ID. Deris provided his disguise while Daris manufactured proper Alliance ID. He'd boarded a ship from Refizan after Vardil's warlock transported him there; he'd purchased a ticket to Le-Ath Veronis afterward.

"Your purpose for this visit to Le-Ath Veronis?" The agent asked, checking Magul's image against that on the ID.

"Vacation. I want to see the glass castle," Magul declared.

"Everybody wants to see the glass castle," the agent replied in a bored voice. "Here's your ID. Have a pleasant stay."

Vic'Law

Terrett

Quin? I leaned in to place a kiss on her temple. Her head was on my shoulder—where it belonged. I'd let her sleep late—it gave me time to watch her while she was relaxed. I hoped her dreams didn't contain remnants of her worries; those were piling up at an alarming rate.

"Terrett?" her eyes hadn't opened yet, but she stretched within my embrace. Her body brushed against my cock, which was already quite hard.

My heart, I want to love you, I informed her. I watched as her eyes opened. She didn't appear frightened, as she had before.

"Will you teach me?" Her voice trembled slightly.

Whatever you want to know, I moved aside so I could kiss her easily. *I will go as slowly as my impatient body will allow.*

~

Quin

"Tomorrow, lessons will resume," Caylon informed me when Terrett and I wandered into the kitchen at midday. Working to hide the blush that threatened, I poured a cup of tea for myself and offered one to Terrett. He nodded and smiled—we'd just had what he called *fun in bed*.

It had been fun. Although the climax wasn't as intense as my first experience, Terrett had given me pleasure. Daragar was correct—there was no pain with my first physical coupling.

I was grateful.

It had also taken my mind off many troubles, and I was grateful for that, too. Terrett smiled and saluted me with his cup before drinking. I ducked my head and smiled, too.

~

BlackWing I

Bear Wright

"We have two ships bound for Vic'Law today," Ace set a comp-vid on my desk. He and his wife, Wynn, wanted to join the crew; they'd arrived with Marco and Cori DeLuca the night before after getting Ashe's permission to leave SouthStar and come with us.

The one who'd surprised me by coming on his own was William Winkler.

"So we follow at a reasonable distance and engage Cayetes' ships when they show up?" I asked.

"That's the plan," Ace grinned. He'd allowed his pale, blond hair to grow longer; a lock fell over an eyebrow as he nodded. Ace was a rare, white wolf when he shifted. Wynn, his mate, was even rarer—a unicorn.

Marco was a black wolf—Cori a panther. Winkler was perhaps the ultimate werewolf—for years, he'd acted as the Dallas Packmaster on Old Earth.

"What if we need backup?" I asked.

"We have something planned—a fleet of six is at our disposal at the Le-Ath Veronis space station, all painted, named and numbered *BlackWing Two* through *Seven*. I talked Lissa into it yesterday. They're hidden in a private hangar."

"What if we need them immediately?"

"Then it's my job to transport them," Winkler chuckled.

"Outfitted with crews, I take it?"

"Most of them. I believe Farzi and Nenzi have command of number two."

"They can transport themselves," I pointed out.

"Less for me to do," Winkler shrugged.

"Never thought I'd be a pirate," Ace slapped Winkler on the back.

"All we need now are eye patches and a parrot," Winkler quipped.

Vic'Law

Quin

"You think Cardino and Churg are holed up in Puntia? That's less than a hundred clicks away," Sal said.

We were deep in our meeting to determine how to keep the people of Mundia warm and supplied through what looked to be a terrible winter. Snow fell outside the library window; I watched large flakes swirl and eddy as the wind blew them against the mansion. While I'd slept through the night, snow had already accumulated that would cover my boot-tops. More was coming before the night was out, too.

"They'll attempt to cut off our supply of natural gas, now that their efforts to destroy the plant and burn down most of the city have failed," Caylon tilted his head in acknowledgment. Already we understood that they'd anticipated this storm and had timed their attack on the power plant before its arrival. Without our intervention, many in Mundia would be frozen by morning.

"It's likely that food deliveries are already interrupted, although Shim will bring that information with him when he and his twenty arrive tonight," Berel pointed out. He and Bel Erland had already discussed this, I could tell.

"I've had word from Winkler—they're tracking two ships that left port bound for Vic'Law today," Sal said. "They intend to stay a safe distance behind until Cayetes' ships show up to take the cargo and leave both crews dead."

"What's the cargo?"

"Textiles, clothing and specialized orders for the families on one ship," Sal said. "The other has wheat, imported beer, electronics, that sort of thing."

"Because the warehouses between here and Puntia are supposed to supply Mundia with food," Kaldill tossed up a hand in frustration. "I can arrange for exports from elsewhere to feed the city—at least for a short while. We need something long-term."

"Greenhouses and hydroponics? Mundia is beside a river," Bel Erland said. "We have plenty of water, even if supply ships are stopped."

"What about the manufacturing concerns, here?" Justis asked. "What does Mundia make that can be marketed elsewhere?"

His observations made me think of Puntia and what Barstle Cardino and Nardes Churg could be manufacturing to sell elsewhere. If my suspicions were correct, those two had been in league together for several years. Somewhere, too, was the distribution point for the drakus seed. That intensified my desire to look at Barstle, Nardes and their connection to someone from the Xilva family—I'd know exactly what they were plotting and how deep their betrayal of Vic'Law ran.

"If there are any existing buildings that aren't in operation or are manufacturing something that isn't really needed by the residents, then I suggest repurposing them," Berel said. "I feel we can have a thriving greenhouse section quickly if we work toward that goal."

"We can ask for enough wheat to keep the city in bread for a few weeks after we take those two ships," Lafe suggested.

"I think same," Yanzi agreed.

"I want to find the source of the drakus seed," I blurted. "Whether it is grown here or delivered at Cayetes' command. We need it gone. I worry that Barstle and Nardes are intending to use it to take Vic'Law. What Cayetes has planned for them afterward I don't wish to know."

"What evidence do you have for this?" Caylon asked.

"All those men—who were firing at Justis and me—all of them had drakus seed in their systems. I believe that Cayetes or someone else has devised a way to keep from killing the drakus seed addicts, but with the intention of keeping them under their thumb through their addiction."

"How did those men die, Quin?" Caylon asked.

Hanging my head, I struggled not to weep. "I killed them," I whispered. "I called to the drakus seed in them. It overwhelmed them immediately and stopped their hearts. I killed them."

Turning, I ran from the room, barely able to see through my tears as I sought my suite.

Bel Erland

"At least we know, now," Caylon sat heavily on a sofa near the fireplace.

"I hope you understand that this talent is something she will use only as a last resort?" Kaldill's voice was low and filled with anger. "Justis' last protection jewel had fired before she did this. She was protecting his life."

"You act as if I'm Quin's enemy," Caylon snapped back. "I assure you I am not. The Orb, on the other hand—I do not trust it. As long as it has control of Quin, then I will be suspicious."

"Then be suspicious outside her hearing," Lafe growled before leaving the library.

Justis was already gone—he'd raced after Quin following her disappearance. I'd risen to follow, but Justis beat me to the door.

Therefore, I stayed in the library to listen to the others.

Quin

"You saved my life." Justis' arms were wrapped tightly about me. I'd wanted to weep my heart out alone, but he'd found me anyway. "The first time you have to kill may be the hardest, but it's never easy, my love. I'm grateful for your intervention, or I wouldn't be here with you now."

I hated having to do it, I sent. I couldn't speak the words aloud, so I chose mindspeech.

I hate that you had to do it, too. We're hunting criminals, beloved. You must be prepared to protect yourself and those you care for.

I would do it again—I can't lose you a second time, fresh tears fell.

I'm sorry you thought me dead, he replied.

"How is she?" Lafe arrived and took a seat on the bed on my other side, his weight making the frame creak softly. His hand ran gently down my feathers, soothing what had been ruffled during the dash to my suite.

"Upset about killing those who deserved it," Justis responded.

"My love, they would have killed you without a second thought—you'd be dead if Kaldill's shield hadn't held. He explained that to me afterward, over a bottle of very strong wine," Lafe straightened another feather.

"Most trainees aren't faced with such terrible opponents so early in their instruction," Caylon appeared. "You have my apologies, young virsee."

"I want to fold space," I quavered the moment Caylon disappeared.

~

Le-Ath Veronis

Magul stood at the railing of the tour boat, staring at the glass castle. The structure was enormous. Certainly larger than he'd imagined after seeing the images on his comp-vid. If he were used to appreciating such things, he'd have thought it breathtaking. Instead, he glowered as he imagined how much trouble it would be to get into it.

Swimmers were lifted regularly from the waters by vigilant Black Wing guards and deposited wet and shivering on the deck of the boat they'd leapt from. They'd drown otherwise—the current surrounding the castle was much too strong to swim.

Vardil Cayetes had sent him to accomplish an impossible task. He wouldn't accept any excuse for not getting the job done, no matter how valid Magul's reasons might be.

"Do you suppose the Red Wing King ever comes out?" a woman sidled up to him. Magul recognized her face and preened at her interest—she was quite becoming. Perhaps a dalliance before the day was over? It would take his mind off his task and help convince her at the same time.

"I have no idea," Magul offered a false smile. "Perhaps we can find out. Together."

~

BlackWing I
Bear Wright

"They're here," Marco pulled up a map of our immediate surroundings. Cayetes' ships—three of them—had slipped in behind the two freighters. They were now between us and the intended targets.

152

"What kind of defense system do the freighters have on board?" Ace asked.

"Just the standard laser cannons—in case they're fired on," Winkler replied after studying a comp-vid he held. "These shipping lanes are generally safe."

"Not anymore," Amos Thompson observed dryly. "Who's up for target practice?"

∼

Vic'Law

Quin

"Mr. Thompson is in charge of BlackWing's weapons," Sal said. "He was a sharpshooter when he was in the military. He doesn't miss his targets."

"You mean Cayetes' ships are under attack now?" Mell asked.

I'd been lured to the kitchen after Justis and Lafe stopped my tears, with the promise of hot tea and a fresh cookie. We'd found Sal already there, eating a plate of cookies.

"That's what I heard," Sal nodded. "Winkler called in another ship—the BlackWing II, so that ought to do it. They'll redirect the freighters after they take care of Cayetes' crew."

"What will they do with them? The crew?" I asked. Sal handed me a cookie off his plate with a grin. "Other than leaving them in an escape pod or two, nothing—I hear Kooper and the ASD will just happen along and take them into custody. If we can get Alliance newsvids here, I figure we'll see them hauled off to jail. Cayetes will be livid."

"He'll try to kill what we've captured," Justis pointed out. "So they won't talk."

"True. If they're taken to Le-Ath Veronis, I'd like to see Cayetes' assassins try to get past Lissa's guards."

They may have Sirenali with them, Terrett said. *My love, are you all right?* He and Berel walked into the kitchen together.

I'm all right, I replied.

"Lissa knows to post guards who aren't susceptible to a Sirenali's obsession," Sal said. "Although they can cause enough trouble to make up for that between the space station and the palace."

Let's hope they can't speak, then, Terrett frowned.

"Cayetes needs to stop making them," I muttered. "He's abusing them, if my guess is right."

He would, Terrett agreed. I blinked at him before turning away. Yes, I understood some things about Terrett's past—things he didn't like to recall. I didn't want to cause him pain by bringing them up.

"Our guests will be here in an hour," Kaldill folded into the kitchen to remind us. "Dress casually so we won't upset or offend our visitors."

Our guests arrived together, although they had a difficult time getting up the hill in the snow. They should have accepted our invitation to pick them up, but they weren't sure they could trust us.

Not yet.

Kaldill, Berel and Bel Erland greeted them at the door and brought them into the dining hall, which Mell, Pellen and Jeslin had managed to make as plain as they could. The food was also plainer than might be found on many a table belonging to those in power on Vic'Law—by design.

Still, the food was very good, with a few additions that our guests would certainly appreciate. They were brought to the table; Shim made introductions and the meal went well.

"I think we can have things well in hand by the end of an eight-day," Kaldill explained. "You must understand that Mundia is a special case for us, and we don't want it falling into the hands of Barstle Cardino and Nardes Churg.

"Because this is the largest manufacturing city on Vic'Law," one of our guests complained.

"Once our mission here is complete, we will leave the city with its citizens," Bel Erland interjected.

"What is your mission?" Shim asked, his eyes narrowing in speculation.

"We're from the Reth Alliance," Kaldill explained. "We're trying to keep Vic'Law out of the hands of Vardil Cayetes. If you don't know who that is, then you are fortunate. As bad as the crime families are on Vic'Law, Cayetes is worse. Five years ago, he destroyed an entire planet with a ranos cannon because he was angry with one man."

If we hadn't captured our guests' full attention before, we had it now. They'd heard about Siriaa's destruction through bootlegged interceptions of Alliance news.

"You're from the Reth Alliance?" Shim whispered, as if one of Vic'Law's crime families might be listening to our conversation.

"Yes," Kaldill replied.

"Why are you here? Nobody ever helps Vic'Law."

"Because we hunt Cayetes, who is not only a danger to you, but to all people. Normally we wouldn't interfere with any non-Alliance world, but as you can guess, this is a special case."

"What about the crime families?" Our disgruntled guest spoke again. "Will you leave us to them when you go?"

"They're doing their best to kill each other," Caylon snorted. "Once the Juffa family was destroyed, they're fighting to take Drood's place. Juffa killed most of the Cardino family when he learned they were plotting against him; much of Birtes Churg's family is now dead by Nardes Churg's command. At this time, Barstle Cardino and Nardes Churg have allied and appear to have the upper hand."

"They'll come here," several whispered. "We're as good as dead."

"Don't be frightened; there is more here to defend you than you know," Sal said. "We are arranging for food and supplies to be brought in to keep the city going, while we work at making it self-sufficient."

"Puntia is less than one hundred clicks away," Shim pointed out. "Nardes Churg is in charge there. It may serve as a base for him to attack us."

"We're anticipating that," Caylon shrugged. "He won't get far, I assure you."

"You expect us to believe that you, here," the skeptic swept out a hand, "will be able to fight off the army that Cardino and Churg can send against Mundia?"

That's when the realization hit me. Shim and his skeptical friend were right to be worried. I could see in the gleam of Caylon's eyes that he wanted to draw Cayetes attention—not just to us, but to the city we defended. He wanted Cayetes to attack us here. He wanted to destroy whatever Cayetes could send against us.

Is this what Director Griff wants, too, Sursee? I sent to him.

Kooper is prepared if we can draw out much of Cayetes' forces, yes.

What about these people? My mental voice conveyed my worry for them.

It is my hope that all will survive unscathed.

We will have to defend them against what is here, first, I pointed out. *They have no reason to trust us. They may find no reason to trust us.*

All the vermin in one trap, Caylon responded.

I didn't reply. Clamping my wings tighter to my back, I stared at the food on my plate. Mell and Jeslin had made pasta for me; it would be tasteless past this point. Was this the reason they'd chosen Mundia from all the cities we could have picked after our exit from the Juffa estate?

Were the efforts being made to feed the people and keep them warm merely a way to placate me? Yes, I'd read people all my life, but I'd never been surrounded by so many who held so much power before. Were my readings of them faulty as a result?

I couldn't tell.

Other worries crowded my mind. My fear was growing and I had no explanation for it; I merely had a foggy notion that I should be afraid.

I feel sick, I sent to Kaldill.

"Please excuse me," Kaldill rose from the table. "I shall return shortly." He walked to my chair, helped me up and together we left the dining room.

Jayna stayed with me when Kaldill left my suite to return to the meeting. Still, I couldn't shake the fear that had come over me, although I had no explanation for it.

"Is it the cramping?" Jayna asked softly as I hugged myself and paced by the window. Outside, snow continued to fall, silent and uncaring that people were huddled in their homes against its chill.

"No—I don't have that," I mumbled. I'd never had that. I hadn't been born—as she had. Shoving those thoughts aside, I searched for the reasons behind my fear. I found nothing and the longer I paced, the worse my fears became.

When the Orb appeared, I was terrified.

Bel Erland

I listened without comment while Caylon talked of arming the people of Mundia—those who were capable of handling weapons—in case Cardino and Churg led forces against the city.

Clearly, their attention was directed elsewhere for now; they had to wrest Vic'Law from the grasp of their rivals first. Then Mundia would become their target.

In their estimation, we'd be starving and willing to allow them to walk in unchallenged when that time came. Caylon knew differently. For years uncounted, he'd been General to the Crane Warlord on Falchan. His aim in this was to allow the enemy to weaken itself in battles against other enemies, while he reinforced his army and waited for the eventual attack.

The plan was solid.

I worried that there could be something we weren't expecting in all this. A knife to the back, while we were busy protecting the front. My fears were realized when Jayna ran into the dining hall, weeping.

"Quin is gone," she wailed. "A shining light came and she disappeared."

I was standing before I realized it.

The connection we had to Quin had failed to take us with her.

CHAPTER 11

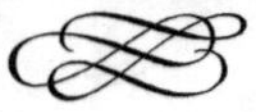

Le-Ath Veronis

   Lissa

It took three Larentii to calm Kaldill down. Bel Erland, who'd brought Terrett with him, had followed Kaldill straight to my palace. Bel was pale as a ghost and barely speaking, while Kaldill continued to mutter curses.

Terrett appeared lost.

If the others hadn't been meeting with twenty residents of Mundia, they'd likely be here, too. All asking the same question.

Why had the bond failed?

To make matters worse, Erland's carefully placed chip wasn't working either. We had no way to track Quin—wherever or whenever—she was.

～

Killshot

   Bleek

We'd parked Killshot just outside sensor range of Harifa Edus, waiting for several ships to join us. With our laser cannons charged

158

and aimed at strategic points outside the city and smaller towns we intended to take, we settled in to watch the planet, eat and make plans.

With my boots resting on the helm as I watched the planet far below us, the winged girl appeared from nowhere and slammed onto the rub-metal mat beside my chair.

Quin

I was so terrified I almost lost consciousness. Although I'd never seen him before, I knew I stared into the eyes of Bleek, Cayetes' general. Two right arms wheeled his captain's chair around while booted feet hit the floor beside my head.

When he stood, he towered far above me, while I could only cringe at his feet. He could crush my head with a well-placed kick; we both understood that.

Black hair swept about his face; black eyes studied me while I lowered my own. I didn't wish to see my death coming.

"You're the girl from LaFranza's shop. What in the bloody god's name are you doing here?"

Reaching down, he grabbed one of my wings and jerked me to my feet, causing me to cry out. For a moment, I could only work my jaw while nothing came from my mouth. "I'm so sorry, Master Bleek. Please, don't kill me."

He laughed.

Where are you? Queen Lissa answered my call.

In the brig aboard one of Cayetes' ships. I couldn't keep the quaver from my mental voice.

Do you know where?

Outside Harifa Edus. I saw it in Bleek's face—Cayetes wants to take back what he lost from Vogeffa II, and he also wants to take New Fyris. He's waiting on more of Cayetes' ships to come and help.

Do you know when they'll arrive?

I think tomorrow.

Are you in immediate danger?

No—he laughed and tossed me in the brig. *I don't present a danger to him —in his estimation.*

Then stay there for now—let him think we don't know. I'll arrange for our forces to meet him and the other ships when they arrive.

All right.

Clamping my feathers about me—it was cold in my small prison—I resolved to wait for rescue. I should have known better. Really.

Whip, Bleek's second-in-command, came for me. He demanded that I serve dinner to him and the crew, while they laughed and made fun of me. He'd informed Cayetes, too, of the apparent stowaway aboard the ship.

He could think of no other way I might have gotten there.

What he didn't realize was this—I knew where Cayetes was, now.

Zephili.

I informed Queen Lissa of that fact while Whip pulled me by a wing toward the ship's galley. At least my wings didn't hurt so much when someone pulled them. I reminded myself of that every time Whip jerked on it while we walked.

Le-Ath Veronis

Terrett

If I'd been with her, I would have killed anyone who touched her. Then I'd probably have been killed in return.

It made me sigh—and hope she stayed in the brig. I knew what kind of torture Cayetes' crew was capable of. I'd seen Bleek's handiwork too many times to count. Bel Erland had gone back to Vic'Law for Berel after the meeting was over with the Mundians. All three of us now sat in morose silence in Queen Lissa's arboretum, contemplating Quin's danger.

All of us had relied on a bond that so obviously hadn't worked. I still couldn't puzzle that out in my mind.

"I just heard from Bree," Queen Lissa arrived and took a seat next to her grandson.

"What did she say, Gran?" Bel asked.

"She said she nullified the bond temporarily—so you wouldn't be tossed onto Bleek's ship while in the middle of a meeting with the people from Mundia. It was a hard choice and a delicate situation."

"So Quin is there by herself, because Mundia might be offended?" Bel rose and stalked toward the tall windows. Outside, Lissia and Casino City glittered in the constant twilight covering this half of Le-Ath Veronis.

"Honey, I don't think it's that simple," Lissa rose to follow him. She placed an arm around him when she reached his side and leaned her head against his shoulder.

For a moment, I felt the old desire for loving parents. I knew who my mother was; she'd sold me when I was five and watched as my tongue was cut out. I never knew who my father was. When I'd passed my first fifty years, I understood that loving parents would remain a dream for me.

I was Sirenali, though, so my father had to be Sirenali as well. I cursed him and my mother—thoroughly and silently as I watched grandmother and grandson share their fears and their affection atop a high palace.

Bel Erland

Yanzi brought Justis and Lafe to Gran's palace late that evening; if Quin's information was correct, then we could be needed on board BlackWing ships. I wanted nothing more than to thwart Cayetes' bid to take the refugees from Vogeffa II as well as those from New Fyris. Getting Quin to safety was foremost in my mind, however.

Cayetes felt he was entitled to the refugees from Vogeffa II. They weren't people to him—only fodder to feed his addiction to life. Dad and I had already had a conversation about warlocks talented and powerful enough to perform Cayetes' transferences—there were many. Of those, some hadn't been seen for years. If we could find the site of one transfer that hadn't been cleaned or disturbed, we might be able to perform a reverse spell to discover who'd cast it.

There'd been nothing left behind on Vogeffa I; we'd already checked. This warlock was smart enough to remove any evidence so he couldn't be tracked, besides having at least one Sirenali at his elbow to hide him from those who held power.

Dad and Grampa already warned me about calling them if we found the warlock—in case their help was needed to contain him. As much as I wanted to take care of him myself, I understood the necessity and the logic behind their request.

"Would you like to visit Avii Castle?" Justis interrupted my thoughts. "Jurris wants to see me, so you may as well go with me if you'd like to see it. I imagine Gurnil would be happy to show the Crown Prince of Karathia through the place."

"Yes," I answered immediately. I'd take anything to relieve my worry for Quin and the thought that she could be at the mercy of terrible people.

"Good. Yanzi, Berel, Lafe and Terrett are coming, too; you'll be welcomed by my brother, as befits your station. I hear he's granted an interview with a journalist this morning, but we can see him immediately afterward."

"How is everything in Mundia?" I asked as I followed Justis toward the door. He'd found me moping in Gran's library; a hovercar would be waiting for us at the side door near the palace kitchen.

"Sal and Caylon have everything under control. They're providing body armor and extra weapons to the ASD agents there. I suggested bringing Jayna here, but Sal says not yet."

Nodding at Justis' statement, we walked down two flights of steps at a fast clip; Justis was military, after all, and used to commanding an army of winged troops. He wouldn't accept anything but my best effort—much like Sal and Caylon.

I admired him for that—that he could effortlessly take charge and set our pace. Dad and Grampa could do the same thing—just by walking into a room.

It took nearly an hour to reach the glass castle at a reasonable speed; we landed inside the bowl, where few outsiders were allowed to land. Terrett was amazed at the sheer size of the bowl, where orchards grew and sheep grazed.

"It amazing," Yanzi confirmed as we stepped out of the hovercar and looked about us. The walls of the outer castle rose high above us, and I couldn't help staring as we made our way toward a nearby door.

Just like the outside of the castle, the inside walls were lined with terraces where grass, trees and flower gardens grew.

Yanzi is correct—I'm amazed. I've never seen anything like this, Terrett marveled.

"The legend says that Liron built it from the sand of the seabed beneath it in a day," Justis shrugged. "I wasn't there, so I can't say for sure."

"Has it always been this color—of the sea, with other colors mixed in?" I asked.

"It tends to reflect much of what is around it—appearing more gray on stormy days," Justis said. "I like to fly about it on clear days, when the blue-green shines best."

"I fly around too—if possible," Yanzi agreed.

Killshot

Quin

Three of my feathers littered the floor—pulled from my wings by cruel men who thought it funny.

I set plates before them; roasted fowl with root vegetables in a rich sauce. I was elbowed away as often as not after setting a plate down— it reminded me greatly of my time in the guard's dining hall of Avii Castle.

A Sirenali of perhaps twenty years sat silent in a corner—on the floor, which wasn't comfortable. Thin he was, and sickly, with knees drawn to his chin and his arms wrapped about himself in a struggle to warm a frail body.

The moment I served the last plate of food and received an elbow in my ribs for my efforts, I made my way toward the Sirenali's corner.

"Where do you think you're going?"

Bleek had arrived and held me back with one of his four hands.

"He's sick—I can help him," I breathed. "Please allow me to help him, Master Bleek."

"See, she knows what to call me," Bleek chuckled and let me go. "He's dying, but sure, if you think you can help, go ahead. It'll save me having to put a bullet through his brain."

I was already glowing when I knelt beside the Sirenali; something in his genetic makeup was skewed and causing his body to die. Glowing brighter and bringing all my talent to bear, I set about fixing what had gone wrong with the poor soul.

"What in the bloody god's name did you do?" Bleek demanded, thumping two fists on his desk. I'd been dragged straight to the captain's quarters after helping the Sirenali to his feet. Yes, his body was still wasted, but he rose, smiling and hungry for the first time in several eight-days.

After a brief examination by the ship's doctor, he was pronounced healthy.

He couldn't speak, just as Terrett couldn't, but he eagerly nodded his thanks to me before Bleek hauled me away.

"I can heal the sick," I mumbled, staring at my shoes. One was covered in gravy, when one of Bleek's men shoved me while I carried plates of food. My body was beginning to ache—none of the punches, pinches or blows had been gentle.

"What happened to LaFranza? Is he dead?"

"No. I healed him," I admitted. "The last I saw him, he was having dinner with friends in Mundia."

"Mundia? On Vic'Law?" Bleek's voice had gone quiet. Deadly.

"Yes, Master Bleek."

"We'll come back to that. Come with me," he grabbed my wing again and dragged me out of his quarters toward the freight-vator. The ride down to the freight deck seemed to take forever, with my wing held in Bleek's hard grip. I worried that he'd snap bones if he didn't let me go soon.

I was pulled relentlessly across the deck toward a door on the far side. Bleek opened it with a handscan and shoved me inside.

I'd seen it in his face already; here was the reality. His son lay in a glass-topped coffin with a heavy, jeweled base. A large, formidable lock on the outside prevented anyone from opening it to interrupt the spell on the boy.

Bleek's son had been placed in stasis by a warlock who couldn't care less about either. It was merely a gesture to keep Bleek in line and in service to Vardil Cayetes. The coffin, though—the same warlock hadn't spelled the lock sealing the coffin.

Someone else had done that.

"Can you heal him?" Bleek's voice was rough as he pointed toward his son.

"I have to bring him out of the coffin and place my hands on him— like I did the other one upstairs," I said. "I think the spell on the lock prevents that."

"You can see the spell?" Bleek demanded, roughly swinging me around to face him. This time, I heard one of my wing bones snap and I cried out from the pain of it. At least he let me go when I dropped to the floor, shuddering in agony.

"How the bloody fuck do we get him out of there, then?" Bleek shouted. He was only beginning to understand that the boy was never meant to come out of the coffin. He was trapped in there forever, unless the one who spoke the proper words removed the spell on the lock. There was one other possibility, but I didn't want to impose on Queen Lissa for a criminal's child, as much as I wanted to save him.

After he'd broken my wing, I didn't want to help Bleek, either. That's when the vision hit me. Before I knew it, I was standing and grasping one of Bleek's hands in mine while latching onto a handle of the coffin with the other. The Orb, which appeared in a blast of light, flung us away from the *Killshot*.

~

Avii Castle

Bel Erland

"We'll have a peek into the throne room where the interview is taking place," Master Scholar Gurnil smiled as he led us down a hallway. Justis had delivered us to him, first, before going to the throne room himself—by leaping off the library terrace and flying there.

Our journey would be a much slower one.

I'd imagined the inside of the castle to be darker. I was surprised to find it well-lit with solar lights overhead and at knee-level through the halls. The halls were wide enough for three to walk side by side comfortably; the one who'd built it had certainly taken wings into consideration in the design.

I realized that Gurnil was more than curious about the interview and that's why he was taking us to the throne room first. I couldn't fault him for it; I, too, was curious, since Jurris seldom granted interviews.

It took ten minutes of determined walking by the Blue Wing scholar to reach our destination. My first look inside the Avii throne room revealed a woman journalist, who was quite pretty. A hover-mic floated over King Jurris' head as he answered questions for her. Nearby, two crewmembers watched and listened to ensure the image and sound were of good quality for broadcasting.

Except one of them wasn't doing his job. Instead of staring at the comp-vid images on the tablet he held, he watched someone who stood not far from Jurris' side—his young son, Liron. Liron's mother, Wimla, stood behind her son, her hands on his shoulders to keep the boy from running to his father.

I glanced back to the inattentive crewmember, who now wore a hungry look as he gazed at the boy.

Yanzi growled as I raised my hand.

The images from my visit to the Avii throne room will always play in my mind, as clear and crisp as the day they occurred. The camera crewman dropped the tablet and pulled a pistol from a pocket at the same time.

Yanzi flung himself forward. Jurris, seeing where the gun was aimed, also flung himself from the Avii throne.

So many things happened simultaneously, and I recall all of them with such horror-ridden clarity.

A shot was fired at the boy. Jurris and Justis leapt. Yanzi also leapt and turned to lion snake in a blink.

A flash of light.

A four-armed giant.

Quin's cry as she fell.

A glass coffin sliding across the floor and upending the one who'd fired at Liron, turning him in a somersault in the air before he crashed to the marble floor.

Justis' movement to pull Liron and Wimla away.

The bullet hitting Jurris in the forehead as he shoved himself in front of his child.

The shriek of the cameraman as he died in midair.

Yanzi's capture of the fallen Jurris, who was already dead—Yanzi had to force himself back to humanoid to catch the King's body.

If Jurris had allowed his brother to protect his child, he would have lived; Justis pulled the boy and his mother out of the bullet's path a hair's breadth before it would have hit its mark.

Jurris, understandably worried about his child, had also gone to his rescue.

Jurris died protecting his son.

Quin was up and weeping over Jurris' body; she couldn't bring back the dead. She could only heal those who hadn't crossed that threshold. One of her wings was obviously broken, and my guess of the one responsible fell upon the four-armed giant who blinked in confusion around him.

"You will stay where you are," Lafe held a blade at the Blevakian's throat. It didn't surprise me at all that the Falchani carried a hidden blade; I'd have been more surprised if he hadn't.

Justis stalked toward the one who'd shot his brother while the journalist and her soundman cowered away from his anger. Lifting the dead man by his shirt collar, he pulled the body off the floor and shook it before tossing it across the floor as if it weighed little.

Wimla and Liron wept in a corner; Gurnil, who'd stood in shock as the incident occurred before his eyes, gasped as we watched the Orb appear over Justis' head. Justis' wing color changed in seconds—from black to red. He was oblivious to it as he began to stalk the journalist and her remaining crew.

Gran? I sent. *We need you.*

~

Quin

Daragar came to repair my wing.

Bleek was held in a cell in the Avii dungeon, his son's coffin left just outside it so he could keep his eye on the child. Somewhere, in an orbit around Harifa Edus, several ships arrived to take *Killshot* and six other ships owned by Vardil Cayetes.

All those ships bore the *BlackWing* name and logo. For all Vardil knew, he'd been attacked by a newly formed crime syndicate—named after me. Justis, still in the throne room and in mourning while Queen Lissa and Gurnil attempted to help, refused to see any of the Avii Council.

Gurnil had sent news of the Orb's appearance and the wing color change almost immediately. That meant that the castle mourned Jurris' death and breathed a relieved sigh that they still had a Red Wing King.

I had things to tell Justis and Queen Lissa; that I'd killed the one who shot Jurris. I'd made his brain explode by enlarging the cells. I admit to being so angry when I saw him and his intent to kill Liron at Cayetes' command that I'd taken his life with barely a thought.

I blamed the Orb, too, for telling Cayetes that it—he—was Liron.

Too many things were becoming clear, after surviving in murky mystery for years. Some of those things I wasn't ready to say, yet.

Yet.

My body was covered in bruises, thanks to Bleek's crew. At least all of them were sitting in cells, now, although a few had died attempting to escape.

Whip, unfortunately, was still alive—he'd escaped before the BlackWing ships arrived to take the others.

While Daragar ran his hands over my nude body, healing the worst of my injuries after healing the broken wing, I considered what I ought to do next.

Amlis, Rodrik and those from Vogeffa II would likely not know that they'd been marked by Cayetes. Perhaps Lissa should tell them so they'd be on guard against future attacks.

Breathing a sigh, I allowed my head to fall on Daragar's shoulder. He hummed gently as he continued his work.

Lissa

"I met him on the castle tour boat. He said he wanted to see the inside of the castle," Trese Herak wept. "He said he was from Refizan."

Translation—she'd slept with him and allowed him to convince her to take him as a member of her crew when she did her interview. Probably planned ahead of time, but I'd have to check with Quin, first.

I also had questions about the bastard's death—Karzac reported that his brain exploded. I understood Quin's grief at not being able to heal Jurris, but dead was dead and I knew of only one person and six Larentii who could reverse that. They hadn't appeared, so Jurris' resurrection wasn't to be.

Instead, the Orb had chosen to anoint Justis, which, in my mind, was more than fair. My concern, however, was that he'd be tied to Avii Castle from now on, instead of following Quin.

I understood being tied to duty.

Too well.

Quin

"Justis?" I walked softly into his old bedroom, where he sat on the bed, his head bowed.

Red wings spilled across the bed behind him—they were magnificent and of no interest to him at the moment.

His brother was dead.

Without a word, I worked my way beneath one of his arms and settled on his lap before laying my head on his shoulder. His arms wound around me then, and he wept.

~

Avii Castle

Lissa

"When Justis is available, I'll discuss moving that four-armed monstrosity from his dungeon," I sighed.

"What about the child in the coffin?" Merrill asked. "It has a spell on it—the coffin and the lock. The child inside is in stasis, likely placed by Cayetes' warlock."

"Is it his child—the four-armed man's?" Dena had brought tea to Merrill and me inside Gurnil's massive library.

"I believe that's true," Merrill inclined his head in thanks for the tea.

"Do you think that's the hold this Cayetes' person had over him?" Dena asked. "Is your tea to your liking? I have more honey and milk, if you want it."

"I'll have milk," Merrill smiled at her. She blushed at his attention.

No, Merrill isn't handsome or anything. I turned my head so he wouldn't catch my smile.

"It is most of the hold Cayetes has over him." Quin had come, with Justis right behind her. She'd spoken; Justis looked haggard. I couldn't blame him—he'd lost the only brother he'd ever had.

Now he was saddled with the Avii throne while he mourned Jurris and worried about Liron and his mother.

"What do you think we should do with Mr. Bleek, Quinnie Bee?" I asked.

"I think I should heal his son, and then see what Bleek does. I just don't have a way past the spell on the lock or the coffin."

"I can get the boy out," I shrugged. "Without upsetting the spells."

"I'll have to heal him the second he's out," she sighed. "He'll die if I don't."

"What about the one who killed my brother?" Justis muttered, anger in his voice.

"I killed him," Quin turned to Justis and placed a hand on his chest. "I made him die—as he killed your brother. I'm sorry I couldn't save Jurris. I wanted to."

"Who was he?" I asked.

"Cayetes' assassin," Quin turned back to me while Justis placed his arms around her and leaned his chin on her shoulder. "Magul. That was his name. I wish I could send a message to Cayetes, but I know he's already left Zephili—he did that the moment he knew his ships around Harifa Edus were under attack."

"You said he was on Zephili," I sighed, covering my face with both hands. "An Alliance world. Fuck."

"He could be anywhere, now," Quin said. "He's quite good at self-preservation, as we've seen already."

"We found Sirenali aboard each of Cayetes' ships," I dropped my hands and blinked at Quin. "Most of them are dying, and they aren't that old."

"A flaw in the cloning process," Quin explained. "I healed one of them. I can heal the others, too. I don't believe any of them wanted to be where they were. None of them can speak, either, if they're like the first one."

"Yes, we've already discovered that," I agreed. "None know how to read or write—they only know they'll be beaten if they don't obey."

"Like Terrett," Quin closed her eyes and lowered her head.

"Terrett teach himself," Yanzi appeared, bringing Terrett with him.

"Terrett?" Quin jerked her head up and held out her hand.

He took it and kissed it, giving Quin a smile. I'd never seen a Sirenali in love. I'd only seen those who were cold and calculating, who valued no lives except their own. This, I think, was how it was supposed to be.

"Shall we heal a young Blevakian?" I stood and held out a hand to Merrill.

"Why do you want to heal him?" Justis growled. His arms dropped and he frowned at Quin as she turned to look at him.

"Because I want to see whose side his father falls on afterward," Quin replied. "Cayetes is afraid of Bleek. If Bleek agrees to work with us, he will become a powerful soldier in our army."

When did she become a general? Merrill quipped in mindspeech.

No idea, I responded. *Let's heal the boy and see what happens.*

Quin

"Queen Lissa will bring your child out of the coffin," I explained to Bleek, who looked as if he'd been punched in the stomach when we'd arrived to examine the coffin. He was terrified for his son—that was easy to see.

"How?" Bleek's voice was a low whisper. The bars of his cage held him back; he might have tried to kill all of us if they hadn't. All four hands gripped thick, steel bars as he gazed upon his son. "He'll die," Bleek moaned.

"That is not our plan," Lissa snapped. "Quin will do her best to heal him. After all, the boy hasn't done wrong. Just you."

"How can you get him out?"

"I'm a vampire who can turn to mist," Lissa said. "I can mist him out, the spell won't be triggered and the boy won't be harmed."

"Show me." Bleek's grip on the bars tightened.

"All right."

Lissa disappeared before Bleek's eyes. Then Bleek disappeared a moment later, landing outside his cage beside Lissa and not far from the coffin.

"For now, we'll trust you," Lissa said. "Make a wrong move and Merrill here will kill you."

Bleek studied Merrill, whose vampire claws slid from his fingers. I hoped Bleek didn't move—Merrill was swift and deadly. Bleek wouldn't stand a chance against a King Vampire.

I think he knew that. He wanted to step back from Merrill's claws, but was afraid to move.

"I'm going in," Lissa announced. "Are you ready, Quinnie Bee?"

"I am," I nodded. Lissa turned to mist. A moment later, she reappeared, the boy's body in her arms. My healing glow was bright enough to blind those about me; they closed their eyes against its dazzling intensity.

CHAPTER 12

*L*issa
Bleek held his son, Barc, in his arms as the boy turned pages on a book Quin had given him. Bleek didn't know whether to laugh or weep with joy, so complete was the child's recovery.

The child, placed in stasis for nearly six years, should be much older than he was. Time would rectify that. From now on, he would grow normally and come to adulthood as he should.

We'd given Bleek a new prison—a suite inside my palace that was shielded and warded against his escape.

Barc could come and go as he pleased, as could anyone else. LaFranza stood at my elbow, watching Bleek and shaking his head. Bleek had nearly killed him on Vogeffa II, so I doubted LaFranza was ready to trust Bleek, if ever that time would come.

"He's a bastard, but he's wicked with his blades," LaFranza grudgingly admitted.

"I'm waiting to see what Quin does with him," I said.

"It didn't take her long to pass judgment on Drood Juffa. I think he stood on the edge of a knife and ended up falling on the wrong side of it."

174

"That happens," I agreed. What I didn't add was that usually, only the powerful could see such things. I'd gotten mindspeech from Salidar earlier—he said the battle for Vic'Law was heating up. Already, half of Der'Vek was on fire, with refugees pouring out of the city in a terrible winter, looking for another place to stay while their homes burned behind them.

Bear Wright had reported two more ships bound for Vic'Law had been taken under Cayetes' nose and their cargo sent to Mundia. Wherever Cayetes was now, he was likely furious.

On the downside, three more worlds were now infected with the poison. Jurris' memorial service would be held in two days; Quin would stay with Justis until then, unless the Orb had other plans.

I, on the other hand, had an appointment with an old friend— Bryan Riley, the vampire in charge of the news stations in Lissia and Casino City. He'd asked for an interview with Trese Herak, who was in my dungeon, charged with conspiracy to commit murder. She'd taken Magul right into the glass castle with her, because he was a good lay.

Her skills as an investigative journalist were questionable, in my opinion. Bryan asked me to be present when he questioned her, to ensure that nobody thought him guilty of laying compulsion during the interview.

It didn't matter; she'd already answered Gavin and Tony's questions, under *their* compulsion.

People should learn not to commit crimes on my planet. Le-Ath Veronis was filled with vampires, all of whom could place compulsion, warranted or not. Laws were in place forbidding unwarranted compulsion, but if you were involved in any crime, inadvertent or not, compulsion placed by law enforcement became legal on Le-Ath Veronis.

"Will you ask Quin to come while we interview Ms. Herak?" I turned to LaFranza. "I'll find someone to transport her, if she agrees."

"I'll ask."

Quin

"I want to come, too," Justis said. I could tell by his frown that he wanted to lift that woman by the throat and shake her. Without her perfidy, Jurris would be alive.

"That is acceptable; Lissa said you'd ask."

Queen Lissa had sent her Falchani mates to take me to her castle. Justis wanted to come with me. Drake and Drew were amenable to the change. I grasped Justis' hand in mine; he laced our fingers together and nodded to our guests. In moments, we were inside Lissa's private study.

"You will be allowed to stay only if you remain silent," Lissa warned Justis. "If you have questions you'd like asked, send mindspeech to me. I'll make sure Bryan asks, as long as they're reasonable."

"I'll do my best," Justis nodded. He still gripped my hand, as if it were a lifeline. His pain ran deep, as he was older than Jurris and had helped raise his younger brother. He'd stood by his brother, too, even when he'd made less than wise decisions. At least Jurris was better at those things after Halthea's death.

I didn't want to speculate on my involvement in any of that—I'd healed him after she'd tried to murder him. Another vampire walked into Lissa's study, offering a warm smile to the Queen.

"Bryan, this is King Justis and Quin of the Avii," Lissa introduced us. "Justis, Quin, this is Bryan Riley, head of the news network in Lissia and Casino City."

Bryan turned a brilliant smile on me, squeezing my free hand while Justis held onto the other. Justis, his right hand free, shook with Bryan, as was proper. I could see in him that he wanted to interview Justis as the new monarch for the Avii, but was willing to wait until a better time to ask.

Ask him in a few months; things will be better, then, I sent mindspeech to Bryan, whose eyes widened imperceptibly at the unexpected communication.

I will, Bryan replied, surprising me with his own mindspeech. I understood then that Queen Lissa had seen to it that he could walk in daylight, send mindspeech and eat normal food if he wanted. It helped him in his profession and proved to me that she held him in high regard.

The Queen chose carefully those who received her blood.

"Shall we?" Lissa interrupted my thoughts. Within a blink, she'd transported us to her dungeon.

~

Puntia

Vic'Law

Barstle Cardino glared at Vardil Cayetes' back. He'd appeared suddenly, accompanied by his witch and warlock, half a dozen captives including a set of twins, his personal assistant and a bevy of servants. More of Cayetes' crew wandered through the house, taking stock of available space and planning Vardil's takeover of Barstle's compound.

Cayetes was now in the process of claiming Barstle's private suite of rooms for himself. Nardes Churg, who'd thought to argue with Cayetes, was now a pile of charred ash and bone on the floor. While it saved Barstle the trouble of killing Nardes himself (he'd planned to do it much later), he still needed Churg's allies for now, especially in light of this new threat. If they discovered that Nardes was dead, they'd fight against him instead of with him.

Vardil Cayetes had played them all; Barstle realized his error in trusting Cayetes. Barstle now worried that his worst mistake from involving himself with Cayetes was yet to come.

~

Quin

"He was handsome and good in bed. I was a fool," Trese wiped tears away. Her cheeks were raw from frequent bouts of tears. I could see that she was stunned by the violence of Jurris' death, and shocked by how quickly it had happened. One moment her lover had stood at her elbow and everything was fine.

The next moment, she was involved in a heinous crime; one she still couldn't comprehend.

"You have to believe me—I didn't know," she quavered.

"Yet you violated the terms of your agreement with your employer, in addition to the journalist's agreement you signed upon your arrival on Le-Ath Veronis. Every journalist knows this rule and follows it; it can damage the reputation of their company if they fail to comply. You ignored all that and allowed a stranger to pose as one of your crew in a private interview with a reigning monarch," Bryan Riley pointed out.

"I thought it only meant Queen Lissa," Trese wept fresh tears.

"The agreement says reigning monarch," Bryan stated. "No names are mentioned on the agreement by design. King Jurris made his home here, and often, other monarchs visit the palace. The agreement covers all of them."

"I guess that makes sense." It didn't to her, but she wanted Bryan's questions to stop. She worried about how she looked while the vid-cam was recording the interview. She worried about losing her job. She worried what her punishment would be.

She was least worried about Jurris' family, who were left behind to grieve.

I didn't want Justis to know what I saw in her—he wanted her punished severely for what she'd done. I gripped his hand tighter and wondered how I might get him out of the dungeon if it became necessary.

"Will it interest you to know that your news agency has already taken steps to terminate your employment?" Bryan asked. "King Jurris was something of a celebrity across the Alliance, and many people have called to express their dissatisfaction with the company, because of your involvement in his death."

Bryan Riley wasn't letting Trese get by on her looks, which is likely what had mattered most when she was hired.

Queen Lissa, do you suppose that somewhere, Cayetes has a financial interest in her news agency? I sent.

It's possible, but his involvement could be buried so deeply we might never find it. It could explain why Magul went looking for her, or, more than likely, knew where she'd be at the proper time.

This is terrible, I responded. *I know Jurris wasn't the main target, Liron was. That means Cayetes will still be hunting him.*

What in heaven's name for?

The Orb, I gave a mental sigh. *It appeared in Cayetes' dreams. Told him it was Liron and was bringing his death. The paranoid criminal nit doesn't know the difference between a god and a child.*

How do you know this?

For a moment, while it was flinging me from the ship to Avii Castle, I saw parts of its memory—some of its intentions. It happened so fast, the information about Cayetes was just about all I saw.

It really wants Cayetes that bad? How did it manage to invade his dreams?

I don't know, I said. *I wish I did. If I could, I'd invade his dreams and tell him I'm bringing his death—for what he did to Siriaa and to Jurris.*

This bears thinking about, Lissa said. *Let me know if you discover anything else about the Orb. I'm beginning to worry that it could cause even more trouble than it already has.*

That makes two of us, I replied.

Lissa

"I'll edit what I got and we'll air it on the late news," Bryan flopped onto a chair in my study. Justis and Quin had already left—Drake offered to return them to Avii Castle. Justis was grim during the interview and didn't speak afterward—I felt Quin would have her hands full trying to calm him down when they got home.

"The more I learn about Cayetes, the more I worry," I said. "At least Magul is dead and that airhead didn't really know anything about him —or Cayetes."

"You say Quin and the others are going back to Vic'Law in a few days?" Bryan asked.

Yeah, I shouldn't have told him that.

"Why do you ask?" I said, although I already knew where this was going.

"I want to go back with them, to report on what is happening there. What other Alliance news agency has access to a non-Alliance world like that, and can report on a coup in progress?"

"Are you sure you want to go yourself?"

"I absolutely do. Usually I'm stuck at the office, handling this problem or stomping out that fire, and I want back in the field. I'll leave somebody in charge—they'll have to figure it out because there isn't much chance of getting regular communication on Vic'Law."

"It's colder than a gravedigger's ass there, right now," I pointed out. "Winters in Mundia are pretty awful."

"I have a coat."

"If Caylon says okay."

"I'll ask."

"You do that."

"I will."

"Good."

"Fine."

Bryan was grinning as he passed Gavin on the way out of my study. "What was that about?" Gavin demanded.

"Banter," I said. "Want some?"

Quin

Drake dropped us off in Gurnil's library. We found the Master Scholar waiting for us. "Dinner with your Council is waiting," Gurnil said softly. I looked up at Justis' face. "We'll fly down," I turned to Gurnil. "Give us a few minutes, all right?"

"I'll tell them the King is on his way," Gurnil rose from his seat at a library table. I recalled eating meals at that table, with Dena, Ardis,

Amlis and several others. I had no idea that those times would become the happier times of memory.

Things had gone strange—and evil—since Siriaa's destruction.

Justis flew around the castle twice before landing on the balcony outside the throne room. I landed right behind him. Without speaking, he strode toward the door while I struggled to keep up with his longer, determined stride.

He was walking into a Council meeting for the first time as King of the Avii. I didn't know what to expect from anyone waiting for his arrival, other than Gurnil and Ordin.

Those two would welcome him as their King.

Every member of the Council was waiting as Justis walked toward the throne. Ardis, now Commander of the Guard, went to his knee and bowed his head when Justis approached. Everyone else in the room followed suit, as if they were waiting for Ardis' cue.

Perhaps they were.

Justis sat on the throne, breathing a ragged sigh. *My love*, he said, *tell them to rise.*

"Please rise and acknowledge your King," I said aloud.

Justis jerked his head at me in a swift nod as those around him stood and awaited the King's words.

"I want you to stay for the coronation—it'll be held the day after Jurris' memorial." Justis shook his head at the transformation of the King's suite. Jurris' belongings had been removed—Wimla and Vorina now had possession of his personal things. I imagined they'd set many of those aside for Liron when he was older.

Justis' things had been moved into the King's suite, although much of his clothing had been left behind—he'd have to stand still to be measured for a new wardrobe.

Both of us were still trying to deal with the derailment of our lives. I didn't tell Justis what I'd known the moment I'd set eyes on Liron—there would be no red wings for the boy.

He'd have his mother's brown. Already, he was showing a talent for drawing. I understood why Justis was made King—he was the best candidate for the throne. I knew it, as did the Orb.

"What are we going to do?" Justis strode toward me and pulled me into his arms.

"Justis," I took his face in my hands, "You know I love you. We will take things as they come, moment by moment if we must, until this sadness and unease passes well enough that we feel like ourselves again."

He snorted, and then half-smiled. "You are the one with black wings now," he pulled me closer.

"Black wings mean nothing unless I'm prepared to challenge my enemy," I whispered against his chest. I'd seen the way the Council stared at my wings—once again I was the hapless standout, because my wings were different.

Justis didn't bother to explain why I had black wings; he'd attended to business instead. I could predict what the gossip would be the moment the Council left the throne room, however.

My wings, and the fact that I'd stood as Justis' advisor in the throne room.

~

Lissa

Bleek stood in the open doorway to his suite, watching as I brought Barc back to him. The boy wanted to see the rest of the castle; I'd arranged for a live feed on a screen for Bleek so he could see that we meant Barc no harm.

I'll admit that four arms could mean four times the potential mischief, but Barc was well-behaved and more than happy that he had no pain—that's what he recalled of his former life—the illness and the pain it brought.

He'd been excited to see everything, especially the kitchen, where Cheedas offered him a cookie. He'd eaten it with a smile and a glass of milk.

"Pap," Barc crowed. "I sat on the throne!"

"I saw," Bleek pulled Barc through the door. "How was the cookie?"

"Good. Cheedas wouldn't let me have two, because dinner is coming."

Thank you, Bleek mouthed at me over Barc's head. I nodded in reply.

Quin

"Gurnil wants to see you," Dena said. She'd arrived at the King's suite and asked to see me.

My breath caught. I saw it in her eyes, which held guilt immediately. I was about to receive bad news. Well, perhaps not bad, but not the best nor the most ideal.

"Walk or fly?" I asked.

"Fly," she shrugged. With my shoulders sagging, I followed her to the terrace, where we lifted into the air and headed for the library.

Far below the castle, I could see three tour boats, with tourists gaping at the enormous glass structure and no doubt recording images of a Black Wing and a Yellow Wing flying from one terrace to another.

When we arrived, I settled my feathers as I followed Dena into the library. There, Gurnil and Ordin waited for me.

Neither looked happy.

"Tell me," I said, without sitting down. After all, I might fly around the castle twice after receiving the news they bore.

Terrett

What do you mean, he has to protect the positions of Jurris' wives? I demanded. Quin had fled the library moments earlier, landing in the bowl somewhere to weep as lambs gathered about her. Daragar was with her—he'd sent mindspeech to reassure the rest of us.

"Same go for Queen, if husband die," Yanzi muttered. "Former mate must marry new King or Queen. To protect rights—theirs and child's."

"So they can't just be tossed out like yesterday's garbage," Bel Erland arrived to join our conversation. "It's to perpetuate the line, too, in the eyes of the Avii. I believe it was originally intended to ensure a succession of Red Wing monarchs, but the law was interpreted to include anyone married or aligned with a King or Queen."

"Only red wing get to be Queen or King," Yanzi added. "No other color elevated."

"So Quin will be one of the herd instead of special," Bel sighed. "In the eyes of the Avii."

I doubt that's how Justis thinks of her, I complained.

"It how she feel," Yanzi growled. "She see it in all faces of Avii."

The King's Suite
Justis
"It didn't go well," Gurnil admitted.

Ordin sat by the overly large window in my sitting room, staring at the sea and refusing to speak.

"Did you tell her it's only a formality? Neither will be in my bed. They're my brother's mates, for pity's sake," I flung out a hand.

"I don't think that's what upset her," Gurnil hung his head.

"What is it, then?" I demanded. I didn't need problems with Quin— I needed her beside me so I could get through this mess without breaking down.

"She knows what the others think," Gurnil sighed before turning away. "She feels outcast again. The others will be expecting Wimla and

Vorina to be with you, rather than an upstart who wasn't born to any Avii."

"She was created by Liron himself," I hissed, my anger rising quickly.

"We know that. Most of your Council fails to understand it. They don't know where she's been the last five years, or where she'll be in the next five. To them, that is an unsuitable mate for their King."

I wanted to hit something, then. Or haul the Council back to the throne room and shout at all of them. I'd be forced to accept Wimla and Vorina as mates after my coronation. I wanted Quin to be first to say the vows, so she'd know she was the only one in my heart.

Liron I would adopt to protect him as he matured, but any King worth his feathers would do the same. Wimla and Vorina would be free to take other mates—in fact, I hoped they'd find someone soon. I wanted them to understand they would never be with me, although I think they already knew that.

"Where is she?" I demanded. "Quin?"

"I heard she was somewhere in the bowl, surrounded by sheep while Daragar attempts to console her."

"I'll go," I snapped, stalking toward the door.

"Take a guard with you," Gurnil reminded me softly. "Last time, you flew with Quin. This time, you cannot go alone."

I cursed, then. In Alliance common and Avii.

Quin

"I'm back where I started," I mumbled while scratching a ewe behind an ear. "With the Avii. They don't trust me. Don't understand where I've been for five years. I wish I could explain where I was, but I don't know either."

"Dearest, don't let this upset you," Daragar soothed. "Justis loves only you."

"I don't want to be the next Halthea in everyone else's eyes," I said.

"They hated her—if Justis listens to me and my words are at cross purposes with theirs," I didn't finish.

"Never compare yourself with that selfish bitch."

Justis had arrived; Ardis, acting as his guard, was right behind him.

"You should go," I said, rising and dusting off the seat of my pants. "You're the King. I don't have red wings. That's all that matters."

"Quin, that's unreasonable and you know it." Justis frowned at me. Yes, he was right. I just felt as if I'd been punched in the stomach and wanted to hit back for a change.

"Commander Ardis, perhaps we should give them some space," Daragar stood and lifted a blond eyebrow at black-winged Ardis.

"I'll fly to the guard's mess; I can see you from there," Ardis nodded and snapped his wings open. Moments later, he flew straight for the door in question, without looking back.

"I'll be listening for my name in mindspeech," Daragar said before folding space.

"So we're to have our argument where the entire Avii race can see us?" I snapped. I knew Justis didn't deserve my vitriol; it spewed out anyway.

"You're the one who left the library."

"You weren't there. You let Gurnil and Ordin tell me what *you* should have," I pointed at Justis' chest.

"I was with Wimla and Liron—the child is having difficulty coming to terms with his father's death."

"Fine." I tossed out a hand and turned my back on Justis. "You could have told me afterward."

"I thought you'd hear it better from Gurnil."

"I'm not sleeping with Gurnil," I turned back and shouted.

"And you bloody well won't," he shouted back.

"I quit," I yelled. "I'm not an Avii. Everybody thinks that. They'll be happy to get rid of me, so you can make babies with somebody who is."

"What in the name of Liron?" Justis went still.

"It makes sense, doesn't it? I can't have children. You're the King.

You'll need an heir. Liron will have brown wings." I dropped to my knees and wept.

∿

Terrett

Justis appeared haggard as he followed Daragar into the library. Quin, unconscious in Daragar's arms, looked as if she'd been weeping.

Avii laws, Bel Erland snorted in my mind.

∿

Puntia

Vic'Law

"Is it operational?" Vardil demanded.

"Not yet," Barstle replied while lowering his eyes. He couldn't look at Cayetes. Not after what he'd just witnessed.

Deris, Cayetes' warlock, had performed a transference while Barstle was forced to watch. There was a purpose in this—Barstle's body would be taken by Cayetes if he didn't do exactly as the bastard wanted.

Barstle had watched, horrified and unable to turn away, as the victim wept and shook while his spirit was stripped from his body. When the body Cayetes inhabited dropped to the floor, limp and lifeless, Cayetes' gaze—from the eyes of the new victim—focused on Barstle. Those eyes promised a terrible retribution if Barstle failed to satisfy Vardil's smallest whim.

"How soon will it be ready? I have a planet to destroy," Vardil growled.

"We are recalibrating the firing mechanism," Barstle's voice shook. "I will see it done as quickly as possible."

"Is there enough drakus seed to ensure compliance with your allies?"

"I think so. You understand the fields were small where we grew it, south of Der'Vek. Xilva owned the land and it was hard work,

187

converting overgrown fields to something that would provide a decent harvest the first year."

"I don't give a fuck about your problems. Where is the store of drakus seed?"

"Here, in Puntia, under heavy guard."

"I'll replace your guards with mine."

"As you say," Barstle muttered, lowering his eyes to conceal his hate and anger.

"What about the takeover? I want the latest reports."

"I will show you what I have," Barstle stuttered, keeping his eyes down.

"Do so. Immediately."

~

Le-Ath Veronis

Lissa

"I don't believe this," I muttered. I had a headache and it was getting worse. Bel Erland sat across from my desk, a troubled expression marring his features. "Couldn't it have waited? What was the purpose in all this?"

"The Council wants Jurris to accept Wimla and Vorina as mates immediately after his coronation. He wanted Quin to be first, so she wouldn't worry about her place with him. It went south in a hurry. The minute she woke, she wanted to leave. Terrett and I have been trying to talk her out of it. Justis is not happy, and this is happening on top of Jurris' death and planning the memorial."

"Ask her to come here," I sighed. "She can stay across from Bleek. He broke her wing and she still wanted to save his son. I hope there's something good in him other than the love for his child."

~

Quin

"Gran says you can stay at her palace. I think it would be polite to stay for the memorial at least," Bel Erland coaxed.

I'd asked him to take me to Vic'Law. Perhaps I could spend my anger and distress while sparring with Caylon and allowing him to knock me to the floor.

"I'm not staying for the coronation."

I think it was my first fit of stubbornness.

Ever.

Until now, I'd shoved my feelings aside and done what I'd been told. Even after being beaten. Angry thoughts of Rodrik crowded my mind. He hadn't hesitated to raise his hand against me.

Hadn't argued with Amlis over its necessity.

Anger that I'd kept bottled up throughout my life was bubbling to the surface, and it was ugly and nauseating.

"I'll stay at Queen Lissa's palace," I snapped. "Don't," I held up a hand as he reached for me. "There's no need to transport me. I'll fly there myself."

CHAPTER 13

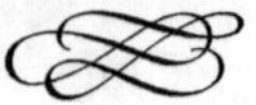

*L*issa

"I think something happened. Something she's not telling us," I said. Erland, my warlock mate and Bel's grandfather, had come at my request. He watched me pace inside my suite.

"Where is she now?" He asked softly.

"In the suite across from Bleek's. She flew here, by herself, all the way from Avii Castle on the light half of the planet."

"That's rather rash—to go that far without a guard," Erland muttered.

"No kidding," I snapped. "If anybody gets wind of the fact that Bel Erland is interested, she'll become a target. Not just with the media, but anybody else who'd like to kidnap her and send a ransom note."

"I think the same goes for Justis, don't you think?" Erland pointed out. His calm made me frown—how could he act so rationally in a crisis like this?

"If Justis wants a child, he can find a surrogate, as we did to get Rylend," I added. "I know the Larentii would help in mixing their DNA, all they'll need is someone willing to carry the baby for them."

"I have no idea how the Avii Council will see that. Bel said they're grumbling about her legitimacy again and questioning her whereabouts for the past five years."

"You know," I shook a finger at Erland, "I'd like to have a conversation with whoever is behind that crap. You know somebody there is whispering poison in the others' ears."

"That happens everywhere," Erland observed. "Stopping that is like halting a planet in its orbit. It can't really be done, for a multitude of reasons."

"Will you stop behaving rationally for a minute and be outraged?" I snapped.

"Will it make you feel better?"

"Absolutely."

"Then I'll be outraged. Can we be outraged while we're naked on the bed?"

"Seriously?"

"We can blow off steam."

"Well, since you put it that way."

"I know exactly how I want to put it."

Quin

Barc almost ran across the hall and into my arms. I wanted to weep as I held him. Even the worst people could have children. Four arms tightened around me as I kissed the top of his head.

"How are you feeling today?" I smiled at him as he let me go. Bleek, confused, watched us from the doorway of his prison suite.

"I feel good," he laughed. "I don't remember feeling good before."

"You'll feel good from now on," I said. "If I have anything to say about it."

"I like your wings," he grinned.

"I like them, too."

"Can you fly?"

"I can fly."

"Can I fly with you?"

"I think your pap would have to say yes, first," I tapped his nose. I heard Bleek release an indrawn breath. He'd been terrified for Barc.

"He's your son," I led Barc across the hall and stood far enough away so Bleek couldn't reach me, although the shield held him back at the threshold. I hadn't forgotten that he'd broken my wing.

Barc looked at his father and then back at me, curiosity in his gaze. "My lamb," I said, ruffling my fingers through his hair, "your pap doesn't know that he can trust me, yet. He is a wise man. You should learn from him. Not everyone is worthy of your trust."

"She hasn't learned to trust me yet, either," Bleek sighed and raked the fingers of one hand through his hair.

"Will you have dinner with us? I'm starved and it's almost time," Barc pleaded. My breath caught as I looked up and into Bleek's eyes. He could break my wing again. He could hold me until Lissa let him and his child go.

He could kill me.

"No harm will come to you by my hand from now on, I swear it on my wife's grave," Bleek held both right arms over his heart.

I hugged myself, squashed my fear and nodded my acceptance.

"It's gishi fruit—from Avendor," I explained. I knew that; I'd just never been to Avendor. I understood it was beautiful, there.

"I like it," Barc declared.

Bleek ate in silence while Barc talked away. At times, he wanted to rush away from the small table where we ate so he could show me something. His father told him to stay and finish his meal, and then he could show me his things.

Lissa had been generous, providing toys, games and more books for the boy. "Do you read?" I asked Bleek.

"When I have time." His eyes were on his plate; he didn't look up at my question.

"I'll have some sent to you," I said. "It's too bad you can't read the Avii language; there are history books in the Master Scholar's library concerning Siriaa."

"The planet Cayetes destroyed." Bleek's voice was flat. "I had nothing to do with that."

"I know."

"You don't make others pay for the mistakes of one enemy," Bleek's two left fists curled tightly.

"I agree," I said. "Marid of Belancour betrayed the people of Siriaa, just as he betrayed Vardil Cayetes."

"The way I see it, Marid and Vardil have betrayed everybody. I heard the poison is spreading."

"I'm glad to hear you say that. I think they betrayed everybody, too."

Bleek's gaze turned to Barc, who pushed green peas around on his plate. I wanted to smile at his aversion to green things and weep at Bleek's worry for his son's life—after all, if the poison destroyed all worlds, Barc would be destroyed with them.

"I intend to kill Vardil Cayetes," I said.

"I'd like to help," Bleek nodded.

Bleek

I watched her walk away, my child waving at her as she left our suite. I hadn't had a civilized conversation with anyone for eight years; I always treated my companions as if I expected them to shoot me in the back at any moment.

This girl had given Barc back to me, and then informed me that she wanted to kill Cayetes.

I wanted to kill him, too, for lying to me. He, his warlock and his witch had fooled me all along—by making me believe that someday Barc would be released from his coffin and made well.

They'd made sure it would never open.

Without the help of the Vampire Queen who could turn to mist, Barc would still be locked inside that box.

Without the help of Quin, who had healing talent that surpassed the fantasies written in books, he'd have died shortly after.

Many years had passed since I'd considered redirecting my rage.

I was doing so now. Cayetes and his Karathian twins should tremble. If Quin asked, I would kill them for her.

And for myself.

Lissa

"What do you mean, she had dinner with that wing-breaker?" Justis was already exercising his authority as the Avii King. He'd arrived in a snit after finding Quin gone from Avii Castle.

At least he'd allowed it to distract him from his brother's death and the memorial service the following day.

Yanzi had transported him from the glass castle, and now sat silently in a corner of my study, watching Justis just as I did.

"Don't worry, I had eyes on them the entire time," I attempted to calm Justis down. "I think it worked, too. Bleek is coming around. He wants Cayetes dead just as much as we do, now."

"Tell her that I will not allow her to break away from the Avii," Justis hissed. "She is Avii. End. Of. Statement."

"Then perhaps you need to convince your Council," I offered dryly. "Somebody's spreading poison, I know that much. Besides, Quin is her own person. Neither of us own her."

Justis' red feathers lifted and rustled at my statement, but he didn't reply.

Smart of him.

"Who's guarding Liron?" I asked.

"Daragar and Terrett," he mumbled, shaking himself and flattening his feathers.

"Cayetes doesn't give up, once he finds a target," I pointed out. "He'll be back, rest assured."

"Then tell me how to protect the boy," Justis huffed. "I'm doing the best I can."

"You know, I think I have an idea," I said, waving a finger at the Avii King.

Quin

"Come with me," I said to Bleek.

"I can't pass the threshold."

"You can this time," I held out a hand. Barc was already holding my other hand while I stood in the hall outside Bleek's suite. He was ready to go to breakfast with me. I wanted Bleek to come, too.

I could tell Bleek didn't trust my words. "I asked the Queen. She says you're welcome at the table this morning."

Bleek wanted to close his eyes as he extended his hand—he expected to be shocked the moment his fingers passed the door's edge. He'd already tried walking out the first day of his captivity. He'd received a mind-numbing shock as a result.

I gripped his hand when it passed through the door.

Nothing had happened.

Bleek's dark eyes widened in disbelief.

"I won't lie to you," I said. "I promise on my white wings."

"You don't have," he began.

"This is just a disguise," I said. "Ask Berel when you see him—he has images on a comp-vid."

Bleek stepped out of his prison. Barc giggled and grasped his father's hand. I led them to the dining hall.

I can find things, after all.

I ate breakfast, sitting between Barc and Terrett. Bleek, who sat across the table, was deep in a conversation between a former Dragon

Warlord and a former Falchani General. They were discussing blade fighting.

If my eyes and ears weren't fooling me, I'd think Bleek was actually enjoying himself. I doubted he'd had the opportunity to talk sword skills with anyone since going to work for Cayetes.

By the end of the meal, both Falchani had arranged for a sparring session with Bleek using wooden practice blades.

"Don't kill anyone," I said when Bleek, a smile on his face, rose from the table.

"Yes, commander," he held one right hand over his chest while saluting me with the other.

"Now that's convenient," Lissa smiled. "Barc, do you want to go to the library or the arboretum?"

"Both," Barc grinned.

"Good choice," she held out her hand.

~

Avii Castle

Justis

Lissa warned me not to tell Wimla or Vorina of our plans.

I was finding it difficult not to do so. It would protect Liron; to me, that's what mattered most.

I'd already asked Ardis to investigate the rumors about Quin.

He never left my suite; he already knew.

Dena told him.

Farisa, Brown Wing Guild Master for the Artisans, had been pouring out her dissatisfaction with Quin since Jurris' death. Until that moment, Wimla, a glassmaker and Brown Wing artisan, had provided the heir to the throne.

Now, Farisa worried that the prestige that Wimla and Liron brought to the Artisan's Guild would evaporate.

Therefore, Quin had become a target. Farisa wanted to discredit Quin in any way she could, in order to push Wimla back into her elevated position as mate to the King.

I was King and I despised politics.

Therefore, I was adding to the plan Lissa had developed to protect Liron. Since Farisa was so obviously suspicious of where Quin had been for five years, I decided that she would accompany Wimla and Vorina when they left Le-Ath Veronis with Liron.

Yes, that would satisfy me and get the mouthy bitch out of the way at the same time. Her second-in-command, Gerig, would serve in her place until Cayetes was dead and it was safe to bring Liron home.

She'd be able to communicate with those she'd left behind, as would Wimla and Vorina. Where they were going, Cayetes could never go. Lissa had assured me of that much. We only had to employ a bit of subterfuge, first.

Then, all I had to do was convince Quin.

That, in my mind, might be harder than moving a mountain with my bare hands.

Puntia

Vic'Law

"How many of them are there?" Barstle whispered.

"At least twenty, so far, but I think—I think more may be coming," Barstle's valet whispered back.

"How? How is he making them?"

"I don't know. He has your entire wing locked and guarded day and night. Who knows what he has in there, now? It's uncanny—they all look exactly the same."

"If the others learn he's here," Barstle shuddered.

"Is there some way we can escape?" his valet pleaded.

"I have no idea. If you think of anything, tell me immediately."

Quin

I was at the back of the crowd at Jurris' memorial—by choice. Terrett, Berel, Kaldill, Lafe, Yanzi and Bel Erland stood with me.

Queen Lissa, as an ally and royal guest, stood near the front with Bel's father, the King of Karathia, showing their support for Justis.

I noticed Bryan Riley, the journalist, at a discreet distance, recording the event. Justis allowed him to come when he would allow no other.

I could see that Justis had respect for Bryan the vampire journalist. Bryan would only show to the Alliance what Justis approved.

A mound of flowers covered the coffin, but beside it lay a single, red, primary feather. Justis had plucked one of his to be sent to the crypt with his brother.

Wimla, Vorina and Liron stood to the left, Justis, alone, to the right. Yes, I should have been there with him, but so many Avii would have disapproved. Pulling my wings tighter against my body, I placed my hand inside Terrett's and sighed.

Terrett

Jurris' coffin was flown out of the throne room where the service took place, and downward, to a lower terrace. From there, he would be carried to the crypt where Avii royalty were entombed.

Any who could fly followed from a discreet distance, once Justis, Jurris' two wives and Liron followed the coffin.

Justis carried Liron himself, as if he feared for the boy.

Perhaps he was right to do so.

Do you wish to walk or fly? I turned to Quin.

"I'll walk with you," she said.

She led me out of the throne room and down wide passageways for what seemed a very long time until we came to a narrower tunnel. "I was here once before," Quin said. "I remember fainting in this tunnel after a healing," she said while touching the wall.

Someone behind us shrieked.

Quin fell through the wall, her hand jerking away from mine as the solid glass met my fingers.

~

Lissa

"I'll mist past the wall," I said. "If she's there, I'll bring her out."

Justis was nearby, attempting to hide his panic. Terrett did his best to remain calm; he'd informed me the moment Quin's hand was pulled from his. Still, I could see the terror in his eyes.

Bel Erland, however—he begged me with his eyes to bring her out. Like the others, he was terrified he'd never see her again.

What was it about this infernal castle, anyway? The gate lay at the bottom of it and this—nobody else could put a finger through this wall.

Somehow, Quin had fallen right through it—or, I worried—she'd been sucked into it.

"I'm going," I breathed, squaring my shoulders and turning to mist. I went right through a very thick, glass wall and into the strangest room I'd ever seen.

~

Quin

At least I hadn't lost consciousness this time, but I had no idea what the room's purpose was.

Piles of glass—like that the castle was made of—lay all around its smooth walls. Each piece was a perfect sphere. Like stacks of boulders, shaped round and smooth, they lay everywhere, in all sizes. Some quite small, others very large.

I knew I should go back—people would be looking for me. I knew where the exit was—it was quite apparent from this side of the room.

From the other side, nobody else could enter.

Except a Vampire Queen who could become mist, I discovered.

"Quin?" Lissa's voice disturbed the stillness of the room.

"Look at all this," I gestured with a hand. "Do you think it was leftover glass from the castle's making?"

"Perhaps, although I have to say, it's more than strange," she admitted, sweeping the piles of spheres with worried eyes. "I need to get you out of here—the others are panicking."

"I can leave anytime—through there," I pointed toward the wall.

"What? I don't see it," she said.

"It's right here. See the line of white?" I pointed. In all the glass that formed the castle, I'd never seen a white streak, before.

Perhaps it had been made just for me.

"That's strange," Lissa went to study the thin line of white. "You can go through it?"

"Yes. I can find it on the outside, too, since I can find things."

"Well, I hope you won't mind if I mist through again—I doubt it'll let me through," she blew out a breath. "Come on—you first. I'll be right behind you."

"All right." Bending down, I lifted a glass sphere half the size of my fist. "I'll take this with me, since it looks to be extra."

Lissa

I watched Quin walk right through the wall, as if it were nothing more than air. Placing my hand on the wall where she'd walked through, it was as solid as the rest of the castle.

"No idea," I muttered to myself before turning to mist and getting the hell out of there.

Quin

"Drink this," Justis thrust a glass of wine in my hands. "You probably need it. I know I do." He lifted his glass of wine and downed half of it in two swallows.

I sat in the King's sitting room where Terrett, Lafe, Lissa and the others had gathered after my reappearance in the castle's narrow tunnel leading to the royal crypt.

Alcohol had been ordered by Dena, who hovered nearby with Ardis, no doubt worried that I'd disappear through another wall.

I'm fine, I sent mindspeech to Dena. *Really.*

I knew tongues were wagging throughout the glass castle. Dena knew it too; I could see it in her face. My fall through a glass wall was another thing that separated me from the others. One more reason to claim I wasn't Avii.

I wondered if it would ever end, even when I was gone.

Yes, I planned to leave before Justis took his crown and the vows required by Avii law to bind him to Wimla and Vorina the following day.

I knew I couldn't bear to watch.

If I had my way, someone would take me back to Vic'Law and allow Bleek and Barc to go with me.

"Master Gurnil is here, my King," a guard appeared in the doorway.

"Good. Get him in here. Now, before she flies away again." Justice handed his empty wineglass to Dena.

"Come," Dena stood before me.

"Why?" I asked. It was a stupid question. How had this slipped past me? I felt dizzy, suddenly.

The wine.

"What did you put in here?" I demanded, my voice sounding slow. I felt as if my mouth suddenly found it difficult to form words.

"You'll be my first wife—I command it," Justis snapped. "If you fly away from me again without telling me where you're going, I will demand a feather. Of my choosing."

"No," I said.

"Tell me you don't love me. You said you did two days ago," Justis frowned.

"No," I repeated.

"Do you love me?" he asked.

"Yes." I hung my head. I think I'd loved him the moment he'd interfered when a guard pulled one of my nubs. Sadly, that came right out of my mouth after my admission of love.

"Do you want to marry me? Tell me truly," he demanded.

"Yes." I couldn't meet his eyes as I spoke the hopeless wish that was lodged in my heart.

"Then you will be my first wife. Gurnil, begin the ceremony."

I think he knew better than to ask me to share his bed. He'd drugged the wine with something that forced the truth from my lips and I was angry, even in my less-than-lucid state.

Instead, Berel was with me inside the suite next to Justis'—it was reserved for the King's favorite wife.

Once, it had been Halthea's. I'd cleaned her closet and arranged her clothing. I hoped it was all gone, now. I had no desire to see anything of hers.

"Do you know what was in that room?" I leaned back and turned wine-fogged eyes on Berel. He'd tucked my head against his shoulder while we lay, fully clothed, on the wide bed.

"No. Tell me." His smile was gentle as he leaned in to kiss me.

"This. And many more like it," I pulled the small sphere from my pocket.

"The same glass as the castle?" He took the sphere from my hand and examined it.

"I think so. Maybe it was extra," I shrugged, snuggling against him again. "Some of the spheres are nearly as tall as I am."

"Will you wear my ring, too, one day?" he asked, taking my hand and fingering the gold band I wore. I nodded, which made him smile.

"Justis is full of shit," I mumbled, closing my eyes.

Berel's chest vibrated as he laughed.

Lissa

There are times when things happen just as they should; when the guilty get their comeuppance and the ones they've harmed are there to witness it.

Those times don't come often, but they do come.

Quin was there to witness the ceremony between Justis, Wimla and Vorina. Liron was watched over by Farisa, Guild Master of the Artisans.

Justis asked Quin's permission before taking those two as wives; it was his way of telling them that Quin was first and always would be.

Quin was still upset with Justis and I didn't blame her, but I watched in satisfaction as Farisa's anger grew.

When the short ceremony was over, Justis informed Wimla, Vorina and Farisa that he was sending them to Wyyld II to protect Liron's life. During the ceremony, their things had been packed and were now ready to load onto a private ship headed for Ildevar Wyyld's home. He, as founder of the Reth Alliance, had offered sanctuary for the child, his mother and two others.

Farisa was ready to explode. If she hadn't worried that she'd be sent to a cell deep in the castle, she'd have argued with the King.

I wondered what she'd say when she learned what we truly had in store for her. I wanted to laugh, but held back. My Falchani twins were with me, though, and they turned heads now and then to hide a snicker.

I could see the strain it placed on Quin, however. She could see every bad word and thought in Farisa's face.

If Farisa could have killed with a look, she'd have done exactly that.

"Hold on for a minute," I held up a hand to let my twins know not to follow me. I pitied Farisa if she attempted to strike me.

She held back—vampires terrified her, I suppose.

As they should.

"You," I said, pointing at her and placing compulsion in a soft voice, "Will never bring harm to Quin or Justis. That includes any lies you think to tell about them. Do you hear me?"

Her eyes had gone blank for just a moment before she nodded.

"Good," I said. "I think we're done here."

Quin

Justis convinced me to share his bed that night. I think he knew the rest of us would go back to Vic'Law the following day.

We'd gone to the space station orbiting Le-Ath Veronis after the ceremony, to see Wimla, Vorina, Liron and Farisa off. I was grateful they were going, if I were honest. Justis didn't need another attack at Avii Castle. Bryan Riley had come, too, making sure that the Alliance was aware that Liron was going to stay with Ildevar Wyyld to preserve his life from future attacks.

"My love," Justis half covered my body with his. "Did you really love me then?" He meant when I'd first seen him.

"I think I did," I closed my eyes with a sigh. "I could see the light shining in you."

"I think I've dimmed it a few times since then," he said, leaning in to kiss me. "For that, I apologize."

"Do you apologize for drugging my wine?" I opened my eyes and frowned at him.

"I will never apologize for making you mine. You may complain all you want about that. An apology will not be forthcoming."

"I told Berel you were full of shit."

I expected him to be offended. Instead, he flopped onto his back and laughed.

Propping myself on an elbow, I watched as he guffawed. *He needs to laugh*, I reminded myself.

Afterward, he made his apology known by loving me senseless.

"Don't worry," Justis wrapped arms about my shoulders. He held me close as we watched the news-vid concerning the private ship carrying Wimla, Vorina, Liron and Farisa.

"But," I sputtered. The ship, according to the vid, had been taken by pirates.

"Wait for it," Justis breathed against my ear. We stood naked in his suite, my back to his front, as we watched a clip from the ship's camera before it was cut off, showing the attack ship's logo.

It bore the name *BlackWing II*.

CHAPTER 14

*Q*uin

"They've been taken to Avendor," Justis chuckled. "Queen Lissa tells me that none get past the shield around SouthStar. Cayetes can break himself against that barrier, if what I hear is correct. Farisa can attempt to run away whenever she wants. The shield will stop her escape."

"This was done to inflame the war we've started with Cayetes, wasn't it?" I asked. Justis took my hand and led me toward the bathroom—he intended to get a shower before Yellow Wings arrived with our breakfast.

"Exactly," Justis tapped my nose. "Liron's testicles, how I love you."

Lissa

"If I had my choice, Barc would stay with me," I informed Bleek. "Your child will never be held accountable for your sins; I will decree it. I hope you come to realize that, someday. I will say this," I said. "Harm or betray Quin and I will hunt you down and destroy you."

"I made a promise to her already," Bleek sounded as if I'd offended him. "She gave my child back to me. Please don't ask me to be separated from him so soon."

"Then I will ask Kaldill and Daragar to protect him while he's on Vic'Law," I said. "He will be welcome on Le-Ath Veronis anytime. I've already approved his citizenship."

I watched as Bleek went still. "He's a member of the Alliance?"

"He is, now. You, on the other hand, have many sins to atone for. Show me you're worthy of my approval, and I'll consider citizenship for you as well."

"They're here," Grant announced, interrupting my conversation with Bleek.

"I want Cayetes dead," Bleek said as I led him toward my study door. "I will prove myself, I swear it."

"Start by apologizing to LaFranza," I said. "You nearly killed him. If Quin hadn't been there, he'd have died."

"He's a master swordsman," Bleek sighed. "It was like destroying a work of art when I cut him."

"Then tell him that, too," I snapped.

Quin

Justis didn't want to let me go.

I felt empty after leaving him behind at Avii Castle. As the hovercar flew us away, I saw tour boats on the waters below, where people crowded the rails and watched as Ardis led his troops in battle formation training.

I wondered if Justis watched them from his window, too.

Bleek

There was no threat coming from LaFranza or any of my new companions as we gathered in Queen Lissa's arboretum. "I'm giving you mindspeech," Lissa gave me a pointed look.

Don't piss me off or I'll remove it, her voice sounded in my mind. I jumped; I hadn't been that startled in sun-turns.

Two trunks were to go with us—one filled with clothing for Barc, the second for me. I was stunned by the Queen's generosity.

It's because Quin believes in you. Don't break that trust.

I promise, I replied, testing my new ability.

She nodded to let me know she'd heard.

I'd been transported by Deris and Daris before. This trip, the journey was much smoother. Yanzi, whose speech seemed broken, had transported us. I may have stared at him in wonder when we landed inside a mansion outside the manufacturing city of Mundia on Vic'Law.

He's a shapeshifting lion snake, Quin informed me. *Tread carefully, he is quite powerful.*

And poisonous, no doubt, I responded.

She smiled. It made me glad—she hadn't smiled once since she'd arrived at the Queen's palace that morning.

~

Quin

A meeting was in order shortly after our arrival at the mansion; Daragar had been busy providing solar power for the power station and to larger buildings. He and Kaldill had arranged to replace natural-gas pipes with energy lines and outmoded stoves with heating panels, or perhaps they merely transformed what was already there.

Either way, houses were now heated with light from Vic'Law's sun, and cooking was done by employing the same type of technology.

"We've received no further communication from Cardino or Churg," Caylon said. "Deliveries to Mundia were already interrupted when you left; nothing has changed since then, so we've been building an army from the population. Their first duties include distributing food to the city."

"We've collected bounties offered by the ASD for turning over the crews of Cayetes' ships—the ones he sent to interrupt the shipments we took," Sal grinned. "The coffers of Mundia are growing nicely, so they can order what they need from legitimate channels. One of us can transport supplies with no trouble."

"Nice," Bel Erland grinned. "Have they elected their leadership, yet?"

"Shim is in charge; his companions are falling into place around him," Caylon nodded. His eyes, dark and enigmatic, turned to me. "Quin, I want you and Jayna to train with those I've chosen as officers in the army; I want more women in the ranks and I think you'll be able to bring them in."

It's because you keep getting up when you've been knocked down, Terrett informed me. *You don't give up. Caylon admires that greatly.*

"All right," I nodded to Caylon. He almost smiled.

Bleek

I wasn't sure of my welcome when I knocked on LaFranza's door; his suite was far from the one Barc and I shared.

Dark eyes examined me when he opened the door. For a moment, I couldn't form the words.

"I will fight beside you from now on," I whispered. Those words were difficult enough, but the next ones I almost didn't get out. Not because I didn't want to say them, but because I did.

"I will owe a debt to you until you tell me it is repaid," I said, bowing my head.

"Stand with me to guard Quin, and that will be payment enough," he said.

"I always heard the Falchani were honorable. Now I know it to be true," I sighed. "Thank you."

Puntia

Vardil was vicious when he was angry.

Barstle felt fortunate to be alive. Four of his servants weren't—their bodies, like that of Nardes, were charred piles of ash on the floor where Deris had killed them.

He didn't understand Vardil's cursing at first; eventually he learned that a new criminal element had joined the ranks—one who'd chosen to attack ships bound for Vic'Law, snatching them away from Vardil's grasp. Barstle realized the depth of Cayetes' betrayal then.

Vardil intended to starve or kill any on Vic'Law for which he had no use. That, in essence, meant all crime families and anyone else who stood in his way. He intended to intercept any ship bringing supplies to Vic'Law in order to achieve his warped goals.

Too, in the midst of Vardil's fit of anger and subsequent murder of four servants, Barstle learned that an assassination Vardil ordered had gone awry. His assassin had been killed and now the intended victim had been taken by the same pirates who were preying on the ships he'd sent his own to take.

The name *BlackWing* was mentioned with regularity while Vardil cursed.

"I want the ones behind those ships," Vardil hissed at Dorgus, his valet and personal assistant. "Find out who they are. They will regret the day they crossed my path."

Quin

The following morning, Jayna and I went with Caylon, Sal, Lafe, Bleek and Terrett to a former hovercar factory, where the Mundian army was now quartered.

Those Caylon had chosen as officers he would train, with Jayna and me participating. Sal was training the rest, but he now had help from Lafe, Bleek and Terrett.

Mell agreed to watch Barc during training time, with help from Kaldill, Berel and Bel Erland.

Bleek was slowly beginning to relax. I think he enjoyed teaching new troops eventually; Sal was impressed with his knowledge of hand and blade fighting.

Jayna and I were two of only three women in the group Caylon trained. Afterward, Caylon had another four who wanted to try for an officer's position.

Jayna and I were allowed to leave at lunchtime to return to the mansion; Caylon stayed to eat what was served to the army and then drilled the troops during the afternoon.

Yanzi came to take us home; all the others stayed with Caylon.

"How was it?" Berel smiled and opened his arms when we appeared in the kitchen.

"I'm covered in sweat," I warned him.

"Don't care," he pulled me close and kissed my forehead.

"It's humbling," Jayna admitted. "That those people are willing to fight for their families, against such strong enemies."

"She's right," I pulled away. "They don't know what they'll face, and they're training anyway."

"Come on, I'll get you into the shower," Berel pulled me away from the kitchen. I could hear Jayna laughing behind me as we trotted down the hall.

Le-Ath Veronis

Lissa

"Is the shield up around Harifa Edus?" I asked. Connegar and Reemagar, my Larentii mates, agreed to do this for me.

"It is," Connegar smiled.

"If more of Cayetes' ships arrive, we will know," Reemagar agreed.

"He won't let this go—just as he won't let Liron's assassination go," I sighed. "The sadistic swine."

"He is much like his brother, as you recall," Connegar said.

"I haven't heard that he's a pedophile, but that's not much to recommend him over his brother Hordace."

"I marvel that he is so difficult to find," Reemagar pointed out. "If

Quin cannot find him with her talent, then I suspect a cause we haven't discovered as yet."

"Kooper found his compound on Zephili, but there's little evidence left behind. Certainly nothing that would tell us where he went. He's likely holed up somewhere, waiting for Vic'Law to destroy its population, then he'll attempt to waltz in and take everything that's left with little effort. Bleek told the truth when he said he didn't know which way Cayetes would go," I added.

"I wonder if Cayetes will make the trains run on time," Gavin appeared with a nod. Occasionally, he'd tell a joke. I bent over laughing.

~

Vic'Law
  Quin

I discovered that Berel and I could teach Jayna and Barc at the same time. Jayna sat with an arm around the boy while they pored over a book, both reading slowly through it. Barc had been so ill the last two years of his life before being placed in a sealed coffin, that he'd had little time for lessons.

He and Jayna were nearly at the same stage of reading ability as a result.

That's where Bleek found us, after he and the others returned to the mansion. "Pap, Quin and Berel are teaching me and Jayna," he crowed, running into his father's embrace.

Bleek's eyes settled on me in grateful surprise.

"You should wash up, my lamb," I rose from my seat and ruffled Barc's hair. "Dinner is nearly ready."

"We'll wash up together," Bleek lifted the boy and carried him out of the library.

~

Puntia

"Here is the list of those imprisoned on Le-Ath Veronis," Dorgus handed a comp-vid to Vardil. "You look most handsome, my Lord."

"I do," Vardil agreed as he studied himself in the mirror. "We're keeping the original twins alive to provide blood; this is the first of their clones. I like this very much," he said, turning from side to side to admire the new body. "No more buying different sizes of clothing —from now on, a single wardrobe will do."

"This color is perfect for you, too," Dorgus gushed.

"I've always liked red, but I never wore it in my original state as it washed out my skin color. This is perfect," he straightened the collar on the red leather jacket.

"I will make sure you have more red in your wardrobe," Dorgus said.

"Why is Bleek not on this list?" Vardil glanced at the comp-vid. "He wasn't listed among the dead—that list came yesterday."

"I cannot say, my Lord. Perhaps it was an oversight."

"Perhaps he escaped—he is quite talented, you know. Attempt to contact him."

"I will do so, my Lord. Immediately."

"Something else is missing, too," Vardil studied the list more closely.

"What is that?"

"The Sirenali. None of them are listed. It's fortunate that Bleek's crew was taken by the ASD instead of those filthy BlackWing pirates. At least we know what happened to them—or most of them."

"Why wouldn't they list the four Sirenali aboard the ship?" Dorgus took the comp-vid back and thumbed his way down the list of names.

"Perhaps they don't see them as anything except animals, since they can't speak. Two of them were dying, anyway."

"I heard from Whip just this morning," Vardil continued. "He's on Cloudsong—his escape pod would only travel so far. I've sent someone to pick him up. I'll hear his version of events when as he arrives."

"I will make sure that happens, my Lord," Dorgus bowed his head. "Will there be anything else?"

"I feel like a swim. Bring my suit and make sure the water in the pool is warm enough. It's freezing outside."

"When we take Der'Vek for you, my Lord, you will find it warmer and the view of the sea much more to your liking."

"Then it can't happen soon enough, can it? Send that fool Barstle Cardino to me. I'll ask him questions while I swim."

"I'll see to it right away."

~

"I don't know who Caylon Black is, or how he's managed to keep Mundia alive," Barstle mumbled.

"Have you had contact with him again, after he made short work of you and your intended attackers?"

"No." Barstle hung his head, refusing to meet Vardil's eyes. "We've shut off the natural gas going to Mundia—they should have frozen to death by now. I can't get drones into the city, either. They're stopped on the outskirts; how I don't understand. The vid goes blank, as if it's been shut off in midair."

"I'll have my witch and warlock devise something, then," Vardil growled. "We will penetrate the perimeter of Mundia, rest assured."

"Thank you, Lord Cayetes. Those miscreants must be taught a lesson. Mundia will be ours," Barstle breathed.

"Mundia will be mine," Vardil corrected, his eyes narrowing as he glared at Barstle. "Tell me, how goes the recalibration on the ranos cannon?"

"It looks quite promising, my Lord. A few more days at most, I think."

"Good. I have targets to destroy. Go. Make sure everything is done correctly. I have vengeance to exact."

~

Quin

"I hear that the common quarter is nearly empty in Der'Vek," Sal said at dinner. "Parts of the city are still burning from the battles between crime families. Refugees are crowding into the fields twenty clicks south, hoping to stay warm and keep from starving. The winter is bad enough there, but it's worse here. At least they knew to travel in a southerly direction."

"We need to keep those who aren't part of the army busy," Bel Erland suggested. "Perhaps we can put them to making emergency food packets?"

"Like trail rations?" Caylon asked.

"Yes. Gran calls them em-are-ees for some reason, which I've never figured out."

Sal snickered.

"You know, don't you?" Bel turned toward Sal.

"It's an old Earth term," Sal grinned. "An abbreviation for meal ready to eat."

"The letters don't match up," Bel Erland snorted. "I know that much, at least."

"Because old Earth doesn't speak Alliance common," Sal said.

"Wait—I feel something pinging my radar," Bel Erland stood.

"What?" Caylon asked, immediately on guard.

"A warlock or witch is trying to get past the sensory shield I have around Mundia," Bel explained.

"Hmmph. They won't get past what Kaldill and Daragar have put up," Sal snorted.

"That's not what worries me. We've killed all the drones they've sent. Now, somebody is asking a witch and warlock to try to get through by scrying. When they discover they can't get in, they'll realize we have someone with power living in Mundia."

"I say let them come if they want to," Caylon muttered, lifting a roll from a nearby basket. "I'd appreciate a good fight."

"That may convince them to band together against us, rather than fighting each other," Lafe said.

"Good point," Caylon nodded at Lafe.

"They won't know how much power is here," Kaldill said. "Only that someone is blocking them out."

What are they talking about? Bleek sent mindspeech to me. *Who is Daragar?*

You have godlings, a Sirenali and a warlock at the table, I replied. *If Daragar were here, you'd have a Larentii, too.*

Bleek, attempting to hide sudden concern, lifted his wineglass and drained it after my explanation.

You have no need to worry, I sent. *Unless you have evil planned, they will protect Barc—and you—because I ask it.*

Bryan Riley had listened quietly to the conversation, no doubt making mental notes to record later for his article. He moved so quietly through the mansion that he didn't interfere or bother anyone with his presence.

"How do you plan to get the food to the refugees?" He asked, speaking for the first time.

"I can do it," Bel shrugged. "It's a simple relocation spell."

"I help," Yanzi offered.

"We'll need the supplies," Berel said. "Where and how much? I can contact my father—he'll put a list of sellers together. We may need more than one—we'll be feeding many."

"Perhaps we should provide solar-powered camping stoves," Sal mused. "They'll serve two purposes—heat and a cooking surface."

"Tents?" Berel asked. "If Father contacts outdoor recreation companies, they may be able to supply most of what we need, including powdered milk and water purification canisters."

"What about the fighting in Der'Vek?" Bryan asked.

"They're lobbing small explosives, with a few minor skirmishes between private armies at the moment," Caylon said. "Salidar and I spent an hour there yesterday, watching. Every family compound has been hit in some way—a few families have warlocks protecting the vital portions of their homes, but these warlocks aren't the most powerful."

"We should be grateful for that," Bel said. "The good ones cost too much."

"Bleek?" I turned to him.

"Quin?" His dark eyes became wary.

"Who is Cayetes' warlock?"

Bel Erland drew in a breath—this was news he and his father had searched for—I could see it easily in him.

"He has two," Bleek sighed. "Twins. Deris and Daris."

"No," Bel Erland breathed.

Le-Ath Veronis

Lissa

"What do you mean, they're distant relatives to me?" I snapped.

"Well, to Wylend—your grandfather, and your father, too," Erland winced. "Several times removed. They were notified when Wylend abdicated, putting our son on the throne."

"So you're saying that those two are in line for the throne—if everybody else dies?"

"You're in line for the throne before they are," Erland offered.

"Right. What the hell are they plotting? Is that what Cayetes promised them if they did this illegal shit for him?"

"I have no idea whether Cayetes promised them anything, except a mountain of money plus living expenses," Erland spoke evenly in an attempt to calm me down.

"I swear, if they attempt a coup against Rylend," I hissed.

"He can protect himself, remember? He doesn't need his mother swooping in for the likes of those two."

"What are their levels?" I asked.

"To perform a transference, you must be level three or higher. It's my guess that at least one of them may be a level four. Wylend tested both when they were young."

"I don't like this," I muttered. My arms were crossed tightly over my chest as I gazed out the arboretum windows. Yes, I felt defensive. How could I not? Cayetes could destroy everything, and I was only now learning that distant relatives could be helping to accomplish that.

"Do you think they're helping to hide him? Is that possible?" I whirled to face Erland again.

"There is a small possibility that they've found a way to amplify Cayetes' Sirenali's talents," he frowned after mulling my question for a moment. "It would be draining, so if they've found a way, one of them will have to spend most of their talent and power on that, while the other focuses on the transferences and anything else Cayetes wants."

"And you're telling me that Ry can take care of himself," I tossed up a hand. "If they come at him with enhanced Sirenali, who is going to see them coming?"

"That means they'll have to amass a great enough fortune to afford to launch a coup, and take the Sirenali with them when they leave Cayetes. He's not going to let that happen as long as he's alive, you know."

"How will he stop them?" I almost shouted.

"If I know Cayetes, he has another card up his sleeve," Erland huffed. "Let me look into this. Bleek reported what he knew. Perhaps he didn't know everything."

"You think Cayetes has something—or someone—to hold over their heads? What if it or they go rogue, too?"

"We have to find out what it is, first, before we can make any assumptions," Erland soothed.

Puntia

"We couldn't get through the barrier around Mundia, my Lord," Deris said. "We have searched for Bleek as well, but we found nothing. If he were dead, we could locate his body by scrying. Perhaps he was destroyed and his ashes scattered. That could keep us from knowing his whereabouts."

"What about the coffin?" Vardil demanded.

Deris exchanged a swift glance with his sister, Daris. "We know where it is," Deris sighed. After all, they had no care for the child inside the coffin. Their only concern was what lay beneath the child's bed within the coffin.

It had been sealed against them as well—Vardil had snapped the lock on right after they'd placed the boy inside. Only one could open the lock, and he held the words and voice necessary—unless they found the one who'd placed the spell on the lock to begin with.

Deris and his sister knew how impossible that was; Marid of Belancour was dead—Cayetes had seen to that.

"Well?" Vardil said, "Where is it, then?"

"It lies in the dungeons of the glass castle on Le-Ath Veronis. It is my guess that they placed it there since they cannot remove the child or open the coffin."

"Well, well," Vardil frowned. "Let me know if anyone moves it. If Bleek were alive, he'd have contacted me and gone after the coffin—he would never have left it in the hands of an enemy. The child can stay where he is forever. Continue to serve me and I will keep my bargain with you—to return what is yours when the time is right."

He thinks we only want the jewels on the coffin. He means to take Karathia for himself, Daris muttered into Deris' mind.

He cannot hold it. He will need us.

We do not need him.

We need him to get us there, Deris responded. *We have time, sister. We will have our due.*

Just make sure your location spell for the coffin works; we cannot lose it, she warned.

Never fear. The spell is strong.

"Back to Mundia," Vardil said. "Why can't you get through? What sort of barrier?"

"One placed by a witch or warlock, my Lord," Deris explained.

"A stronger witch or warlock," Daris nodded.

"You're fifth level," Vardil narrowed his eyes at Deris.

"I am, but that doesn't mean I'm the strongest fifth level. Someone is keeping us out, after we attempted full force against it. You have an enemy, my Lord. One with a powerful warlock at his back."

"BlackWing," Vardil muttered. "I want information," he shouted. "I want this BlackWing and I want him to die in front of me. I assume you can handle that much, can't you?" His gaze leveled on Deris.

"Yes, my Lord. It will be as you say."

Quin

Production of camp rations for the displaced of Der'Vek began the following day. Bel Erland, Yanzi and Berel had worked through the night, making contacts and placing emergency orders.

After our training session that morning, Jayna and I, with help from Mell, Pellen and Jeslin, helped a small army of volunteer workers clear out an old warehouse and set it up to assemble meal packets.

The initial packets would also include a health and hygiene packet, with soap, a comb, a small first-aid kit and other personal items.

One section of our volunteers put other, larger packs together, which contained a tent and a camp stove.

"I heard Caylon say that some are fishing for food while others search through the fields looking for anything left from the last harvest," Jayna informed me.

"I worry that many may need medical attention," I said, although her words concerning the last harvest worried me. Berel said the growing of food was done near the equator. The short distance the refugees had traveled south of Der'Vek was still not close to the equator. I wanted to go there and see this for myself, in addition to healing those I could.

"Please, don't place yourself in danger," Jayna lifted her eyes from the packet she was assembling.

"Caylon and Sal went to Der'Vek. Someone can take me to the refugee camps," I asserted.

"You'll exhaust yourself," Jayna lowered her eyes.

"Lives are worth exhaustion," I said. "To me."

"I'm worried," Jayna said. "About you."

"I'll ask Daragar," I said. "If he is with me, I should be fine."

◈

Avii Castle

Justis

"It's become something of a novelty—like a museum piece," Gurnil said. "I suggest moving it into one of the locked cells or placing it in the library."

We were discussing the glass coffin that lay where we'd left it after removing the boy. I learned only that morning that curious Avii were visiting the thing and poking about it. According to Ordin, it was covered with Avii hand and fingerprints already.

"I say put it in a cell," Ordin suggested. "That way they can look without touching it. I'm concerned about the spell on it, and how it might react if one of ours gets, shall we say, *creative* in an attempt to open it."

"You think somebody may try to break the thing?"

"It has gold and jewel inlays about the edges of the base—what if they get curious to see whether more gold or jewels are in the bottom of it, beneath the silk bedding?"

"I see your point," I agreed. "Very well, clean it up and place it in a cell. Ardis," I called out. "See that Gurnil and Ordin have access to a cell and help them lock that infernal coffin inside it."

◈

Puntia

"You have things to tell me?" Vardil narrowed his eyes at Whip, the only one to escape from the Killshot and evade his captors.

"Strange things," Whip nodded. "Bleek probably should have killed the girl when she was dropped inside the ship, but he didn't."

"What do you mean?" Vardil demanded.

"I reported to you when the girl appeared suddenly. I erred when I failed to give you her description. I have her image on my comp-vid— I was able to take it with me in the escape pod." Whip pulled up the vid in question—he'd downloaded it from the ship's security system shortly after her arrival.

He'd masturbated to the images, too, but he didn't intend to tell Vardil that.

Whip's first clue that Vardil was furious was when he stood, dropped the comp-vid to the floor and then lifted his chair to fling it toward the door.

"BlackWing is a woman," Vardil shouted. "Why didn't someone fucking tell me that?"

"Here is what we have from Vogeffa II," Dorgus placed a comp-vid in Vardil's hand. Dorgus worried about this comp-vid; Vardil had broken the one Whip brought earlier by tossing it on the floor. He'd then thrown his chair and anything else inside his suite he could lift.

Vardil, still seething but more controlled, accepted the comp-vid and stared. "Before LaFranza was killed by Bleek, this one served as his assistant in the tattoo shop. I am beginning to believe that she is seeking vengeance for LaFranza's death."

"Where did she get the money to build ships?" Vardil hissed. "We've seen four so far."

"I only have a theory," Dorgus backed away discreetly.

"What theory is that?"

"That she has allied with other criminals, with you offered as the ultimate prize."

CHAPTER 15

uin

"My love, you may not be able to tend all who need help,"
Kaldill said. "I know you want to, but there are limits.
Besides, you must be fully rested before you go."

He was right. I didn't want him to be right, but he was. Perhaps
this was why gods and godlings didn't interfere much of the time.
Whom do you choose to help? My shoulders drooped and my wings
drooped with them.

"Will you take me tomorrow, then?" I pleaded.

"I think several of us will go. Caylon will keep Jayna here to drill
with the troops, but I imagine that most of the others will come with
you—to ensure your safety."

"Thank you," I sighed. I felt guilt for taking all of them away from
duties or other plans, but something troubled me about the refugee
camp.

We'd be close enough for attack from the crime families left in
Der'Vek, too, so we had to be as secretive as possible. While Kaldill
would likely shield us, I was concerned for the scattered refugees,
who'd be left behind and vulnerable to an attack.

If the families bothered to fly over the camp, either themselves or by sending drones once the tents went up, they'd know someone was helping the refugees.

Still, we couldn't leave them to starve or freeze to death, and it was easy to see that the crime families had no sympathy for any but themselves.

"A helping hand can often do harm without intending to do so," Kaldill said softly.

"Damned if you do, damned if you don't—that's what Gran says," Bel Erland nodded.

The morning brought bad news, just before we were scheduled to travel to the refugee camp. Caylon brought a comp-vid to me and set it on the table at my elbow while I had breakfast.

"Cayetes works fast," Sal said.

My photograph, with a wanted notice, had been posted on a site frequented by criminals. "Kooper sent this to me a few minutes ago," Caylon said, taking a seat at the end of the breakfast table. "He wants you bad—many would sell their own mothers for fifty-million Alliance credits."

"You can't go to the refugee camps—people there will see you," Bel Erland pointed out. "That means they can sell information to anyone who asks, or report it to keep their lives if they're threatened. It's easy enough to shield us from outside eyes, but inside, especially if you're healing them," he shook his head.

Breathing a troubled sigh, I turned back to the comp-vid. The image of me had been recorded while I was on Vogeffa II—that was easy to see. I was grateful Terrett wasn't visible—I worried about his safety—as well as mine.

He it was, however, who came up with a temporary solution. *Change her wings back to their original color while we're visiting the camp,* Terrett suggested. *I doubt any would know it to be her.*

"Terrett needs a disguise, too," I said. "I don't want him placed in danger because of me."

He started to protest, but Kaldill agreed with me. "Quin will be herself when we visit the camps," Kaldill decreed. "Terrett will wear a disguise."

~

"Kaldill, his disguise must be permanent—until a time comes when he is no longer in danger from Cayetes," I said. I'd asked Daragar and Kaldill to meet with me before we went to the refugee camp.

"But why?" Kaldill asked. "I don't understand."

I didn't want to tell him what I knew, but Terrett's life could hang in the balance. "That image of me on the comp-vid—from that criminal site?"

"What of it?"

"That was recorded on Vogeffa II, while I was with LaFranza in Gungl. You don't see it—likely Terrett's image was cut off so only I would be shown. He stood beside me in the marketplace when that image was recorded. I didn't know—and those shopkeepers didn't know either—that the camera was there. That means Vardil Cayetes was spying on Gungl the whole time, from who knows how many vantage points."

"But still," Kaldill argued.

"No, you don't know what I do," I said, rustling my feathers. "Before Terrett was given to Marid of Belancour, he was enslaved by Vardil Cayetes."

~

Terrett

"You will choose the image yourself, because it will be permanent until you and Quin are deemed safe," Kaldill informed me. "She will wear her BlackWing disguise to fool him and draw his attention—as long as we can keep her safe that way. When necessary, she will wear her white wings. You, on the other hand—Quin says you were standing beside her when that image was recorded—the one Cayetes has placed on the site with her bounty. We worry that your image was edited out, but Cayetes will also be searching for you."

He was right, but perhaps not for all the reasons Cayetes would have for hunting me. I nodded my understanding. *I will choose*, I agreed. *Something to my liking—and to Quin's liking.*

"Then send for her—you can choose together."

~

Quin

His hair was longer; eyes dark, hair darker. Skin slightly darker as well. "He looks like someone from Wyyld II," Sal observed.

Terrett grinned at me—he was taller, too.

"New ID," Kaldill handed an identification chip to Daragar, who employed power to place it beneath the skin on Terrett's wrist.

"Are we ready to go?" Sal asked.

"I'm coming," Bleek elbowed his way into the crowd surrounding us.

"You won't be so easy to hide, Master Blevakian," Daragar said.

"I refuse to hide from Cayetes."

"Suit yourself," Kaldill agreed. "Let's go."

~

Avendor

"Liron! Where are you?" Wimla sounded desperate.

"He's here." Someone walked through the trees carrying the boy. Someone tall, with light-brown hair and wearing a grin as Liron rode high on his shoulder.

"Who are you?" Wimla demanded. "That is my son, the heir to the Avii throne, I'll have you know."

"And that's my son carrying yours," another man stepped forward. "I named him Ashe when he was born. Most people refer to him as the Mighty Hand."

"Well," Wimla huffed.

"It's all right, Dad. She has no idea who we are. Liron does, though, don't you?" Ashe swung Liron off his shoulders while the boy squealed in delight.

"Come on, it's time for dinner at the big house," Ashe said. "You'll be our guests tonight."

~

Quin

My heart sank when we landed in the fields the refugees had chosen for their temporary homes. Yanzi and Sal knew it, too, by the scent.

This was where they'd grown the drakus seed.

"How much could they have harvested?" Caylon asked as people in the distance only now noticed our arrival. "Could any have been left behind?"

"Not seed—they careful not to drop any," Yanzi whispered. "Roots —they grow again in spring if not stopped."

"Drakus seed is worth more per ounce than gold or platinum," Sal breathed.

"Is the food and tent drop ready?" Caylon turned to Bel Erland.

"Yes," he nodded. We watched as people in the fields were gathering to walk in our direction—we'd appeared from nowhere, so I couldn't blame them for being suspicious.

"You're sure none of it will drop on anybody's head?"

"It's designed to float gently to the ground—where there's enough space for it to land," Bel grumbled. I could see he didn't appreciate Caylon's doubts.

Without another word, we witnessed the drop—the sky above the camp was suddenly filled with floating food packs, and in between, the larger stove and tent crates. They couldn't have landed any better or caused more delight once the people learned what was inside, than if it had been planned for months. Shouts of joy could be heard everywhere as food packets were opened—the people were starving.

"Nice work," Berel grinned and high-fived Bel Erland.

"Now to tend to their other needs," I said, squaring my shoulders. I was surrounded by Lafe, Yanzi, Terrett, Kaldill, Bel Erland and Berel, with Bleek coming behind us, blades strapped to his back, his eyes watchful for any attack as we made our way toward the gathering, increasingly noisy crowd.

Puntia

"Tell me what you saw," Barstle demanded. He spoke via comp-vid with Reede Xilva, an ally in Der'Vek.

Nearby, Vardil and Deris listened in. They'd positioned themselves so they wouldn't be seen behind Barstle while he communicated with one of the younger Xilva sons.

"I was afraid to get close; I went to check on the fields," Xilva sputtered. "They were covered by the filth that ran from Der'Vek. I wanted to kill them, but didn't have a suitable weapon with me. I was turning to go when something happened."

"What was that?" Barstle, his eyes narrowing with suspicion, asked.

"I recorded images for you. You can see for yourself," Reede said. "You must tell me what to do—food and tents for the refugees dropped from the sky. Perhaps weapons were included in the drop; I cannot say. Is someone arming the commons against us?"

Terrett

"The drop was recorded," Sal said, flopping onto a chair at the kitchen table. "It's only a matter of time before Cardino learns we were there."

"You think he'll try to kill those people?" Quin asked.

"I think the one who recorded us may have been planning that before he saw us. He's a coward—he was a long way off when I scented him. Probably with a high-powered weapon so he could shoot from a safe distance and brag about his kills later."

"Is that why you got us out of there so fast?" Berel asked.

"It is. I'm sorry you didn't get to heal anyone," Sal held up a hand to hold Quin off. "I think we need to relocate that camp. Who has ideas —we need to make a plan."

Puntia

"You tell that Xilva filth that I have plans for some of those bodies," Vardil hissed in Barstle's face. "They're not for target practice, do you hear me? Go. Tell your friends to round them up immediately; I have testing kits. Those who meet my requirements I will keep. The others you may destroy in any way you see fit."

"But what about the food drop? Doesn't that concern you?"

"That is insignificant to me. It merely means that those I want won't die before I get to them." Vardil gripped Barstle's collar and pulled his face to his. Barstle's feet almost left the floor—Vardil in his newest incarnation was much taller and stronger than Barstle.

"But what if it's the same ones from Mundia?"

"We have people in Der'Vek, waiting for you to tell them to collect what is mine. You think those fools in Mundia can get to them faster than that?"

"No, Lord Cayetes."

"Good. Scurry. Tell that Xilva ass to move quickly. I want those bodies transported away by tomorrow."

"At least he's not looking at us," Barstle's valet whispered after Barstle ended the communication with Reede Xilva.

"What is he looking for?" Barstle whispered back.

"I overheard someone saying the proper blood type, but that sounds strange."

"Hmmph. I think he's as crazy as a lunar sloth-bear."

"Then he's a dangerous lunar sloth-bear," the valet muttered. "Has there been any other information from Mundia?"

"Messages aren't getting through," Barstle shook his head. "I know some of my spies have to be alive, still, but like the barrier keeping the drones out, I can't get any information to them."

"I'm concerned by the fact that Cayetes' warlock can't penetrate it, either."

"That only means they have a more powerful warlock. Easy enough to buy if you have sufficient funds."

"Perhaps we should buy one, then," the valet suggested.

"Take this," Barstle shoved a comp-vid into his valet's hands. "Go to the site. Offer whatever it takes to bring a fifth-level warlock to Vic'Law."

"Me?"

"Yes. Go. Do it now, while I let Cayetes know that Reede and his brothers are rounding up the commons from Der'Vek."

Bel Erland

"Grampa?" He'd appeared inside my suite shortly after dinner, giving me a smile and a hug before I could even say his name.

"Don't worry, I'm not checking up on you," Grampa Erland informed me. "Your father and I found something just released on one of the criminal networks."

"If it's Quin's wanted poster, I already know about that," I said.

"Nah—your gran and I already talked to Caylon about that. No, this is something new, and from somebody who sounds desperate. We need to find out how desperate, and exactly who they are."

"What's that?" I asked.

"Here." Grampa has a certain flourish when he *Pulls* anything into his hand. Gran calls it his *voilà* gesture. The comp-vid he held bore an advertisement for an incredible amount of money—for a fifth-level warlock. "We've traced the sending to Vic'Law," Grampa added. "Usually the sending is blocked, but it looks as if the sender either didn't know what he was doing or was interrupted before he could block it."

"You know," I tapped a finger on my chin, "somebody recently pinged my shield around Mundia, but they didn't have enough power to get through it. You think they're looking to get past my shield to see what we're up to?"

"That makes sense," Grampa Erland agreed. "I can't figure out why they seem so desperate, though."

"What are you thinking of doing?" I asked.

"Corolan has offered to go undercover," Grampa said. "So he can report back to your father and me."

"But," I said.

"He's fifth level," Grampa held up a hand. "We're concerned that Cayetes may be putting pressure on his allies here, and placing Corolan in the mix will give us information."

"But what if Uncle Cory is walking into a trap?" I said.

"What if that's what you're doing?"

"You have a recall spell on me, don't you?" I accused.

"Just as I'll have one on Corolan, if he gets the job. You get hurt, you'll be pulled away. Simple as that."

Bel! I heard Sal's mental shout. *The refugee camp is under attack!*

Quin

People were running. Some were screaming. A few were dead.

That memory of the attack will remain with me always. I'd saved the people of Vogeffa II from a similar fate.

This attack began before I was aware of it.

Armored hovercars flew overhead, attempting to herd the refugee population, while their occupants fired weapons at the running crowd. I wanted to weep—several small ones had been trampled in the rush to get away.

Farther away, armed men forced captured refugees into a hovervan.

Berel stopped beside me, pulled the pistol Queen Lissa had given him from his jacket and fired at the hovercar I'd seen shooting at the running crowd.

"No," I shouted, before realizing that he and Bel Erland had planned the maneuver. Berel shot the vehicle; it exploded, the loud boom bouncing across the fields. Bel Erland then placed a shield, keeping the exploding bits and resulting fire from raining down on the people below.

Somehow, too, Bel made the thing disappear.

"I have us shielded, except for the weapon," Bel shouted over the noise. "Fire away."

The explosion of the second hovercar sent the attackers into a frenzy, however. The kidnappers loading victims into the hovervan pulled hostages away from the vehicle and hid behind them.

Other hovercars began shooting indiscriminately.

Time stopped for a moment as once again, I did what I hated doing. This time, it was so much worse. If Kaldill, Sal and Caylon hadn't come, and if Terrett hadn't held me up while I did it, more would have died.

Drivers died at the controls of hovercars.

Those using hostages as shields dropped behind their victims.

Every vehicle nosedived toward the ground—Kaldill, Caylon and Sal took over, collecting them with power and tossing them toward the sea.

When my knees buckled as the last attacker died, Terrett held me up. I discovered I was weeping.

No time for tears, beloved, Terrett whispered in my mind. *There are children to heal.*

~

Terrett

The refugee camp was moved to an open space near the river in Mundia. The dead were left behind—they were beyond our help.

Quin wept for some of those she'd killed.

Not all.

Kaldill told me that Reede Xilva had forced the teenage children of his servants to drive the vehicles and shoot at the refugees, after threatening them with the lives of their parents.

Dead was dead. Quin couldn't bring them back. She'd had no choice; they'd have continued to shoot otherwise.

Bleek and I followed her now, as she went from cluster to cluster of refugees, healing the ones who'd been hurt. Kaldill and the others were clearing a factory to house the crowd, although only half of what had originally been in the camp had arrived in Mundia.

Xilva had gotten away with several hovervans filled with refugees before our arrival.

News had come, too, that Barstle Cardino was redirecting food and supply deliveries to Puntia—from the warehouses that provided for the commons on Vic'Law. We'd intercepted the ships delivering to the criminal element; their answer was to steal from the commons.

It was likely that the same was happening in Der'Vek.

Quin moved as if she were caught in a dream—a nightmare from which she couldn't escape.

Bleek felt helpless—as did I. All we could do was keep Quin moving. We had no talent for healing and little for comforting the sick or wounded. There'd been no time to turn her wings white this time; she walked through narrow lanes to get to the next ones needing her help, black wings trailing in the snow behind her.

We're ready to move them, came from Sal.

Good. Quin is exhausted and ready to drop, Bleek responded before I'd had time to form a coherent thought to do so.

Bel Erland

Shim arrived with nearly fifty at his back. I learned quickly that these were the medical personnel who could come—those not currently on duty at the poorly equipped med-center of Mundia.

Their assistance inside the cleared-out factory freed Quin to treat the worst of the lot. I was grateful there were only three of those left.

"What do you suppose they'll do with the people they captured?" I asked Terrett.

Add to their army? You think they're desperate?

"They had children driving those hovercars," I said. "And older ones shooting weapons at the refugees. That seems desperate to me."

"If Cayetes were here, I'd have a guess as to what the people were for, but your explanation is better," Bleek said.

"If they pull troops from the commons, it will extend the war," Sal joined our conversation. "This is fucked from beginning to end."

"And the commons not in the army will be left to starve. That's motivation to join one faction or another," Berel observed.

"We need a better medical facility and medical supplies," Caylon walked up beside me. "Want to help?"

❧

Quin

When the last one who needed my help was healed, I only wanted to collapse in a heap where I stood.

Bleek, who'd followed me while I worked, hauled me over a shoulder before nodding to Terrett. Someone transported us back to the mansion, but I was asleep when we arrived and didn't care who it was.

❧

Karathia

Brenten Arden

"I don't think this is a good idea, Corolan. Not for you, anyway."

"I told him that," Wylend, my father and former King of Karathia, agreed. Five years earlier, we'd settled in Wylend's former summer palace, with permission from Rylend, my grandson and current Karathian King.

We sat at breakfast in the kitchen while two servants cooked and served our morning meal. As a former king, Wylend had advantages many others didn't, including enough wealth to afford servants.

"Why?" Corolan's eyes settled on me from across the small table.

"I have a bad feeling about this, that's why."

"I've already said I'd go," he began.

"I'll go instead," I said. "I still hold power. You know that. Besides, I doubt there's anyone who would recognize me. You, on the other hand," I shook my head.

"You're concerned about any rogue warlocks employed on Vic'Law, aren't you?" Wylend said. His butter knife scraped across toast as he considered what I'd offered.

"Yes. Too many of them can recognize the warlock who once stood at King Wylend's elbow," I said. "Stay here and protect Wylend. I'll go. This sort of thing used to be my work, you know."

"Very well," Corolan sighed before looking away.

I felt the danger in the assignment—he didn't. Something was terribly wrong, here, and he likely wasn't prepared to handle it.

"I'll leave tomorrow," I nodded to Wylend, who gave the slightest of nods in return.

Puntia

Xilva was a coward. Barstle was beginning to see that. Reede had stood on a high vantage point, recording the debacle on a comp-vid while armed children drove hovercars and fired upon panicked refugees.

He'd told Reede to keep them alive; that's what Cayetes' instructions were.

Now, not only were many dead, but more than half had escaped. Barstle sat uncomfortably in front of Vardil Cayetes, whose eyes were hard, his mouth drawn in a scathing frown.

"This is how your underlings follow orders?" Vardil demanded after watching the beginning of the carnage.

"I recorded my instructions to him—you have that evidence," Barstle defended himself, his voice trembling.

"Did you see the entire recording?" Vardil went on.

"No, Lord Cayetes. I brought it to you immediately, when I received it."

"Then look at this," Vardil shoved the comp-vid across his desk. Barstle barely caught it in his hands before it fell over the edge.

Barstle's breath caught at the frozen image. Cayetes had caught the perfect one and enlarged it for Barstle's benefit.

There, on the dark, frozen ground of the drakus seed field stood three people who shouldn't be there. One was a woman with black wings. Barstle recognized her easily enough. The two men who stood beside her, Barstle didn't recognize. Vardil's fury was evident; Barstle prepared himself for the worst.

Terrett

I was in the room when the call came. Caylon still carried the comp-vid he'd taken from one of Barstle Cardino's moles in Mundia, hoping that Cardino would contact us again, leaving us clues as to his location.

Barstle placed the communication, but two stood behind him as he spoke with Caylon. *Get Quin*, Caylon's voice hissed in my mind.

I shouted her name mentally as I rushed out of the library; if she weren't awake yet, she needed to be. I understood that Caylon wanted to know who stood behind Barstle.

Bel Erland

It took a while to get Quin to the library, as she was asleep when the communication was placed. Caylon did his best to keep Barstle Cardino talking, but it wasn't long enough. Cardino made threats.

Said he had images of BlackWing and two others, from the refugee camp. He demanded to know whether we had any dealings with, in his words, that filthy winged pirate. Then attempted to soothe Caylon's anger by offering one-hundred-million Alliance credits for her and the people she'd stolen from Vic'Law.

"I don't deal with criminals," Caylon snapped. "You, or any other," he added.

"Yet you've stolen Mundia from me," Barstle hissed.

"I've stolen nothing. Mundians run Mundia, now, instead of that filth Drood Juffa."

"You're fighting with them?" Barstle was unconvinced.

"I understand that this is a foreign concept to you," Caylon responded. "Nevertheless, it's true."

"I'll pay for you to drop your warlock's shield around Mundia," Barstle turned to wheedling. "I'll give the entire city to you if you'll only let me in."

"You only—or the army at your back?" Caylon asked. I knew that look he offered Barstle Cardino—Sal, who stood beside me, nodded. Caylon would kill Cardino the moment he was close enough.

"You are a dead man," one of the men at Barstle's back pointed at Caylon. "Come out of that bubble you've built for yourself and face me."

That's when the screen went dark—the communication was terminated. Terrett and Quin arrived moments later—too late for her to identify anyone.

CHAPTER 16

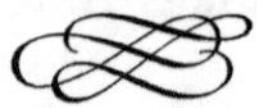

*Q*uin

"We tried to trace and record the communication, but something blocked it on their end," Caylon growled.

"Probably a warlock," Bel Erland replied. "I can do it—it doesn't take much. And no, I didn't recognize either of those men behind Cardino. If he had a Sirenali nearby, the warlock's spell could be amplified, preventing the powerful from tracing it."

"Could have been anybody, but the one making threats—Cardino should have shut him up or refused to let him speak," Sal said.

My brain was still addled from the day before, and I'd been wakened long before I wanted to be. Morosely, I nursed a cup of hot tea and closed my eyes against the plate of food set in front of me—my stomach wasn't ready for food, yet.

Milk, Terrett set a glass in front of me. *Better than tea*, he added.

He was right; the milk was good—I drank all of it in very little time.

Puntia

Brenten Arden

"Master Cardino is engaged elsewhere, Sir Warlock," Phorr, Barstle Cardino's valet, claimed. He'd asked me to meet him in a barn on the outskirts of the Cardino estate—not the usual venue for the arrival of a powerful warlock.

The moment I saw Phorr, I could see he was desperate—for himself and his employer.

"Payment?" I demanded. It was the question any warlock working on the wrong side of the law would ask.

I didn't give a rat's testicles about payment. Something had bothered me for a very long time about what was going on. The obsession I held was kicking in, when I least wanted it to.

No, it wasn't an obsession placed by a Sirenali. It was an obsession that psychiatrists might want to treat. Somewhere, deep inside my brain, lay a need to make things right, no matter the cost.

I'd fought battles with it in the past, and lost every time.

"I have this," Phorr lifted a small satchel at his feet and handed it to me. "Gold. There will be much more if you do as we ask. I only want you to disguise yourself—like this." He handed a comp-vid to me, which bore an image.

The one depicted was dead—I could see that by *Looking*. Barstle Cardino was desperate enough to kill in order to cover his actions.

I wanted to ask whom Barstle was afraid of. That information, like so much other information needed or wanted, was fogged and out of reach.

That spelled Sirenali involvement—*strong* Sirenali involvement.

"What does he want first?" I asked.

"He wants to get away," Phorr hissed. "With me and a few others."

Le-Ath Veronis

Lissa

I know you don't want to hear from me, he sent. *But I have the criminal*

Barstle Cardino within my grasp, if you or those parked in Mundia want to see him.

I knew in a moment that instead of Corolan, who was supposed to answer the ad from Vic'Law, my father had gone in his stead.

You have him right this minute? I demanded.

I will have him shortly. I'm currently disguised as a servant that Cardino killed in order to explain my presence in Puntia, he replied. *I'm staying long enough to see who now holds the upper hand against him, making him want to leave and promising a ridiculous amount to do it.*

Just grab him, I said. *I'll have Kaldill and Daragar modify the shield around Mundia to let you in. We can question Cardino and find out what we need to know.*

Yes, you're probably right, he sighed mentally.

Daddy, please. Just do this my way. If you stick around, too many things can go wrong, I pleaded.

Baby girl, I'll do this—for you.

Mundia

Bel Erland

Honey, you have to let your great-grandfather through your shield—Kaldill and Daragar have already modified theirs to let him in, Gran said.

When is he coming? I returned.

I don't know—he says he hasn't laid eyes on Barstle yet, so we have to wait until he does.

I had difficulty accepting that Great-Grampa had actually contacted Gran. They never talked. Both wore a pained expression whenever the other was even mentioned. Grampa said Corolan was answering the ad. When had Great-Grampa intervened?

Why had Great-Grampa intervened?

I'll fix it so he can get through, I said. *Let me know if you get any updates.*

I will, Gran promised. *Take care of yourself, honey.*

Quin

The sphere I'd taken from the hidden room in Avii Castle was in my hand as I stood at the library window, watching as more snow fell.

Caylon, Sal, Bleek and the others had gone to train the troops. I was exempt for two days—at Caylon's command while I built up my strength again.

The sphere fit easily in my palm and would glow if any sunlight struck it, but the day was gloomy and overcast while snow continued to pile up outside.

I couldn't help thinking that I should have carried a larger sphere away.

I had no basis for that thought, so I shoved the sphere in a pocket and wrapped arms tightly about myself—it was colder next to the window.

The feeling of dread that enveloped me was one I couldn't shake; I felt something terrible was about to happen, but once again, a fog blanketed the information and I was unable to reach it.

"My love?" Kaldill appeared behind me.

I turned to him and pulled his face down for a kiss. He was so handsome, my Elf King. He hadn't asked, yet, but soon I wanted to spend a night with him—the first of many to come. I felt I might bloom in his hands, just like the roses he could command to grow in solid rock.

"Do you feel it, too?" he asked gently when he pulled away.

"The cloud of doom settling over everything?" I asked, slipping a hand in my pocket to touch the sphere.

"Yes. It is a burden to carry, when you can't be certain of what troubles you."

He was right. It weighed on me and I couldn't shake it or leave it behind. We turned our attention to the snow outside—the flakes now smaller, their falling thicker, their purpose more sinister.

BlackWing I

"I've adjusted the orbit," Marco sighed. "We won't hit those archaic satellites, now."

"I can't believe that Vic'Law is still living in the dark ages," Winkler nodded. "Salidar says they had to supply the entire city of Mundia with solar power; the population was still using natural gas to power everything. Those people would be dead if they hadn't put up solar panels—the natural gas was shut off somewhere before it reached Mundia. Satellites instead of booster pods," Winkler shook his head. "Ridiculous."

"I don't recall that Earth's satellites were that big," Marco agreed. "These are monsters."

"Likely added onto through the years, employing warlock or wizard power instead of putting a crew up there to modify them, or replacing what they have. They look like floating piles of junk, now. Probably kept in place by a warlock spell, if my guess is correct. Their orbit should have deteriorated by now and they'd be crashing somewhere inconvenient without outside interference."

"Do you know why Lissa wanted us here instead of in the shipping lanes?" Marco asked.

"She said something is going on—I'm not at liberty to explain."

Puntia

Brenten Arden

I'd been retired from the Saa Thalarr for centuries. The work I did now while waiting for Barstle Cardino's appearance was worse than any assignment I'd had then. Cleaning the kitchen by hand was something I hadn't done in a very long time. Back in the day, I'd only cleaned up after myself.

Cardino had a palace filled with servants, guards and others, none of whom apparently picked up after themselves.

Cardino deserved the worst Lissa could give him; he'd killed a hapless, innocent servant so I could take his place. His other crimes were probably many and much worse. After all, he could have ordered the servant to hide or leave—at least he'd have kept his life that way.

Cardino thought it more convenient for the man to die.

Shoving trays of dishes into the dish machine, I turned it on before grabbing a cloth to wipe counters. The cook or cooks, whoever they were, were quite possibly the messiest I'd seen. Flour was everywhere, as was sugar and—*wait.*

Two tiny, red seeds. I was suddenly grateful for the cooks' messy style of baking. Anyone who'd ever been around criminals before would recognize those two seeds.

Drakus seed.

The game had just ramped up to another level.

Le-Ath Veronis

Lissa

This is what I found, my father informed me when the envelope dropped onto my desk. *I think perhaps I should wait a bit to see what the plans are.*

Don't you think Barstle will know all that? I asked.

I worry that he doesn't. He's been in a meeting all day—food was taken in earlier. I'm cleaning the kitchen—that's how I found those seeds.

You think the plans are to place Barstle and anyone else who doesn't willingly cooperate under the influence of drakus seed?

Likely.

Is this a new development, or something that has been going on for a while?

My guess is it's new—but why is this new threat only now reeling Barstle in?

You haven't been able to Look *to find out?*

Something is fogging it, whatever it is. That's why I wanted Cardino—so we could question him.

You haven't seen any Sirenali, have you?

Not yet. I'm sure they're hidden and well-guarded.

I'll destroy the seed, I said.

Thank you. I didn't want to throw it out—those seeds can lie dormant for years and then sprout under ideal conditions. Before you know it, you have it growing everywhere.

Keep me posted, then, I said. *I don't like this—something is worrying me about it.*

I too, he replied. *I'll let you know whatever I find.*

~

"My father found this," I handed the envelope containing drakus seed to Karzac. "Will you examine the seeds to see if this is a new strain? I'm curious about it."

"I'll check," my Refizani mate agreed. "I'll destroy anything left of it."

"Thanks."

~

Quin

I was distracted, but Berel and I taught Jayna and Barc their lessons anyway. Berel carried most of the weight—I stroked Barc's hair as he read from a book, his head snuggled against my shoulder.

"Time for dinner," Bleek announced as he walked into the library. He'd already cleaned up after drilling and training Mundia's army. *How's he doing?* Bleek sent mindspeech.

He's learning at near light-speed, Berel replied. *He wants to know everything, as of yesterday.*

Six lobes, Bleek grinned.

What excuse do you use when things go badly? I teased.

Six lobes, he laughed. *Brain's too crowded to think straight.*

I had no idea he'd be anything except offended by my teasing, and to be honest, I'd sent the message before thinking about it. My mind had been so filled with worry that the humor came unexpectedly.

"I'm starved," Jayna stretched before standing.

"Son, come wash your hands." Bleek was still grinning and he winked at me before turning to leave, Barc right behind him.

Puntia

Brenten Arden

By the time Barstle Cardino appeared while I helped serve dinner, it was already too late.

He was under the influence of drakus seed.

Perhaps it was fate—or punishment—for his misdeeds in the past, when he'd done the same thing to guards and servants alike, to keep them under his thumb.

Phorr, for whatever reason, had disappeared. I suspected he was dead.

Barstle walked right past me, as if he no longer recognized the face of his servant. Whoever had raised this strain of drakus seed had found a new and terrible use for the drug.

Yes—I considered that I could be in danger. I had plans to make and a disguise to change. That would be easy enough—I'd seen the same face, repeatedly. I knew, too—eventually—why that was.

Lissa, I sent. *Someone has found the Lyristolyi drug and is using it.*

Le-Ath Veronis

Lissa

Are you sure that's a good idea—changing your disguise to match a clone's?

They wander everywhere, my father replied. *Nobody stops them. They eat, they sleep and generally do what they please.*

Barstle is a complete idiot, now?

It looks that way. Whoever this is has found a way to tailor drakus seed to do this. His actions are their commands.

Like a Sirenali, only different? I guessed.

Similar, yes.

Frightening.

Agreed.

Who's in charge? Any idea?

I can't say as yet—I'm afraid to ask questions, for the obvious reason.

You'll call attention to yourself.

Yes. There's a section of the palace where most aren't allowed to go—it's my guess that the one in charge is holed up there, with a Sirenali.

Makes sense. Well, I suppose a clone disguise is as good as anything else, I said.

I'll let you know when I get more information.

Thank you. "Grant," I shouted aloud. "Get Gavin and Rigo. Now."

Quin

William Winkler appeared and had dinner with us. Afterward, he, Caylon, Sal and Kaldill locked themselves inside Kaldill's suite to have a discussion.

I did and didn't want to know what they were discussing.

Terrett and Berel pulled me toward the spa; we found Bleek there already, leaning back with all four arms splayed out on the flagstones while hot water bubbled around him. Jayna had put Barc to bed; Bleek wouldn't have left the boy alone to wander.

Now he was soaking sore muscles after a hard day training troops.

Ignoring the fact that he was naked, Berel, Terrett and I climbed into the water. Bleek barely opened his eyes to see who'd joined him before closing them again. "Getting warm?" Lafe, Bel Erland and Yanzi joined us.

"Yes. Hoping to relax," I mumbled, leaning my head back and closing my eyes.

"Which one help most?" Yanzi asked. "I give massage." Opening my eyes, I discovered he was nearby and grinning.

"Massage this way," Bleek murmured.

"Hold on, I'll take care of the four-armed mountain first, then I'll take your massage," I nodded at Yanzi.

"Four-armed mountain?" Bleek opened his eyes and sat up.

"Really? You're offended by that?" I crawled out of the water and went to sit behind him. At least I wore a swimsuit—he was still naked and still didn't care.

"Not really," he sighed the moment I put my hands on him. The healing glow was soft and gentle as I worked the kinks out of Bleek's muscles. He groaned in appreciation as the ache went away.

"I've never gotten any massage this good," he sighed. "Thank you."

"You're welcome. Just remember that if you ever decide to grab one of my wings again."

"I'll kill anyone who tries it from now on. I know now how big a mistake that was," he admitted. "You have my apologies."

"I accept." I swatted his arm. He laughed.

Bleek

I wondered if the healing Quin provided for Barc felt as good as what she'd done for me. Training troops reminded me of how out of shape I'd gotten. With her hands on me, my troubles—as well as my aches—had evaporated.

I marveled that she could do that. Someone else may have wanted to dissect how she'd done it; I accepted it as a wonder and a work of beauty and didn't question it after that.

In fact, I looked forward to getting sore muscles in the future.

She and Yanzi disappeared after Yanzi pulled himself from the water and placed his arms around her. I sighed and closed my eyes again.

Kaldill

"He's there now?" Sal asked.

"Yeah. And before you say it, Lissa is just as shocked as you are that he's trying to help." Winkler shook his head—if anyone would know what was going on with Lissa, it would be her werewolf mate.

Frankly, I think all of us were shocked. I had no idea when Lissa had last spoken with her father.

Before now.

"This is what he told her—that Barstle Cardino is now addicted to drakus seed and under someone's control, and somehow, those dimwits have gotten their hands on the Lyristolyi drug and are making clones."

"What the hell for?" Caylon demanded.

"No idea," Winkler shrugged. "So far, Brenten hasn't gotten close to whoever is in charge—at first he was disguised as one of Barstle's dead servants, but now he's disguised as a clone. He's attempting to get into the owner's suite to see who's in charge, but for now, they're hiding behind guards, locked doors and a Sirenali, most likely."

"I don't think you understand how dangerous the Lyristolyi drug is," I said. "Between drakus seed and that, I'd say drakus seed is less harmful."

"I don't even know what it is," Sal admitted.

"It was supposed to be destroyed long ago," I said. "The drug was an abomination when the Lyristolyi created it in the beginning—all in the name of benign research. Having both drugs in the same hands? That's frightening."

~

Puntia

"Whip, I want you and the ranos cannon aboard one of our freighters waiting outside Harifa Edus," Vardil instructed.

"What about Vic'Law?" Whip asked. "They're not exactly cooperating at the moment."

"They'll cooperate—or else. I've had a last trick tucked up my sleeve for a while," Vardil smiled. "Put in place two turns ago, without anyone's knowledge."

"Then I'm sure it's a good one," Whip nodded. "I'll need transport to the freighter—along with the ranos cannon."

"Deris will take you. Daris will stay here with me; I have a transference scheduled after Deris' return."

"I'm pleased to see you've found such a suitable body that can be cloned," Whip complimented Vardil. "You look amazing."

"It does suit me, doesn't it? Dorgus says the same."

"Dorgus is quite particular, so you know it to be true," Whip said.

"Yes. Go now—Deris is waiting for you. I want Harifa Edus destroyed. If you're successful, then target Le-Ath Veronis afterward."

"I will see it done, my Lord."

Quin

Yanzi hadn't asked for sex. Of course he wanted it, but was content to wait. Instead, he'd rubbed my shoulders and back, then tucked my head on his shoulder and lulled me to sleep.

I woke the following morning with a tingling itch between my wings. Something was going on, but I couldn't get past the fog that concealed it.

"I think same," Yanzi yawned and stretched before sliding off the bed and extending his hand to help me up. "If I snake, scales itch. I send mindspeech to Farzi—he say be careful."

"One of your brothers?" I asked.

"Oldest," Yanzi shrugged. "He keep us together when we young. Keep us alive, too."

"He sounds like a very smart man. Strong, too," I said.

"He is." Yanzi searched for his shoes—and mine. "We have breakfast. You train today."

"Oh. I forgot about that."

"Caylon not forget."

"I understand that about him," I agreed.

"He say women training want winged woman to come back."

"Now I feel self-conscious. Again."

"No. Not do. Come. Have tea and breakfast. Terrett waiting in kitchen."

~

"Defense posture," Caylon barked at me. My hands went up automatically. I had to shut off my brain—it wanted to overload on my lack of exercise for a few days, the fact that I might not be ready to block his blows and the women who were watching me.

Arm up to block the first blow. Turn aside to avoid the second. Turn back to prevent the takedown. Feathers in the eyes to get away. Wing extended to sweep his legs.

I stared in shock as Caylon fell, almost in slow-motion.

"It's almost like having four arms," Bleek said beside me as Caylon studied me from his position on the floor. "Your wings, I mean." He held out one hand and pulled Caylon to his feet with barely a grunt.

"She gives good massages, too," Bleek said before turning away. "After that fall, you might need one."

~

Puntia

Brenten Arden

I watched as Barstle Cardino, now a mindless automaton because of the drakus seed he'd ingested, arrived to pull a clone away.

My suspicions went on high alert; would the clone be taken to the master suite?

Long ago, I'd been vampire, and half Karathian before that. I still held a vampire's gifts—when I chose to employ them.

I did so now, placing compulsion on Cardino and the clone, to take me instead. Whatever was going on inside the master suite, I would discover shortly. Feigning meekness, I followed Cardino out of the massive ballroom where the clones spent most of their time.

~

Quin

Lafe ruffled my hair when I appeared in the kitchen for lunch; I'd cleaned up after my training session with Caylon. After I'd dumped him once on the floor, he proceeded to trounce me soundly in front of everyone else.

I'd fallen three times to his one.

Still, Lafe thought it reason enough to celebrate. I was distracted, though—whatever caused the skin between my wings to itch when I woke was back and worse. A nameless fear nagged at my mind; one I couldn't set aside or ignore any longer.

When the Orb appeared, my fears were realized and my immediate fate sealed.

~

New Fyris

Lissa

"Push now," Karzac directed. Beatris was having difficulty birthing her second child; Tory, who spent much of his time in New Fyris, had called me the moment they'd discovered the problem.

Beatris had already been in labor for eleven hours and was exhausted. I asked Karzac to go with me; he would save mother and child if anyone could.

Rodrik was in the birthing suite with us; he fretted nearby, worried about his wife and child.

"She has no strength left," I informed Karzac before taking Beatris' hand and feeding her some of my energy. "Now," I said. "Push now, honey. You can do this."

The moment the baby's head crowned, the shield my Larentii mates had placed around Harifa Edus took a hit. While the shield held, everything inside it was shaken, including the planet.

Only one thing could do that—*a ranos cannon.*

The second shot it sent in our direction was worse. The child was born amid Beatris' scream of pain and terror.

Puntia

Brenten Arden

Some would have found them grotesque. I only felt pity as I gazed upon the creatures hiding the inhabitants of the master suite from even the most powerful. Twin Sirenali, joined through the tops of their heads to one another. They shared a large brain between them and neither could live without the other.

Someone had found the most effective weapon possible in hiding from those who sought him or her.

As yet, I hadn't seen who that might be.

Wylend, my father, and Erland, father to my grandson, who now sat the throne of Karathia, imagined it might be a talented warlock's spell that ramped up the effectiveness of a Sirenali to create this result.

Instead, the truth was so much sadder. They wore ill-fitting clothing—few comforts had been provided. It was my guess that they'd been used since they were very young for this purpose.

The saddest part was the metal cage in which they lived. I had no idea whether they'd ever been set free of it, once they were weaned. It wasn't even tall enough for them to stand.

Shoving aside my growing anger, I followed the empty-minded Barstle past the twins and into another section of the master suite.

Quin

I fell and rolled on the rub-mat of the ship, right into the midst of the crew on the bridge.

They'd already fired on Harifa Edus twice, and were preparing a third volley when I arrived. Most on the bridge I didn't recognize.

One stood out, however, and the moment he turned toward me, he raised a weapon to fire. Whip, Bleek's second-in-command aboard the

Killshot, was commanding this freighter and determined to kill me before he destroyed Harifa Edus.

Puntia

Brenten Arden

His back was to me when the alarm went off—I watched as he snatched a comp-vid from a nearby table and shouted at it.

"What in the name of the bloody god's ass is going on?" he yelled.

Two more walked into the room while he waited for an answer.

I recognized both of them. They, fortunately, didn't recognize me in my disguise.

That left no doubt as to who held the comp-vid.

Lissa, I sent. *We have trouble.*

Quin

Whip was the first one I killed—he fell, his brain disintegrating inside his skull. I hoped his death would hold the others back.

It didn't.

"Prepare the cannon for a third pass," another shouted into a communicator while the rest rounded on me.

They are here, the Orb informed me, before sending images of every man aboard the ship. *Kill them. Before they destroy New Fyris.*

Without thinking about it, I dispatched all of them—except for the Sirenali chained to the walls.

They were helpless and I wasn't about to destroy them.

Pulling a ragged breath into my lungs, I shuddered at the lifeless bodies surrounding me on the bridge.

"Answer me," Whip's comp-vid squawked.

I have no idea why I lifted it and stared at the one speaking. He could see me in return, after all.

"You," he shouted. "How in my brother's name do you keep showing up? Where's my crew? Answer me!"

"Hello, Vardil," I said wearily. I could see right past the face he wore into the blackness of his soul.

"What?" he sputtered, shaking his head. "How?" he continued. He couldn't imagine that anyone might recognize him outside his small circle of trusted servants and employees.

Three more people walked into view behind Vardil. I drew in a painful breath. Deris and Daris Arden, and a disguised distant cousin stood there. "Never mind," Vardil lifted a small transmitter. "I'll destroy the ship." For a brief moment, Vardil smiled before Brenten Arden dropped his disguise and leveled a power blast at Vardil Cayetes, killing him instantly.

I screamed as the Orb flung me away from the ship, which exploded behind me. Cayetes had managed to trigger the remote detonator before he died.

Puntia

Brenten Arden

If I'd thought Vardil Cayetes the worst of the worst, I discovered how very wrong I was. I now faced Deris and Daris Arden, distant relatives of Wylend—and mine as well.

"Usurper," Daris screeched before *Pulling* a small device into her hand.

"Betrayer," Deris shouted as he hauled Vardil Cayetes' body up with power.

"You die," Daris hissed and pressed a button on the device.

I barely had time to build a shield about myself when the entire planet exploded.

undia
   Quin

The breath was knocked out of me when I hit the Mundian mansion's tiled kitchen floor. I'd held the glass sphere in my hand as I watched Vardil Cayetes die. The fall loosened my grip and the sphere now clicked on tile before rolling across the floor. Mell shrieked in terror at my sudden appearance.

"No," I shouted, reaching out in an attempt to grasp the sphere.

Terrett's foot stopped the sphere from rolling, but it was still out of my reach. I needed it more than I'd needed anything in my life.

In slow motion, almost, Terrett toed the sphere in my direction. A terrible light bloomed as I grasped the sphere in shaking fingers—part of that light came from the Orb.

Harifa Edus
   Lissa

They're all dead, an unknown voice spoke in my mind. *The ship is partially destroyed and the ranos cannon is still aboard the ship. Please release us,* the voice pleaded.

It's an old Larentii trick—to follow mindspeech back to its source. I'd never have sensed the ship, otherwise.

Karzac held Beatris and Rodrik's newborn son in his hands; my Refizani mate blinked at me just as I disappeared. The Sirenali who were still alive aboard the ship needed my help.

I also didn't want anyone else getting to that ranos cannon before I did; the sender of the mindspeech had sent out a blanket message—anyone with the talent to hear mindspeech would know.

I also sent a call to Winkler—to help with a wrecked and drifting ship, likely sent by Vardil Cayetes.

The moment my feet touched the remains of the ship's bridge, I went still.

It was the moment before impact.

The moment when you discover just how vulnerable those you cared for might be.

No! My scream was likely heard across the universe.

Vic'Law had just been destroyed.

Le-Ath Veronis
Justis

"What's wrong?" Gurnil asked. He and I stood at the railing surrounding the library terrace.

We were watching the tour boats on the waters far below. Gone were the days when I could leap off the terrace and fly downward to pull a feeble-minded tourist from the rough waters.

Ardis and his troops kept watch, now. It wouldn't do for the Avii King to place his life in danger, just to rescue someone foolish enough to leap off a boat.

"I feel unsettled—like something's wrong," I said. "I can't shake the feeling, either."

"You worry too much, I think," Gurnil replied.

"Perhaps you don't worry enough," I said.

"What is there to worry about?"

The cry sounded behind us. I turned first; Gurnil was much slower than I.

"Quin?"

She'd landed hard on the grassy terrace, the breath knocked out of her with her cry. The Orb, shining brightly, appeared with her. Quin's eyes, filled with terror, locked with mine as she struggled to stand and draw a breath at the same moment.

Something was clutched tightly in her hands, which she refused to release.

Ignoring the pulsing Orb, I ran toward her; she lurched to her feet.

Before I reached her, she'd launched herself into the sky while I shouted at her to come back. Ignoring my call, her wings pumping in desperation, she lifted herself higher and higher on the winds surrounding the castle. In three blinks, she was high enough to fly over the tallest spires. At that point, the Orb disappeared.

Cursing, I snapped out my wings and leapt from the ground to follow her. Gurnil followed as quickly as he could to guard me. I had no idea where Quin intended to go; I was following her blindly, hoping neither of us were in danger.

Her wings had grown strong; I discovered that much as I worked to keep up with her. The glass at the top of the castle gleamed in partial sunlight—clouds had gathered overhead, predicting rain for the afternoon.

Once Quin was past the inside edge of the glass top, she dropped immediately, heading for the grass inside the bowl.

Quin? I inserted my voice inside her head.

She didn't reply. I'd shortened the distance between us—if she intended to fly away from me, then I intended to follow.

Black Wing guards rose from the bowl like a scattering of crows; their King was chasing something. They were determined, therefore, to chase it as well.

Stand down, I snapped, hoping they'd hear my mental voice. I didn't need or want Quin injured.

I was still yards from touching the grass of the inside bowl when Quin set down. It was probably just as well.

With an explosion of light and sound—mostly screaming, I noticed—the entire bowl was suddenly crowded with people.

～

Quin

Dazed. Addled. That's how I felt. I'd dropped onto the grass of the bowl while thousands talked, cried or shrieked around me.

I still held the sphere in my hand, but it had spent its usefulness, after the Orb and I had crammed the whole of Mundia's souls into it. Now it was dark—dead; its inner light gone. Sadly, we couldn't save all the innocent lives on Vic'Law—the sphere could only hold so many. The people we'd gathered in Mundia barely fit.

"My love?" Justis knelt beside me.

"Quin?" Barc had found me, his father following close on his heels. "You all right, Quin?" Barc leaned over, his head almost upside down as he gazed at me with concerned eyes.

"Barc," I opened my arms and pulled him to me. "Are you all right?"

～

Lissa

"A ranos cannon, hidden inside one of those outmoded satellites orbiting Vic'Law," Winkler growled. "Fuck."

"Who knows when Cayetes placed it there," I sighed. "It was a way to keep them all in line—after all, he could leave them to their fate if they failed to do as he asked."

"I killed Cayetes," my father spoke. "But I'm concerned. Before they disappeared, Deris and Daris took his body, the twin Sirenali and most of the clones."

"What would they want with his body?" I asked. It didn't make any sense.

"Hmmph. You should ask Erland about the reconstruction spell. It's outlawed for a reason."

"What does it do?" I asked.

"I think you'd refer to the recipient as a zombie, but that's putting it mildly," he shrugged. "I'm more interested in what Quin was able to do with that sphere."

"Don't ask me," I said. "I'm just as puzzled as you are. My question is this—what about Deris and Daris?"

"Oh. That. You may have to have a few drinks and an uninterrupted hour for that story. Wylend tells it best—perhaps you should ask him."

I wasn't sure I wanted to see my grandfather, but if he could clear up the mess with distant relatives, I'd dress up and invite him to dinner if he'd come and explain it.

"Soon," I said. "For now, Kooper and I have a ranos cannon to destroy."

Terrett

Justis thought to ask the question; it hadn't occurred to me.

"Why didn't you wait for me? I would have helped you," he lifted an eyebrow at Quin.

"I had to get them out of the sphere quickly," she rustled her feathers and stared at her feet. "If I'd waited, they'd have died—from lack of air."

We sat inside Justis' royal suite; he'd ordered that our dinner be served there. It had just arrived and we were ready to sit and eat.

Once they'd been gathered from the glass castle's bowl, the people from Mundia had been transported to Harifa Edus—Quin had somehow fit all one hundred sixty thousands of them, plus the inhabitants of the mansion we'd taken for ours, into the Orb.

It had been an uncomfortable experience, and she was right—I knew I was trapped somewhere and didn't remember breathing during what felt like an eternity.

Kaldill still marveled that she could stuff him into the sphere with everyone else. Perhaps he and a few others may have gotten themselves out again, but most of us depended upon Quin's talents to do that for us.

"How did you know you could do that?" Caylon asked her.

"I saw it in the Orb—just before I landed in the kitchen in Mundia. The Orb pulled everybody into the sphere, but people miniaturized and stuffed into it will only survive as long as they can hold their breath," she added.

"Strange," Justis shook his head. "Come, my love, let's eat. You must be hungry."

"I am," she agreed and took his hand.

Quin

Since our escape from Vic'Law, the Orb hasn't reappeared. It is my hope that Cayetes is forever dead, but after seeing Queen Lissa's father for the first time since our return to Le-Ath Veronis, I began to have my doubts.

Without seeing Deris and Daris again, I wouldn't know for sure. What I did know was this; Brenten Arden needed my healing. A part of his mind was misshapen. He often did the wrong thing for what he believed to be good reasons. Somewhere in his past, he'd been damaged.

I hoped to make him whole, but that would take time.

For now, I enjoyed my time at Avii castle. Without Farisa to pour poison into waiting ears, I had a much easier time fitting in as Justis' mate. Still, though, I wore black wings and I wondered at that. It made me think—again—that the troubles requiring my attention were far from over.

Sitting on the grass in Avii Castle's bowl, I watched as Caylon drilled the troops from Mundia, Jayna included. He said—and Queen Lissa agreed—that to interrupt their training would be doing them a disservice. They'd be allowed to protect Harifa Edus, once their training was complete.

I think Jayna was looking forward to it. Her disguise had been dropped—she no longer needed it. It made me smile, too, to see some of Ardis' Black Wing troops assisting with the training.

"Quin," Caylon turned toward me and barked my name. Rising from my sitting position in the way he and Sal taught me, I released my wings, lifted from the ground and glided toward him. Sursee Caylon intended for me to become an elite warrior.

I didn't know whether that was possible.

Only time would tell.

In'Frias

"It's worth a try," Deris muttered, preparing the syringe of blood. "At the moment, he's a drooling fool. We won't get those words to open the lock unless we do something. We have the money and the network to get what we want, now. We only need the spell and the coffin."

"If this doesn't work?" Daris glared at her brother.

"Then I hope Marid of Belancour told his son what the locking spell was before he died."

"I hear Morid is on Grey Planet," Daris huffed.

"There are ways to get around that," Deris held up a hand. "Come, help me inject Cayetes and pray to our royal ancestor that it works."

The End

www.ingramcontent.com/pod-product-compliance
Lightning Source LLC
Chambersburg PA
CBHW070518100726
47907CB00004B/881